THE NAKED TRUTH

As the front door closed on the delivery man, Frank said into the phone, "Sorry, what can I do for you?"

"Look, I'm sorry to call you at home, or even call you at all. I'm the last person in the world I know you want to hear from. But . . . I'm Jean. From Baltimore?"

Frank took a moment for it to register. When it did, he gripped the phone tightly and ducked his head away from the door to the kitchen. In the kitchen, his wife and kids were loudly discussing the issue of his sick father.

"Can you talk?" she said. "I don't have a disease; I am not pregnant." She chuckled, despite herself. "I am not calling because I have thought only of you since we met or because I must see you again. But today, just now, I got a call, some guy who is trying to blackmail me about that picture that was taken. I wanted to warn you. I think he's going to chase you, too. Have you heard anything?"

"I haven't." Not yet, anyway. Then it struck him who had just been standing in his front hall. He stared at the envelope he'd just accepted from the delivery man. Hands trembling, Frank tore open the flap. Inside were a note and a photograph. Even before turning over the picture Frank knew what it was . . .

FAT CHANCE

CHARLIE SHELDON

POCKET BOOKS

New York   London   Toronto   Sydney   Tokyo   Singapore

This book is a work of fiction. Names, characters, places and incidents are either the product of the author's imagination or are used fictitiously. Any resemblance to actual events or locales or persons, living or dead, is entirely coincidental.

An *Original* Publication of POCKET BOOKS

POCKET BOOKS, a division of Simon & Schuster Inc.
1230 Avenue of the Americas, New York, NY 10020

ISBN: 0-671-73591-8

First Pocket Books printing December 1991

10 9 8 7 6 5 4 3 2 1

Printed in the U.S.A.

Acknowledgments

For the call out of the blue and the unexpected push, George Foy; for pushing some more and leading me to my agent, Paul Kemprecos; for encouragement after suffering the first drafts, Sten Carlson and the Bonnell Clan; for support and cheerfully living through those weekends when the computer was king, my wife Martha and children Justine, Jack, and Oskar; for his conviction, faith, and example to follow, Bill Hohle; for all her assistance and fantastic ideas; my agent, Meg Ruley; for liking it enough to go on, Dana Isaacson, my editor; for providing the structure, the setting, and the fantasies that led to this story, the inbound head car, 7:30 and 5:20 Gladstone Express; and for keeping it all in perspective, smoky basements everywhere.

FAT
CHANCE

Chapter One

TUESDAY NIGHT

The lounge lizard made his move about eleven, just when Frank was closing in for the kill. Frank, that was the name he'd given. He was new at this sort of thing, Jean could tell. In fact she'd had to work pretty hard to get him this far. But now that he was ready, he wasn't about to let this character steal her.

She'd seen the other guy slide into the lounge just after ten, shooting his cuffs as he came through the door, the faded blue blazer and red pocket handkerchief a nice contrast with the open white shirt. He was about thirty, thirty-five. Standing at the bar he checked out the talent in the mirror above the racks of bottles.

Jean knew right off he was one some women went for. Handsome, a little seedy, he would draw out the cuddling instinct. Here it was Tuesday night in the airport Holiday Inn outside Baltimore where Jean was staying and she believed this guy was on the make. He might be after the well-traveled flight attendants getting loaded in the booth by the door. He might be after the two businesswomen hiding along the wall, facing a night alone with HBO or a six-dollar erotic film which was nothing but a porn movie with the good stuff cut out.

He might be after Jean. They often were. But Jean had

1

seen this Frank much earlier, leaving the lounge on the way into the motel dining room for dinner alone. She had caught his eye, given him a smile. When he'd arranged to sit just two tables away, Jean had smiled again.

Earlier, at dinner, a hesitant Frank took the safe approach. He leaned over and asked, "What do you recommend here?" He faced her, smiling sincerely.

This allowed her to take a look, check him out, make up her mind, let him make up his mind. He had this fantasy: There'd be a smile back and after a couple of exchanges they'd take their meal at the same table. "Silly to shout back and forth, isn't it?" After dinner, coffee and cognac. Frank would suggest the bar for a nightcap. Then, after several drinks in a darkened lounge with a three-piece dance combo sawing away in the corner, after a few dances to get used to being close, Frank would suggest moving to his room where the air was a little less smoky. But unlike any fantasy, here he was, just about there this Tuesday night. And she was very nice, very sexy, even before the five drinks since dinner. Jean-something was her name.

The snake had appeared about ten, up by the bar all this time trying—and sometimes succeeding, Frank saw—in playing eye games with Jean. Then the lowlife started to make his move.

Frank, though, was ready for it.

"I knew a guy once, at his company's Christmas party," Frank said, completely changing the subject, leaning across the narrow booth table, taking her hand and stroking a knuckle with his thumb. "He picked up his beer like this, see?" And he picked up Jean's mug of beer with his free hand. It was nearly full; he'd just ordered her a refill. "He held the beer up to his chest like this waiting for his boss to come up behind him—he really hated his boss—and when he knew his boss was just behind him he suddenly twisted around..." As he was speaking Frank started twisting, knowing the guy was about one step away from the booth, all set with whatever his line was, probably going to ask her to dance. Frank swung around, pretending to throw the mug of beer. "... he twisted around like this and threw it—oh, Jesus, Jesus! Sorry, fellah!"

Perfect, just perfect, just like an accident, his arm hitting the guy's knee, beer all over his pants, looked like he pissed himself.

"Jesus, fellah, I didn't see you there at all, I'm sorry, oh, Jesus..." Frank tried not to smile watching him standing there soaked. There'd be no invite to dance this song, better to go get dried out. "Listen, I'm here at the hotel tonight. Give me your name, address, and I'll pay the laundry bill." Leaning back to catch how Jean was taking it, he caught her eye, giving a little wink.

Paul Johnson looked down at his crotch, shook his head, smiled at Jean. "No dance this song, huh?" Dripping, he grinned, shook his head again, and turned, heading for the men's room.

" 'Nother beer?" Frank asked, waving to the waitress, pleased with himself.

"On purpose! You did that on purpose!"

"What?" All innocence, watching to see how it went.

"You did do that on purpose!"

Frank knew that now was the time: get out of here before the snake dried off, thought about it, and came back pissed off. Taking a breath, he said, "What do you say we finish up our drinks, move to my room, catch HBO? Got a minibar, ice cubes, the works. Kind of smoky in here, you think?"

"Two-fifty, mistuh." The waitress was chewing gum, bored, waiting to be paid.

Frank peeled off a five, watching Jean. "Keep the change, honey."

Jean raised the beer to her lips, drank, and said, "That sounds fine to me."

Dammit, she looked good, smiling at him, and Frank

thought, hope I haven't had too much to drink here; I've had plenty, that's for sure.

He watched her finish her beer, gazing into his eyes. She looked a little blotto, actually. But then so did he.

Jean-something was actually Jean Progulski Newman, thirty-four, married five years, with a boring but maybe-one-of-these-days rich husband, a computer expert named Norman. She was alone in Baltimore on a business trip setting up a flower growers' convention, which was a dull convention except she loved flowers. Jean worked for a company that arranged conventions and trade shows. By the time this convention started Thursday, Jean Newman would be back home in Maplewood, New Jersey, back in boredom-land with her loving but sexually useless husband, Norman, which was why she was letting this character Frank Benson—probably his real name—buy her dinner and drinks at the airport Holiday Inn where she was staying.

Actually, he looked a little like a horse, those big front teeth, the big head, but his body seemed pretty fit. Maybe he was hung like a horse, too. Watch it, Jean thought, finishing her beer, don't be too eager. But she was eager, waiting for him to settle the bill. She liked his hands, broad, strong palms with big veins on the back. He was much bigger than the far sexier-looking guy who had run off when Frank neutralized his move with her beer. Tonight she wanted big, not pretty, anyway.

Jean giggled and reached for her purse.

"Ready?" Frank asked.

She reached over and brushed his arm.

"When you are." She gathered her purse and accompanied him from the lounge, enjoying the hard stares from the other single women by the wall. When she stood up all the beer went to her head and before they rode the elevator to his room she stopped at the ladies' room. Inside, she washed her hands after using the toilet, inspecting herself in the mirror.

"Not bad," she said. She knew she still looked good, still had the figure, skin smooth, maybe because there were no kids yet. She grinned and reached up under her dress, pulled off her panties, stuffed them in her purse. Give him a nice surprise. If after all this talk, dinner, and drinks this guy let her down, got guilty, she'd reach in her purse and strangle him with her panties.

In the ladies' room, as in many others these days, she noticed the new machine selling condoms. It was the Take Responsibility for Safe Sex, Ladies era, she thought. She carried three condoms in her purse already, lifted from home. Norman always used one. Although she hated them, she felt better when he used them.

He was so fucking fastidious about it anyway.

"Anything wrong?" Frank asked, seeing her scowl as she emerged from the rest room.

"Oh, no hand towels in there," she said.

When the elevator came Frank pushed five. Jean blinked. "That's my floor, too."

"Five-one-eight, that's me," Frank said, facing her now in the slowly ascending elevator, moving in close; she could smell the Scotch on him. It smelled nice, and when she raised her chin he lowered his head and kissed her, mouth open, a real "Miami Vice" kiss. It was very nice, very. He was hung like a horse, she could feel it.

He was just starting to stroke her when the elevator stopped and the door opened. The hallway was empty, stretching ahead, narrow and green. Frank led her past her room, five-oh-seven, which she hadn't told him she was in because of the kiss. At his door he pulled out his key, fumbled with the lock.

When she entered the room in front of Frank she saw it was not too bright, shadows by the bed, the room neat and warm and the soft rock FM station playing in the background. He reached for a light switch and she took his hand and pulled it against her belly, backing against him. Then his hands were on her stomach, reaching up and cupping her breasts, and she felt him push into her from behind.

"Um?" he muttered into her neck, hands busy, now opening the top two buttons and reaching inside. She turned and began to unfasten his pants, suddenly horny as hell, wanting to be naked before him, have him in her mouth, in her body. She began to shake as he bent down and mouthed her breast.

His pants came free and fell to the floor. Jean knelt before him, pulled down his shorts, and he gasped as she opened her mouth and moistened her tongue.

The telephone rang.

On her knees before Frank, Jean was close by the bed. The clock on the nightstand showed 11:31.

"Wake-up call?" she asked, smiling, stroking him, leaning back and gazing up, hair swinging back from her forehead. His head was thrust back, throat veins throbbing. He obviously didn't want to answer the phone, but when it rang again he said, "Fuck it!" Sitting down on the bed, he reached across to the telephone.

Jean moved up to sit on the bed. She sat cross-legged before Frank, dress above her knees, and she saw his eyes glaze as he looked at her crotch. Staring, he spoke into the phone.

"Hello."

Jean could hear some woman on the other end, couldn't make out what she was saying. She knew it had to be his wife. At least he hadn't told her he was unmarried or separated—not that it would have mattered.

"When?"

More talk.

"Christ. It's in the third drawer under my worktable. In the garage. You call me this late for that? Christ!"

The woman began to sound excited.

"Michelle, it's almost midnight. What are you doing looking for the long-handled screwdriver now? Calm down. Haven't you taken one of those sleeping pills Dr. Schwartz prescribes?...Oh, that's right... Yeah, I forgot... Well, if you have any hanging around, why don't you take one?...What a time to start a project!''

Jean leaned back against the pillows, watching Frank get hassled by his wife, knowing as he spoke that his desire, his need, would flag without direct action. She began to stroke herself, an easy slow rhythm, staring at Frank's crotch, tongue against the roof of her mouth.

"Look, honey, I had a hard day today. I'll be home Thursday. I'll call you in the morning, all right?" Frank's hand crept up Jean's thigh, and her motion was faster. "All right? Michelle, I'll call you tomorrow." He gripped himself and began to move his hand. Staring toward Jean, he leaned over, replaced the phone, watching her.

This was the ultimate in Safe Sex, Jean knew, watching him, stroking, stroking, getting right there, oh, right there, watching him, moving faster as he moved faster. Now if only now he goes, now, like that...Frank, panting and a little stunned, stroked her head as she licked his belly, his wet hair. Jean stretched like a cat along his side, getting down and dirty, like this, just like this.

"I'm so bad," Jean said, feeling great.

"You are that." Frank had a big sleepy grin.

So take that, Norman. She knew she would be good for some more in a while. A lot more. She was ready for it. She could tell, feeling around, he'd be ready for it, too.

Paul stood in the men's room patting himself dry with hand towels from the dispenser. He'd tried the hot-air machine but he had to stand funny, belly against the unit, hips cocked to present his crotch to the blowing air. It looked like he was trying to screw the machine.

But the hand towels didn't work too well. After the dispenser ran dry Paul used the machine again. That worked, after a fashion. Cooked his unit, though. After ten minutes he was just about dry.

It was supposed to be a real easy hundred bucks, just get

the lady to dance, nice and slowly, pull her in close, cheek to cheek, hands resting low on her hips, make it look nice, get set up for the photographer. And then only if she wasn't dancing with some other guy. Paul knew it was tied to the package he'd picked up months earlier from Henry Fallon, a real blackmail specialist; get the goods on the little lady when she's on the road, use her to put pressure on her husband, something to do with a new medicine. He'd gotten the call late this afternoon.

"Paul. Henry, here in Newark. Got a job for you."

"Henry." Paul had not heard from Henry for months. He'd begun to think, hope, he'd been forgotten.

"You too busy to work, quick little job? Easy."

"Like what?"

"Oughta be right up your alley, lady-killer like you. I'll get you a hundred bucks if you find this woman, Jean Newman, staying tonight at the airport Holiday Inn down there. I gotta client wants someone to dance with her, real close, you know? Let a picture be taken. I already called the photo man. It's one of the bartenders there. Got his camera behind the bar."

"Hundred, you say?"

"Right."

"Jean Newman?"

"Client said she's thirty-three, thirty-four, black hair, five-six, one hundred fifteen pounds, nice figure, said she's got a wide mouth and looks a little wild, married, likes to wear that silver-pink lipstick. She's staying at the Holiday Inn there, oughta be in the lounge about ten, probably getting hustled by some guy. You just move in, ask her to dance. You wanna let it develop, that's your business, but get close for the photo."

"This some divorce thing?"

"Shit, bigger than that! Remember that package you picked up from me in Newark a few months ago? Her husband works for a big drug company in New York. He's involved with this special project they got."

Paul hung up, showered, changed, fixed himself dinner, watched some ESPN, had a beer, and headed out to the airport. He had nothing going on this Tuesday, and a hundred sounded good to him. Not to mention the chance the assignment might develop bedroom-wise. Paul liked that, although truthfully speaking he had slowed down some in the past year or so. All this AIDS stuff made him nervous, though he thought if he avoided women who shot dope he'd probably be all right. All the same he'd slowed down. He was getting up to thirty-five now, no chicken any longer. Wasn't doing enough sit-ups either.

Gotta be in shape, you want a decent job, get away from driving trucks for Ryan Express, get it together here. It's just like they said: Being a parolee is a hard road to travel. Make contacts, that's what he'd figured out, what some of the magazines told him. Get some side deals going, use the Ryan routes to get little projects, some simple low-grade private investigations. So far he'd worked with this Henry Fallon in Jersey and five or six others, guys he'd met delivering packages or on the road. Now and then they passed some work his way if they needed anything from the Baltimore area.

Like this Jean Newman thing, provide a service for Henry from Newark, except with Henry he didn't have much choice. Henry claimed he had the goods on Paul: evidence of distributing cocaine, all his parole officer needed to send Paul right back inside. Back in June, Henry had paid Paul cash in the mail after a week or so. Paul knew Henry was following some big operation. And if he could, if he had the balls, Paul wanted to force Henry to spread a little of the cash his way if it came to that. But, with Henry, that could be very risky.

Actually, Paul was terrified of Henry.

When he parked in the motel lot he locked his car and entered the lounge from the lobby. It was 10:00 exactly, and on the way to the bar as his eyes adjusted to the light he could pick out one noisy twosome by the door, not bad looking, either of them. Two women sat alone in small booths by the wall. A bunch of men were at the bar. A couple danced to the music.

"Light rum and Coke."

Over the bar a color television was tuned to the basketball game, Bullets and Celtics in Boston. It was halftime, early in the season, mid-December, but the volume was turned very low and Paul wasn't interested in the game anyway. He liked hockey.

"Hockey game on?"

"Here we watch basketball." The bartender didn't even look up from the glasses he was washing.

"Sure."

Only one of the two along the wall was decent to look at, under forty, slender, nose like a blade, though; she wasn't Jean Newman. The other one, midthirties, dark haired, glasses, finishing a sandwich, she was heavy. The dancing couple returned to a small table, the man a big-shouldered guy attentively pulling out a chair for his partner, and Paul could tell immediately, as Henry had suggested, Jean Newman was being hustled in the bar. Even in the bad light Paul could see the glint of silver-pink lipstick, and although she was a little too angular for his taste he could imagine the evening developing.

He'd have to slide by horse-face.

Paul let some time pass, see how bucko was doing. Jean Newman looked like a woman who had made a decision: This is my night out, this man, he beats HBO. He could tell the guy with her was no pro at this, but, now started, he wouldn't quit. As Paul watched the drinks came and went. Having a few of his own along the way, he could see, despite catching her eye once or twice, that she'd be hard to tear away.

Finally, just after eleven, the ballgame on TV winding down to the end, the bartender approached Paul.

"Mister. You here to dance, or what?"

Paul started. The bartender pulled a camera from a shelf under the counter.

10

"You better move it. That guy with her's been on the case since dinner. Just get a dance real close, huh?"

What the hell. Paul started over. If horse-face got nasty, he would be shy the hundred, but by now the twosome by the door, both easy to play eye games with, looked—one of them anyway—better and better.

Horse-face made him a little nervous, to tell the truth. But he was turned away, telling Jean Newman some story, gesturing with a beer. Paul was about to stop, excuse himself, ask for a dance, when suddenly bucko lunged around and drenched him with beer.

Paul was impressed. The guy thought Paul was trying to move in, what a move. Paul was soaked. All he could say was, "No dance this song, huh?" and retire to the men's room to dry his pants.

By the time he was dry and had returned to the lounge he expected to see that Jean and horse-face had left, and they had. The bartender was hanging up the telephone.

"Nice move." The bartender shut off the television. "Mr. Fallon really wants a picture, you know?"

Paul waved his hand.

"Maybe another time," he muttered, suddenly afraid. He asked for another drink. What the fuck, the redhead from that twosome wanted to play. She was smiling at him.

"Listen." The bartender leaned toward Paul. "How would you like to make four hundred? Now?"

"Uh-oh." Paul guessed what was coming.

"Listen." The bartender reached for the camera. "I got passkeys for all the glass doors opening onto the balcony deck. That guy just took that broad up to his room, five-one-eight. It's on the corner, southwest side. All you got to do is take the elevator, this camera, and this key, get off on the fifth floor, go out the fire exit to the balcony, walk around the corner, open the door, take a picture, take off. Guy's gonna be in the saddle, oblivious to it all. No sweat."

"You do it. I'll tend the bar here."

"No, you do it, Mr. Fallon'll up the ante to four hundred. Plus the hundred you already have."

"What hundred I already have? I'm not paid yet. Why don't you do it? You know this place a lot better than I do."

"Where'd I go? Back here? Guy who does this, he's got to shoot the picture, drop the camera back here, leave, be gone. Listen. Mr. Fallon told me his client wanted pictures of her with other men, like dancing, but think of this! In the rack! That's worth four hundred, easy, get a picture like that."

Paul listened. Over by the door he could see the two women were preparing to leave. It was the redhead or the money. Or maybe, both.

"Shit."

The bartender handed him the camera.

"Fifth floor, five-one-eight. Southwest corner."

On his way through the lobby, the redhead approached him.

"You're not very friendly." She pouted. It was a nice pout. "You a photographer?"

Paul, high on adrenaline, nervous with what he was about to do, said, "Yes. I specialize in female models, seminudes." He surprised himself, keeping a straight face, saying this.

"Really! Models?"

"Uh, that's right. Fashion."

"I once wanted to be a model before I became a flight attendant."

Musta been a while ago, Paul thought, and he gave it his best shot.

"Listen, I got an assignment right now. But if you want, if you're a night owl like me, I'll be happy to shoot some shots—framed head and shoulder stuff—in a few minutes. If you got a light background in your room—"

"Three-ten. Sally Jones."

Jesus.

"Five minutes?"

"What do you drink? Beer? Scotch? I'll have something ready."

12

"Uh, Scotch." *If I get out of this one alive, that is.*

There were two elevators. Paul watched as Sally and her friend, who had been scowling at him, entered one of the elevators. He waved at Sally, then as soon as the door closed jumped in the other and rose to the fifth floor.

The fifth floor corridor was empty. Five-one-eight was at the end, on the left. Straight ahead was the fire door to the balcony. To the right, opposite five-one-eight, were the stairs.

Paul knew he had to act fast. The four hundred promised downstairs suddenly didn't seem like enough. The corridor seemed very long.

One last thing: He held the DOOR OPEN button for his elevator and called up the other one. Then he sent both down after hitting all the floors, up and down, and the basement levels, on each. *Keep them stopping for a while so he could beat horse-face down the stairs.*

When he passed five-one-eight he heard faint music and, for sure, groans.

He figured he'd get the shot. By the time the other guy realized Paul had to go down the stairs or elevators to get away he'd be most of the way down. He could either take off in his car or if it was close confuse the guy, zip back upstairs in an elevator, see if this woman Sally was for real.

He was nervous as he went onto the balcony. He knew he was nuts to even consider chasing that redhead instead of driving off. He made sure the exit door was held open by a matchbook; otherwise it would self-lock, isolating him out on the balcony.

He stepped outside. It was cold. There was a little wind this far above the parking lot. He edged toward the corner, looked around. The room faced the balcony with two wall-high glass sliders, both closed. A latch and lock caught light from the streetlights below. Paul saw the drapes had been pulled across the entire wall, except one corner near him where the drapes had caught on the heater.

He bent down and looked.

Jesus. Perfect. Her on her knees, parallel to the window, him all over her from behind. Jesus, it looked like that?

He knew he had to work quiet and fast, though even through the glass he could tell they were pretty into it. He thought about how much he wanted that four hundred dollars, how using the key in the lock would be. It was cold out here.

Four hundred was a lot of money. Inside, the noises rose.

Hell with it, let's go. Do it. And, as the key turned in the lock, he thought: I left my car locked. Brilliant, Paul.

Frank, for the last fifteen minutes practically in heaven, was right in the middle of one of his best fantasies, happening right now, something he could keep and relive for a long time to come, with a woman apparently as bad as he was, and oh, Lord, what fun.

The bed had been thumping against the wall for a while. Jean was making a lot of noise and he could feel it all coming for the second time, by Christ. He hardly noticed the faint clicking sound at the balcony door. She did.

Jean jerked her head up, looked toward the window, pulling free of him at exactly—*exactly!*—the wrong moment. My God! What?

The room suddenly exploded in white light. Jean yelled and rolled away. Confused, Frank, holding himself, turned, naked, to see the heels of someone disappearing from the now open slider. There was a blast of cold air.

"Shit!"

Picture! Someone with a camera! Jesus!

He lunged toward the slider. The balcony was empty in each direction. Then he heard a door in the corridor slam, close by, and he got it.

"Jesus!"

Jean, confused and scared, knew she'd been staring full-face toward the slider when it opened and the guy appeared with a camera that immediately flashed. She never saw anyone get pants and shirt on as fast as Frank. Instantly, it

14

seemed, he was out the door and pounding down the stairs after the other guy.

She sprang from the bed, still throbbing. She'd be sore tomorrow. She pulled on her clothing, desperate to get away, to get out of there before Frank returned.

Holding her shoes, she opened the door, hearing a faint ruckus below in the stairwell across the hall. She pulled her key from her purse and fled to her room up the hall. She would take a long shower, get clean. Thank God she had somewhere to go early tomorrow—the flower show exhibitor breakfast meeting. She never wanted to see that guy Frank again, ever. Tomorrow she'd be the nice professional, low-key, gathering strength to face Norman when she got home. She was never so angry at him as she was right after a night of good sex with another man.

By the time Frank made the ground floor he knew he had lost the photographer. The lobby was deserted. He didn't think to look in the lounge, where in fact Paul was now hiding. Through the doorway to the lobby Paul saw horse-face burst from the stairwell, race outside, then return to the lobby to check the elevators, both empty and standing on the lobby level. Paul thought he was a goner for sure but instead of looking in the lounge the guy seemed to realize he looked pretty strange—no shoes, shirt unbuttoned, no belt, obvious where he'd just been—and he got into the elevator and the door closed.

The bartender, cool as a cucumber, finished washing some glasses. "Think he'll be back?"

Paul didn't know.

"I assume your actions got you a picture."

Paul kept shaking.

"Tell Henry, you speak to him, next time gonna cost more than that."

The bartender nodded.

"Sure."

"See ya." Paul left the lounge.

In the lobby he suddenly got a picture in his head of the big guy standing up on the balcony, watching the parking lot, waiting for someone to appear. He'd get a license number. Paul felt certain the guy was up there and almost without thought he entered the other elevator, pushed all the buttons from one to five, and got off at three.

Sally Jones opened the door of three-ten at once.

"Your drink's getting warm," she said.

She looked nice. Safe. Her room looked safe. Shit, he had no camera, he'd left that with the bartender. But she didn't seem to care.

"No camera, I see." Smiling, she gestured him inside.

Frank stood it as long as he could, shivering up on the balcony watching the parking lot and the street below. Every few minutes a jet flew low overhead, landing at the airport. The cold worked into his bones and eventually he returned to his room.

Jean was long gone.

Frank warmed up with a hot shower, trying to think through his headache. Was he identifiable in the picture that had been taken? He hadn't been facing the camera when the door opened, but he was turning when it went off. Maybe his face did appear. Had that been the reason Michelle called so late with that crazy, silly question about a tool? Probably just making sure his tool was in his room. That was it. He'd been stupid to call her and let her know where he was staying. But that's what he always did, especially now when he wanted to be reachable in case anything developed with his father, who was in intensive care back home, very, very ill.

Maybe Michelle had had it, Jesus knows she'd warned him enough times. Now she was getting the evidence on him. It occurred to Frank that her family might be behind it. They made him nervous.

It did not occur to him that the picture was of Jean. Frank had surprised himself, for all his occasional fantasies and

16

halfhearted efforts with strange women, the experience with Jean had been unique. Not to mention the move he put on the snake. Frank was surprised he had it in him. Now, imagining the horrors at home if Michelle ever did find out, Frank started to feel guilty.

Chapter Two

SUNDAY MORNING

P aul."

"Henry." Paul had been waiting for three days for the cash that had been promised. Instead he had received an envelope in the mail containing a fifty-dollar bill and a second envelope doctored up to look like a Federal Express message. A rough handwritten note had been attached: "I'll call. F."

"Hank tells me you did fine down there Tuesday."

"Hank?"

"Yeah, that bartender. He said you showed class. Tells me you got the guy and the lady at the critical moment, then wandered back downstairs to the lounge cool as a cucumber, dropped off the camera. Cool, he said."

Paul hadn't been cool at all. Not at all. *Scared* was a better term.

"Where's the rest of the money?" Paul asked, turning over the envelope in his hand.

"One thing."

Uh-oh.

"You there?"

Paul thought he should hang up. Knew he should. He'd had two dreams already of being trapped in a stairwell, a big monster one flight above coming down fast in a foaming rage.

"Paul."

"Sorry, Henry, just drifted off there a moment." Paul didn't want to be in this conversation. He stood barefoot in his tiny kitchen staring out over the roof of the garage next door, white under six inches of new snow, still falling. It was a big storm today, the big pre-Christmas storm. The plows weren't out yet. It was supposed to snow over a foot. Paul stirred the soup he'd been heating when Henry called. A big football game was on TV, Broncos and Giants at the Meadowlands. It was halftime, Giants ahead by ten. Paul had settled down. It was his Sunday off. He planned to drink beer, lounge around, watch the rest of the game. Hang out.

"Paul, you did great down there with that Jean Newman broad. Got a great shot, perfect, just perfect. Looks like she was posing, for Christ's sake." Fallon laughed into the phone. "That woman likes to fuck, I'd guess. Ha-ha."

"Where's the rest of my five hundred?" Paul wanted his money.

"That envelope I sent you, you got it, right?"

"Holding it right here. What's this about? Who's this Franklin Benson the envelope's addressed to?"

"How's about you take a little trip up to Philly?"

"Philly! When?"

"Now. Old Jean there, she came out real well, and the guy with her, you got a perfect shot of his face in the mirror, too! Perfect! I did a little research."

Paul, holding the envelope, could see where Henry was leading. "Shit, Henry."

"Listen, Paul. This one here will be you and me, fifty-fifty, how's that? Franklin Benson, Two-thirty Holland Drive, northwest Philly, out toward the Main Line, nice four-bedroom home on a third-acre lot. He's got a wife named Michelle. The guy, it turns out, doesn't want any attention drawn his way, none. Works as a bank security consultant, travels around helping banks set up security systems or evaluates systems already in place. He's a goddamn pillar of the community, Boy Scout leader, even. Turns out, based on a little checking around I did with another couple of clients I got in the banking business up here, there's sort of a coincidence. He goes in, does a bank system, or looks at one, something with alarms and computers, well, a few months later, the bank he does is missing some funds. Started last year.''

Paul remembered Franklin Benson, all right. A guy he never wanted to see ever again, a big strong man with a neck like a post and hands like mallets. He'd been lucky to get away. Drive up to Philly in this blizzard to see him?

"Hey, Henry, this sounds too heavy, you know?" But he was listening; fifty-fifty had to be better than a few hundred dollars.

"No heat yet, not yet, none, the banks are all in different states, different types, some savings, some straight commercial. But I've checked it, you know, through my buddies up here, old 'friends' I made when I was an officer of the law.''

Paul thought, yeah, crooked public servants, crooked cops, getting all the dirt—computer theft, sex, whatever—all for the purpose of blackmail.

"Here's what you do. Drive up there, check this guy's place out, look at his home, let him get a fast look at you when you deliver that envelope. Then you take off. He opens it. Out falls one juicy photograph! That'll soften him up when I call him in a day or two.''

"He'll recognize me!"

"He see you taking the picture?"

"No, but—"

"Listen! If he recognizes you, it'll be as the guy he already put down in Baltimore, the loser he beat out to win his lady of the occasion. By the time he connects seeing you at his door with that picture, you'll be long gone.''

"Henry, I can't drive in this.''

After a long silence Henry spoke again before ending the call. "But you will, boyo.''

Paul thought more about what Henry said he had on him, evidence he had been distributing coke. It might be true, for all he knew. He hadn't known what was in some of the packages he'd delivered. Paul hated to drive in snow. It would take him three hours at least. He'd miss the last half of the ballgame.

"But you will, boyo."

The company Paul drove for leased a fleet of vans, old UPS castoffs someone had rebuilt and repainted. Ryan Express dispatched small packages within one hundred miles of Baltimore, guaranteed same-day delivery if picked up before ten-thirty. Paul had been driving for the company eight months, since his release from Mitchell Medium Security. He'd been in for passing bad checks. Paul had tried to be careful since he got out. He truly disliked the work, but it was a job, hard to find if you were an ex-con. There were some perks. Going into a lot of company offices, he'd meet the receptionist, deliver the package, smile, and if she looked nice, he liked her, her left hand clear of rings, it being by then usually late in the afternoon, he'd get some dates. Also, the way it was working out, he'd met a few people he was now doing jobs on the side for, like Henry. Driving the van got him around a lot, in and out of a lot of places.

Going out the door to the street where the van was parked, Paul wrapped a scarf around his neck. He had brought three packs of smokes from an opened carton for the trip, matches, a pair of mittens, and a hot thermos of the soup he'd prepared on the stove.

Christ, it was just like the Yukon out here. Heavy gusts of snow swirled around the buildings. The street was white and buried. A cold wind blew. It was a black-and-white photograph, all the colors lost in the snow. There were a few cars, creeping past at about ten miles an hour, drivers hunched over their steering wheels, rigidly staring ahead.

The van was parked in the small lot next to Paul's apartment building. He scraped the windows free of snow, got in, started up.

Ryan Express allowed the better drivers to keep the vans at home over the weekend as well as during the week. Every weekday, 7:00 A.M., it was the driver's job to be in the van, close by the radio (each van had a two-way radio), ready for the dispatcher to read off assignments. Paul was Code Eleven. Weekends were off.

It took the truck ten minutes running in place to defog the windows, heat up the cab, get the windshield warm enough to melt off the ice under the wipers.

Paul placed the envelope Fallon had prepared on the seat next to him and stared ahead, mesmerized by the wipers sweeping back and forth. He'd been working for Ryan one month when Ryan asked him to go up to New Jersey to pick up a new van. Ryan himself was a young kid even younger than Paul, real entrepreneur type, always telling whoever was within earshot how he was going to be the next Fred Smith, Federal Express, make a million by thirty, stay with me and when I go public you'll get to cash in a lot of stock if you invest some of your paycheck now back into the company. Paul believed none of it. Ryan, smart as he was, was stupid about a lot of things. Either he didn't know that driving all over for Ryan was like a license to profit or he didn't care. The way Paul looked at it, he had permission to travel most anywhere. It allowed him, in between picking up and delivering packages for Ryan, to pick up and deliver parcels for others. Soon he had a nice little secondary business going moving stuff between different divisions of the big companies they did a lot of work for. Paul was sure he was moving coke or reefer but he didn't look or care so long as the cash kept coming in.

It happened like this, which was why Henry from New Jersey had met Paul, why they were working together. Or, rather, why Paul was now working for Henry. Every Tuesday, Paul made a regular stop at Boothbay Chemicals, a company in south Baltimore. He'd move stuff over to a satellite operation around D.C. There was a nice-looking receptionist there, a slender divorcée named Cheryl. Early spring, just after Paul had started, Cheryl asked him to drop a little envelope to a girlfriend who worked in the D.C. operation. It was real easy, nothing to it, an easy fifty bucks.

Immediately thereafter, it seemed, Cheryl got promoted,

went to work for some fast-rising new business development vice-president. Paul stayed in touch, once even sleeping with her. One day in May she called him, asked him, very mysteriously, if he could get up to Jersey to pick up a package for her. The pay would be ten times the usual fifty. Coincidentally, this was requested the morning after Ryan asked him to retrieve the van.

Paul figured he had tied in to some kind of money tree. He took the bus to Newark, New Jersey, picked up the freshly painted and registered van from a warehouse just outside Port Newark, and before heading back to Baltimore, he drove to an address in Newark to get Cheryl's package.

The man answering the door was huge, about six-four, two-forty, mean looking. He pulled Paul in the door, gripping his arm like a vise. In his other hand he held a thick manila envelope. He said, "You ain't too sharp."

Paul was speechless with pain.

"I'm here for, ah, a package?" he gasped.

The man laughed. "Huh." He looked down at the envelope in his hand. "You think dope, right?"

Paul nodded. Boy, if anyone looked like a bad guy, it was this guy.

The man laughed again, releasing Paul's arm. Paul's fingers tingled.

"You got to broaden your horizon, boyo. Broaden! Good money lies in dope, sure! The big money? The big, big, big, steady and forever, legitimate money? Look to industrial espionage!"

Paul, rubbing his throbbing biceps, knew Cheryl worked for a big drug firm, that she was now working for some aggressive new business guy, that the money she'd offered Paul for this trip here was ten times the usual. It made sense. He shuddered with relief when the guy stepped back.

"Well, this here ain't insulin, either. Bigger than that, I think. I'm passing on this stuff through you. You'll keep quiet, too. Know why?" Paul's spirits sank. "You're an ex-con, buster. You been making coke deliveries for Cheryl since April. You say anything, I tell your parole officer. You're working for me now, sonny!" The man's smile, the long pointed brown teeth, made Paul feel terrible.

"How'd you know, uh, I was a parolee?"

"I'm an investigator. A good one. Henry Fallon." He handed Paul a card. "Listen, I like ex-cons! Love 'em! They make good workers, good partners! Keep their mouths shut! You like money, right?" Paul nodded, afraid of the wild look in the man's eye. Then to Paul's surprise the man shook his hand, nearly crushing it. "We'll be partners on this one! Before I became a dick, I was a policeman! Thing is, I got caught where I shouldn't be, left myself exposed there, same year the mayor was running for reelection. I ended up as a big campaign issue, being as how his opponent was the chief of police. The chief won the election, actually, but by then it was too late for me. But I keep up my contacts, and it was easy to find out about you, sonny."

Fallon pulled Paul into a dark hallway. Paul eyed the package. He wondered, industrial espionage? Worth more than coke?

Paul stared now into the dark gloom ahead. There was snow all over the road. Not many cars. Paul got the van up to thirty and started up I-95 to Philly. He'd only delivered for Cheryl that once. Now she was too busy up in the rarefied reaches of executive corporate strategy. Whatever they wanted, they had it and good-bye to him. But Henry Fallon had stayed in touch, had the lever on Paul, that's for certain. Now Paul was driving north to Philly through the worst pre-Christmas blizzard since 1963, driving to send a message to horse-face.

Halfway there, he was down half a pack of cigarettes and the thermos of soup was gone. Armadas of plows worked the interstate. He crawled, his speed below thirty. There was no radio and he was thoroughly sick of the thumping wipers and their uneven rhythm: *swish...clack! swish...clack!* It would be a long trip.

Paul had it figured this way: He would cruise the area where this guy Frank Benson lived, looking like a delivery man searching for an address. He even planned to wear a messenger service cap he'd found. Then he would take the envelope, deliver it to Benson, and get the hell out of there.

If he played it right, he could get a good look inside the house, see how it appeared, see how this guy lived. How this would benefit Henry Fallon he had no idea, but if he was lucky he could tell right away whether this guy was pulling in money on the side. In his admittedly limited experience, if guys like this guy Frank got on top of some deal that makes them a lot of cash quick, they just got to spend some of it fast: either a new car in the garage, a thirty thousand–dollar fishing rig on a trailer in the backyard, or something like that.

Paul hoped to take a look, hand over the envelope, then leave, with this guy none the wiser until Paul was well away. Paul desperately hoped if the guy came to the door himself, he wouldn't remember Paul. That bar had been poorly lit and his face had never been in the light. The guy had been two sheets to the wind anyway. Later on, when he took the picture, the guy didn't see him.

The drive took forever, almost four hours. Unbelievable. By the time Paul reached Frank Benson's neighborhood it was long dark. After cruising the street a couple of times he prepared to head in. Just before he started up the walk he remembered to place the messenger cap on his head. It looked like someone was home, anyway. Just don't recognize me, all right? Please?

"Norman! Norman! It's snowing!" Jean loved snow. She came down the stairs. Through the storm door she could see snow drifting over the porch. A plow grumbled down the street. The Rankin kids were trying to build a snowman next door. They looked so happy, all bundled up, thick snowsuits, bright red in the snow, laughing and shouting, making sure everyone on the street was awake at nine-thirty this Sunday morning. Jean wanted to go out there, join them, be seven years old again with all her life a promise stretching ahead.

Instead she walked into the kitchen wearing her old nightgown, mixed some orange juice, started the coffee.

Stuck in condoland with Norman. The night before, after they made love, he just rolled over, went to sleep, leaving her hanging. At this moment he was probably doing his sit-ups upstairs next to the bed, his daily regime, thirty sit-ups, twenty push-ups, deep knee bends. Not that it helped. Norman was going to be a whale—no matter what he did—by the time he was forty-five. Each year, another two to four pounds. He'd weighed one-sixty at their wedding five years ago. Now he was almost one-eighty-five. His father, who died at forty-eight, had weighed over two-ten. They'd said when Norman's father had died that his arteries were totally obstructed with plaque. Ever since they were first married Jean had tried her best to keep Norman on a low-fat diet.

Jean poured herself a cup of coffee and sat facing the back porch, the long narrow backyard, shared by the East Ridge Association, their condo group. It was the first and only Maplewood condo, snuck in by a sharpie when nobody was looking, three units in a remodeled Victorian monster on a third of an acre. Each unit, three floors, about one and a half rooms to a floor, like living in a hallway, bought for a hundred and ten thousand when they'd been married six months. Then she'd been almost happy, still confident they'd work out the physical thing, expecting to get pregnant, have children as soon as they'd moved in, nice community close to New York, an easy commute for Norman to reach his job with Bonnell Industries, Finance Division, Thirty-sixth Street and Fifth Avenue. Her friends said Norman was a catch, nice middle-management position with one of the largest chemical companies still remaining in the city. An MBA from NYU, grossing forty thousand two years out of business school, nice family background, he would be a good provider. He was sort of cute, a good catch for a twenty-nine-year-old executive secretary working at a law office with no pension plan. All her friends who were still unmarried, from the group she'd grown up with, gone down to the shore with, Belmar, they were jealous.

It didn't work out that way. Maplewood was a great town if you had kids. But they had no kids. Not enough money in the bank yet, they both felt. Norman wasn't "ready." She thought he'd never be ready.

It was one thing, get married, move out of the city to the suburbs, buy something and start building equity. Jean remembered the urge, the need, to own something, but stuck in the suburbs without the main suburban interest—kids—and a husband who more and more seemed capable of providing only money and nothing else . . . he was so boring . . . well. First the "no kids yet" thing. Then the continued sex disaster. The boredom of being stuck in Maplewood while Norman toddled off to work, rattling around the condo. She soon found herself very attracted to one of the guys repairing the new steam boiler in the basement. Long, lanky, corded body, claimed he once rode rodeo at the Flemington Fair Grounds.

Norman, the creep, he never got it, even after seeing the guy when he stayed late finishing the job one night. Norman was so out to lunch sometimes. After that, Jean realized that some men still found her attractive. There were other times, other men. To this day she never crossed the old rug on the hallway floor without remembering what she'd done there, her and that guy.

Soon after that, she got a job of her own, in self-defense, with the convention services company, first as secretary, later as a project planner. Oh, Norman fussed for a while, it didn't match his idea of the perfect wifey, but after she left around articles proclaiming the status related to "double wage-earner professional couples" he shut up.

Once at a New Year's Eve party at Norman's company, she heard someone refer to couples where both worked, no children, as DINKS—double income, no kids—and that fit. Norman was a dink for sure.

The job was nice, let her travel, gave her a breath of fresh air, occasional good sex, she was making almost forty thousand a year now herself, she and Norman were really salting it away, over fifteen hundred a month. She was good at her work. Lately, though, saving all this money, nice as it was, she was thinking maybe it wasn't enough.

She stared at the snow.

Since the flower convention setup in Baltimore, she'd spent one day, Friday, in New York City at the Javits Center, helping a bunch of companies exhibiting packaging containers. It was a small job, but good pay. She took the train with Norman, except by the time the train reached Maplewood there were never two empty seats left together, which was fine by her and probably fine by Norman. God help anyone who interfered with his Holy Mission, or who got between him and his goddamn briefcase, which he locked even at home, considering it more precious than gold. Whatever he did for Bonnell, there must be a lot of secrets. He had been so weird about his work these last few months, often staying for late-night meetings. And so nervous, his careful diet all gone to hell. He was more uptight than usual, stiffer-jawed about everything.

She knew he worked on things having to do with stocks and the raising of money for the company. For some months he had been working on a special project. He would refer to this by talking through his nose like he did whenever he spoke of business. So serious and formal. It was disgusting.

Jean refilled her coffee, beginning to steam just sitting there. It had been five days since Frank. It had been great until the horrible last few moments and the picture, which she didn't want to think about. But whenever she thought of Frank she thought of the picture, had to.

Upstairs she heard the shower running, Norman getting clean for the day.

When she returned from Baltimore, she got together with her friend Beth for lunch on Friday, like they did if she was in the city. Beth was still single, a year younger than Jean, had a good job, owned an apartment ten minutes by PATH from lower Manhattan. She lived in one of the new yuppie growth areas, Hoboken. Jean would bitch about Norman. Beth would bitch about being single and the clock ticking. They'd both reminisce longingly about the weekends years before down at the shore, when anything was possible and anything, almost, was done.

Beth advised Jean to dump Norman.

"Give the creep up, Jean," she'd say.

"For what? So I can be single again, go through all that shit just to find someone else suitable?"

"But him! He'd be cute, if he lost a little weight."

Then, Norman and Jean's relationship out of the way, Jean would listen to Beth strategize on how to better her campaign to find a husband. It wasn't that she couldn't attract men. It was that they were creeps, or lice, or bastards. Right now she had two on the string, Don and John, playing one against the other. John was now in the lead. He had just invited her to meet his parents.

Beth loved to hear about Jean's adventures on the road. Jean knew Beth felt that, being married, Jean could play around, whereas being single and looking, each situation was so loaded. Playing around was more difficult.

Neither Don nor John rang Beth's bell sexually, which to Jean made them both nonstarters. After an hour or so of this talk, Beth folded her hands and leaned close across the table.

"Any news from Baltimore?" She knew Jean had been down there.

"Well . . ." Jean grinned.

"Yes?"

"Well, met this guy. Big guy." Jean paused. "Big, know what I mean?"

Beth giggled.

"I hit on him at dinner, had to. He wasn't easy to get started, but when I got some drinks in him he got started, all right. . . . I got started, too. . . ."

Beth asked for details. After some prodding Jean gave details.

"But at the end!" Jean shuddered. "Here's what happened."

Jean described how someone took their picture in bed together, how when Frank chased the photographer, Jean took off.

Beth and Jean speculated on the purpose of the photo. They had Irish coffee and a rich dessert after lunch.

"His wife hired this guy to follow him."

"I don't know, Beth, he didn't seem like a guy who did that sort of thing a whole lot. In fact, I got tired batting my eyes at him before he did anything!"

"So maybe his wife is suspicious."

"She called when I was with him, actually." Jean blushed, remembering. "Sounded like a weirdo, Beth. I bet she was just checking up, trying to catch him in a compromising position."

"Wouldn't you consider the doggie position a compromising position, Jean?"

"Beth!"

"How about, he's a spy. The picture is for KGB files?"

"I'll get a call from Boris or Ivan: My dahlink, I saw your face in a picture last night. I simply must, must have you!"

"Maybe the whole thing was a mistake."

"Except, Beth, to do it, the guy had to be given a key to the room by someone. It means the hotel was in on it! I don't know. It must have been his wife. That's the easiest explanation."

"No!" Beth began to giggle. "It was Bob Guccione, or Larry Flynt, getting a snapshot for *Penthouse, Hustler,* 'scenes we'd like to see.' You're going to be in the March issue."

"That isn't funny."

That wasn't funny at all. They both decided it had to be Frank's wife, that Jean's face would not be recognizable, what with her hair across her eyes and lips all swollen, puffy, the light so bad. By the end of the lunch, Jean was almost reassured she'd never hear about the event again.

Almost. Now, though, watching the snow, the shower off upstairs, Norman probably about to make his entrance to the kitchen, she felt a twinge, just a twinge, of uncertainty.

"What's for breakfast?"

Norman entered the kitchen. Jean knew she looked terrible, dressed in her oldest and most comfortable nightgown, no makeup, eyes probably baggy from the wine she'd had the night before. She could see his eyes take her in and find her wanting.

He hadn't found her wanting last night, had he?

"What do you want?" Jean always cooked, or made, breakfast, not because Norman couldn't or wouldn't, but because that way she controlled what he ate. Norman's cholesterol count had been as high as 310, but since they had been married Jean had beleaguered and cajoled and forced Norman's eating behavior to change. Most recently, six months before, his count had dropped to 240. Still way too high. For a while he had accepted her diet conditions—cottage cheese, juice, whole wheat bread without margarine, low-fat yogurt, the standard breakfast. But recently he had resisted. A lot, in fact. Over the past several weeks their weekend breakfasts had become strained. Jean stiffened up as Norman gave her a glance and headed for the refrigerator.

"Norman! What are you doing?"

Norman, saying nothing, pulled out milk, eggs, sour cream, and chilled maple syrup. He reached for a bowl and the pancake mix. Then he rummaged in the refrigerator and pulled out Jean's bacon, placing a half dozen strips on a griddle.

"Norman!" This was the fifth or sixth weekend in a row he'd done this!

"You want some, Jean?" Norman asked, stirring.

"How can you do this! Didn't what the doctor said all those times sink in?" Jean watched in horror as Norman's belly bulged against the counter while he ladled sour cream into the pancake batter. Jean was furious, sputtering with anger.

"Nothing like an ex-smoker to get all high and mighty, Jean," Norman said, calmly continuing to stir batter. Then he turned the bacon. Jean wanted to hit Norman in the face. She couldn't believe it.

Norman started to smile.

"You're being such an asshole, Norman!"

"No, I'm not."

"But, Norman, your poor heart!"

"Whatever." Norman poured three large pancakes on the griddle after removing the bacon. He munched one of the pieces as he watched the pancakes bubble. "Paper here?"

"Didn't check." She wanted to kill him.

He gave her a look, went to the front door. The paper was lying under a small drift on the porch. He shook the snow all over the hallway floor.

The phone shrilled.

"Norman there?"

It was one of Norman's work cronies.

"Hello. Yes . . . yes . . . no." Norman went into his Deference Before Authority pose: his shoulders in and down, head thrust forward, talking to some superior at work. Even on the phone. "Yes . . . yes . . . of course . . . no problem."

Hanging up, he glanced at Jean, then started from the kitchen.

"Get dressed, I need to go to the station."

"What?"

"That was Wentworth at the office. He has called an emergency meeting of the special project team. I must be there as soon as possible."

Jean looked at the snow, now nine inches deep and drifting.

"I can't drive in this!" Norman had not yet arranged to put snow tires on their Toyota. Jean, as a matter of principle, refused to have anything to do with auto maintenance or upkeep. For this reason their automobile was always in the shop, as Norman cared nothing about the car, either. She spoke to empty space. Norman was already upstairs changing into a suit.

There was a train in fourteen minutes. They lived just a mile from the station. By the time Jean had managed to back over the plowed hump at the driveway entrance and negotiated the streets past the park, the train was rounding the corner into the station.

Norman leapt from the car, already wearing his at-work expression, *Sunday Times* Business Section clutched in his hand, slamming the door and racing for the train.

Jean watched him go. He made it just in time, swinging aboard, never looking back. He disappeared into the car as the train headed off toward the Oranges, Newark, New York.

Jean stared as the diminishing red lights of the train were swallowed by the snow. She shut off the engine, left the car, walked across the small plaza to a coffee shop. It would be a long day alone in the house, even longer without having Norman for company. Maybe she'd find a friend or an acquaintance while getting coffee and a doughnut. But there was no one there she knew, just a group of strangers brought together by the heavy snow and their adventures reaching the center of town. After half a cup she left, returned to the car, struggled home.

They lived halfway up a gentle hill behind the park. The car nearly failed to make it to her drive. By now the Rankin kids were whiter than the snow itself. The snow was just wet enough to pack and they had rolled up several two-foot snowballs and were making a fort.

Jean watched the kids from the car. She'd see what movies were on HBO. Maybe Beth was free, but Beth was way off in Hoboken. No, this weekend Beth was skiing up at Hunter with John. Or Don. Whoever.

Jean was getting out of her car when she looked back and saw Norman's precious briefcase. The creep was in such a hurry he'd left it on the back seat.

Back in the unit, a fresh pot of coffee on the stove, Jean placed the briefcase on the table, stared at it a while. Then she tripped the latches. To her astonishment the briefcase snapped open. Norman must have skipped sit-ups this morning and been working upstairs and left it unlocked.

Jean knew very little of Norman's work. In fact, she knew virtually nothing. He refused to tell her much, not that she asked very often, except he "crunched numbers" for Bonnell and was now working on some special project, very hush-

hush. Once he had tried to explain what he did. It was so dull Jean never bothered to ask again. Something about cash flow, net present value analysis, and so forth, very dull. Lately, however, he seemed to be harboring some internal secret or something. He was very self-important about this project and recently she'd become very curious about just what he did.

Actually, she'd been wondering a lot. He made good money, deposited a hefty sum every two weeks into the joint account. Beth had started Jean down this road, wondering about Norman's work. Beth said, dump the creep, divorce him, but first take him for your rightful share, which is half. Find out how much he has, don't you know that?

Jean did not know, not really. Now, standing over the unlatched briefcase, knowing Norman was probably entering Hoboken terminal and would be gone for the day, she smiled.

Opening the briefcase, she saw a savings bankbook, not from the bank they did their joint checking or savings with, but another bank! She flipped it open and scanned its contents. The bankbook contained twenty-four thousand dollars! It had all been deposited on a single day in September.

Jean sat down and gasped.

Then she rapidly looked through the other stuff in the case. Papers and memos, even what looked like blueprints, something to do with some new product. She could not make head nor tail of them.

Twenty-four thousand dollars. In their name. There it was, Norman and Jean Newman. Almost as much as they had jointly saved these past three years.

She stared into her backyard.

Here this past year she'd been so busy being mad at him she'd stopped paying attention. She had plunged headfirst into her own work to offset the emptiness at home. Had she forgotten something he'd told her? Was he a lot more subtle than she thought? Was it possible this account had some perfectly reasonable explanation?

The long day ahead with the snow began to look better.

Hours and hours to figure out just what was going on. That something was going on, Jean was sure.

Michelle looked out the bedroom window, saw the snow, started in.

"Frank, it's snowing. Before you settle down to watch the football game you better shovel the front walk and clear the driveway. Also shovel a good path from the driveway to the back door and shovel the front walk, too. We need to get the snow tires on the station wagon. You didn't do that last weekend even though I asked you and here it is with a lot of snow on the ground and we don't have the snow tires on yet. Remember Suzie has her piano recital at the Legion Hall across town at four today, and visiting hours for your father are one to seven Sundays . . ."

On she went, her gray voice steadily providing instruction, without pause, not stopping until she had dressed and left for the kitchen, talking on and on in that monotone she had been using, it seemed, for years. Where was the bright-eyed, funny, *alive* girl he had been so attracted to, it seemed like yesterday?

Snowing. Like they said it would. No piano recital today, that's for sure. Should be a good ballgame. He was still a Giants fan after all these years. Probably like a lot of men his age who as youngsters watched Conerly, Huff, Grier, Gifford and dreamed. He had been thirteen when he watched the famous 1958 game between the Colts and Giants, overtime. It had snowed then, too.

Talk, *Jesus,* she could talk.

Lying in bed, facing a slow Sunday, Frank Benson gazed toward the ceiling. Their bedroom, crouched under the eaves at the back of the house, felt cozy with the storm outside and Michelle mercifully silent downstairs, fixing breakfast.

This was a decent house. Nice house. Bought in 1972, eight percent interest, the down payment a wedding present from his dad, who even then was starting to fail. He'd changed a lot since before Frank went in the service in the spring of 1963. Right after high school, Frank joined the marines. Fourteen months later, Tonkin Gulf. After advanced infantry training, Frank was overseas. Him and all the other kids, wide-eyed and eager for war, feeling lucky they had the chance, for Christ's sake. That jubilation hadn't lasted long. Back then his dad had been his dad, not sick with the cancer.

Long time ago, over twenty years. He'd been married to Michelle over sixteen years. What had happened to her, to them, to change their life from the joy it had first been to the flatness of today?

Suzie was now fourteen, Brad twelve.

As he now often did, Frank wondered. He wondered how his life came about, whether all men his age secretly felt it was all passed by, going through the motions. What happened to the promise of endless years ahead to grow and alter the world? Would there ever be another heart-stopping moment looking at a girl so lovely it was true love on sight, like it had been with Michelle in 1970? He wondered these days if he'd ever have again the wide-open, alive sense he had on his return to the world in 1968, at least before he got off the plane and saw what a lot of people felt about him. Here he lay, forty-three, going on forty-four, feeling sorry for himself. The only things brightening his life were Suzie and Brad, who were often elsewhere on their own projects or far away from him when he was on the road. Despite the guilt, he'd felt alive with that Jean in Baltimore, felt able to create the self he wanted to be for just a few short hours.

But then he blinked, lying in bed, shook his head. He knew what it was: fear. The financial terror of the past couple of years, trying to make ends meet as the bills for his father mounted and grew, as the insurance ran out and he did what he felt he had to do to cover the difference—his secret. His future doom, he was sure. But what could he do? The scam, he called it. Sometimes he tried to rationalize it as his way of connecting to the energy he had first felt as a good, second all-state linebacker in high school, the aliveness when on patrol before he ended up in a haze at the end of his second tour. But he knew he was kidding himself.

A radioman-rifleman in the marines. Some police experience as an MP in Okinawa. From that, trade school after coming home, electronics, computers. It seemed natural to slide into the security business when he got out of school in 1970. That and computers, he was good at. A good technician, too. And as computers grew and the fear of robbery grew he found himself as a self-employed consultant to banks and corporations in the Middle Atlantic states.

Put anyone near a vault enough times, they get itchy fingers. He watched college costs shoot through the roof. Michelle was unable to go to work due to her nervous condition. He figured it was normal, getting itchy fingers, no big deal. But then in the past two years the costs to carry his dad's treatment changed things.

It started cautiously, shaving hundredths of cents from computerized accounts. Instead of rounding off, move the tenths of cents to a new account accessible from any terminal, any city. At first he just tried it to see if it could be done. He programmed it from his computer in the guest room with just a modem and the passwords he knew from his security assignments with banks. He was amazed how fast the fractions of cents added up, virtually untraceable. He moved the money from account to account before going offshore by wire to a Bermuda bank. Then back to the U.S. in anonymous bearer bonds, to be invested by his friend and broker, Terry, his partner in the deal for thirty percent. He believed it was a secure system. He'd started it very carefully and slowly. Now entering his third year, he was drawing off eleven banks, all widely scattered, no way to trace him, he was almost sure. *Almost.* Lately, though, he had grown uncertain. Yet, as quickly as his secret cash account grew, his dad's hospital bills grew faster. In the last three weeks the bills had escalated again. Although he still had over two hundred grand salted away—enough to cover any contingency with his dad and leave a fund for other things—his fear remained, had increased.

He had this fantasy, more than half serious, to escape, with Michelle, a different Michelle, free from those goddamn little helpers she took morning and night that zoned her out, that turned her into a zombie. Take off to the Pacific Rim, his latest place (earlier it had been Europe, once South America) where money went far, life was easy. Or they could go to Paris. Anywhere, he never could choose. He was amused, and sometimes troubled, by these dreams. But they played on in his head.

The fear ate at him. He thought of the photograph.

He rolled out of bed, shivering as he bent to pull on some pants. Shaving in the bathroom he thought: When's it gonna hit? Phone call? Letter? Jesus, now when the phone rang his heart started pounding. He ran to the mailbox when he spotted the mailman. Someday, somehow, that photograph's gonna come his way. Was it Michelle setting up a divorce action? Was it someone else, trying to set him up, force him to show them the way into the other banks? Another hustler? The feds?

"Ouch." He cut his cheek shaving.

It couldn't be Michelle. She was either a real good actress or she didn't care at all because he felt no heat from her on that end, none.

Frank knew in his heart it was just a matter of time before someone else, along the way, noticed the scam. It was such a simple concept he was sure a lot of other computer guys were on the same game.

"Hey, Dad," Brad called from his room.

"Morning, kiddo."

Brad's room was a lot like his own room when he was a kid, except Frank never had a billion Lego blocks for cars, planes, trucks, space stations, plus a billion more lost from previous structures and stored in a huge box. He'd never had a computer in his room, either, because they didn't have such things thirty years ago. But just like Brad, he liked to make plastic models, hang warplanes from the ceiling, build a regular air force.

"Look." Brad was now working on a big ship model, the *Cutty Sark*. He'd finished the painting and assembly. Now he was working on the rigging. "I just finished the standing rigging. Took me a month."

"That's terrific." The ship looked great. Where'd this kid get the patience, the quiet ability to focus his attention and take the necessary time? Not from Frank, that's for sure. Well, actually, maybe some. He could wait, too, but for a twelve-year-old the kid was amazing. Except when it came to homework.

"Big snowstorm today, huh?" Frank liked snowstorms.

"Radio said fifteen inches! Maybe no school tomorrow!" Brad was carefully, oh so carefully, threading a tiny line through a tiny tackle block, now starting on the running rigging. He'd maybe have the model finished by the middle of the winter, and by then it would be perfect. Frank wished Brad brought the same focus to school, but neither Brad nor Suzie were much in the way of students.

On the way down the hall he thought, I wasn't much of a student either.

Learned enough, though, he thought, secretly proud to be established in this home in a nice suburb, enough money, future looking bright. He'd even have to hire someone soon to help him in his business. He'd been avoiding it too long as it was. With only a high school education, he'd learned a dozen ways to cuff the question, where'd you go to school?

Suzie and Michelle were at the kitchen table, Michelle reading the paper, Suzie plowing through the comics. Watching his daughter, Frank realized it wouldn't be too many years before she'd be a grown woman. He suddenly saw that her lower lip was thrust out, pouting. She and Michelle must have argued about something. That lip he found so irritating on her was exactly the type of mouth that attracted him most to strange women.

"How about French toast, Suzie?" Frank loved French toast. He often made it for his kids and himself on Sunday mornings. It was the only time during the week he allowed himself eggs. For the previous two years he had cut way down on fatty foods and cholesterol. He tried to get healthy.

"I already ate, Dad."

"Frank, I don't know why you persist in eating that food. The eggs will only worsen your cholesterol count and you know what the doctor said!" Michelle didn't even look up from the paper. Frank sighed.

"Maybe later this afternoon the roads'll be clearer, be easier to get to the hospital."

"Supposed to snow all day," Michelle said, staring now fixedly as Frank started breaking eggs into a bowl before adding a dash of milk to soak the bread.

"Well, then I won't bother to go," he said, baiting her a little, stirring the eggs.

"What, leave your father without a visit from you? You know how he looks forward to your visits!"

That's it, damned if you do, damned if you don't, Frank thought. I wish now and then you'd come with me on these visits. He cared for you, too, even if you didn't like him. But he said, "Want to come with me?" knowing what her answer would be.

Frank had breakfast, coffee, read the paper. Then, tired of Michelle's expectant sighs and significant glances toward the snow drifted against the window over the sink, he pulled on a pair of boots, sweatshirt, and went to work outside with the snow shovel.

Practically every health tip he read in magazines found in doctors' or dentists' waiting rooms, collections of the worst magazines he'd ever seen, said shoveling snow was bad for the heart. A weak heart, maybe. Frank actually liked the exercise. It used his arms, back, even legs. He'd get going on the driveway like a steam engine, up one row and down another, warming into it. First he cleared the path from the back door. That stretched him out, got him loose. Then the front walk, which was two shovels wide, and after that, he'd find the breathing pace, a little heavier this day because the snow was wet, heavy, almost a foot thick. By the time he reached the driveway, his sweatshirt was off, just a turtleneck now. He took thirty-seven minutes to do it all, walks, drive, even the mailbox out by the street.

Forty-three, by God, still in pretty good shape, though the steady seven-minute miles were a few years behind him; his knees were no good anymore. He stood for a while, cooling off, watching the snow continue to fall. Most days, mornings, he still did the air force exercises he'd done since he left the service. An old military habit he supposed, though lately he'd exercised to burn off the hangover from the night before. It was a quick, if painful, way to clear the head.

After lunch he drove over to visit his dad.

Michelle didn't come, of course, and he no longer tried to get Brad or Suzie to accompany him. Too painful for them, he supposed. He understood that. It was almost too painful for him, too: the old man shrunken, almost hollow, it seemed. Nothing but chin, nose, sunken bright eyes. All there mentally, though. The cancer was in the final stages. The doctors kept saying anytime now, but anytime now had stretched to six weeks.

Six weeks at two hundred seventy per day, plus twice that much in drugs and treatment. Frank didn't begrudge the private room so his dad could face his pain with some dignity, but the insurance had run out long ago and already the bill was over forty thousand dollars. Frank didn't begrudge that, either, because he had the scam to pay it, but Michelle didn't know that and he had to do a lot of fast talking to explain to her why his dad wasn't on the street and why their bank account wasn't empty now the insurance had lapsed.

Far as he was concerned, he wanted his dad home with him for his last few days, but Michelle had a fit when he mentioned it a week before. She wanted nothing to do with bedpans and caring for him, which Frank knew would be mostly her job with him working. She didn't want anything to do with it. It would be too painful for her, she said. He understood her position, but it hurt.

He was about ready to just drop work for a while and do it

anyway, care for his dad himself, except the doctor kept saying any moment now and the move itself might kill him.

At the hospital he steeled himself before opening his dad's door.

"Dad? It's me, Frankie."

The room was dark, blinds drawn. Huddled under the blankets his father lay on his back, tubes in his arms, down his nose, needing a shave, opening his eyes at the sound of Frank's voice.

When Frank reached the bedside and touched his dad's scrawny hand, his dad gripped Frank with surprising strength. He was in pain, Frank could see that, even though the pain was several layers removed by the Demerol dripping into his arm.

"Frankie."

"How you doing, Dad?" Frank sat by the bed, somewhat toward his dad's feet so his dad didn't have to turn his head to see him, just his eyes.

His dad grimaced around the tubes.

"Bad. This is real bad. Same as ever." He could hardly speak, his voice was a croak. Somehow, though, he smiled.

"It's snowing, Dad, a real blizzard. Want to see the storm? I'll open the blind."

"Snow. Huh, seen a lot of that already. Seen enough. No, don't open the blind. The light hurts my eyes. Michelle, the kids all right?"

"Fine. They're not with me because—"

"I know," his dad said, cutting off Frank's lie.

"Brad's finishing the *Cutty Sark*. Boy, does he have patience, Dad."

"You did okay as a kid, too, Frankie."

"Suzie's got a piano recital today."

"Still on in the snow?" His dad was definitely all there mentally.

"Doubt it. Michelle thinks so. Suzie, no. They had a big argument about it just before I left. Michelle is bound and determined to go."

42

"Huh." His dad tried to change position, feebly scratching the sheets. "Michelle's nervous problem any better?"

"Not really, Dad. You know her doctor, Schwartz? He's prescribed her pills for years. Well, last month he told her to stop taking them for a while, and she's become a real monster."

"Addicted to them."

"Must be." Frank thought it made sense, thinking about it.

"Business good?"

"Fine. Just fine."

After a long silence his dad's hand relaxed. He smiled at Frank and shook his head.

"Tired. Sleep."

He closed his eyes. Frank watched him fall asleep suddenly, limp, breath slow and fluttery. He sat there with his father, holding his hand, for a long time. Later on a nurse came in, checked the tubes, smiled at Frank, and left.

When the day had gone dark enough for the snowflakes outside to be lost in the black, Frank bent over, kissed his dad on the forehead, whispered, "I love you, Dad," and left.

On the way out he ran into Dr. Andros, the guy who'd been treating his father. He was surprised to see him at the hospital on a Sunday.

"Frank. How are you? He's about the same."

"I know."

"These patients in the final stages, some of them let it take them. It runs very fast once it goes systemic, they pass on very rapidly. But others, like your father, they fight to the end. Last week I was sure he was failing fast, but now who knows? He's tough as nails, your father, he could hang on some time."

Last week he was saying any day now. Now it's who knows.

"What about him coming home with me?"

"You asked about that last week, didn't you?" Dr. Andros, a slight, meticulous man, gazed up at Frank. "Expensive, Frank. Intrusive to your family, very intrusive."

"But possible?"

"It's up to you and your family, of course, and it will be difficult, but, yes, possible."

"Good."

"You were very close, weren't you?"

Frank nodded. Close, yes, they'd been close, just him and his dad after his mother died in 1958, the seventh grade. He'd heard about it in homeroom period, his dad standing at the classroom door. *What's he doing here?* he remembered thinking, knowing even before his teacher and dad called him out to the hall it was very bad news.

"Yeah, we were close, you could say that."

"Why don't you think about it, discuss it with your family, give me a call tomorrow?"

"Sure."

Back in the car Frank thought about it. He had three projects coming up, one he could commute to from home, the other two in New Jersey, a very long, but maybe possible, commute. He could at least be home most of the time, care for his father himself, hire help for when he wasn't there, take the pressure off Michelle. Then he remembered Michelle had plans for the family to visit her folks over Christmas, all of them drive down to Atlantic City, stay over there ten days. His idea of living hell was staying in that enormous, glitzy, overstuffed house, feeling all crowded and confined, facing ten days of beady-eyed interrogation from Michelle's mother and father. Frank was certain her father was one of the Bad Guys, connected somehow, a slick and smooth attorney for the goombahs who ran a couple of the casinos. The man made him extremely nervous, like he was always just about to make Frank an Offer He Couldn't Refuse. Frank knew Michelle's marrying him had not been approved. Their relationship, recently, last couple of years, had been terrible, and that had been clear to everyone when they had visited the previous summer.

Frank knew Michelle's father could make life very difficult

if he wanted to, if he had the goods on him, and all of a sudden a light went on.

The fucking picture in Baltimore, of him with Jean. It had to be Michelle's old man. That's why Michelle was so obtuse about it all. She didn't know. Frank could picture it now in Atlantic City, first night there, after dinner, in the study with Roland, as her father consented to be called. Roland would reach in the big desk, pull the picture from the drawer, lay it before him; now let's talk about what you should do.

Skidding around the corner in the snow, entering his street, he thought, on the other hand, I bring my dad home for his last days, have to care for him, I'll stay here. I got the perfect excuse to avoid going to Atlantic City at all, and I got my dad where he belongs. Without Michelle, the kids here being hassled or resentful, everyone out of the way for ten days, maybe my dad's last ten days.

He'd have to shovel everything again. There were five more inches in the drive. Michelle had in fact taken off with the station wagon he'd neglected to put the snow tires on. She was driving to or from the certainly canceled recital.

Getting out of the car, Frank chuckled. Roland, his father-in-law, it wasn't Roland had him scared. He just didn't want to go off to the in-laws this Christmas. Not with his father the way he was. Not with the worries about that photograph.

Shit, he thought, it's four-fifty-five, I missed the entire Giants game. I'll shovel the drive again, settle down, have a couple of real stiff drinks, lay the news on Michelle when she gets back.

She ain't gonna like it.

Chapter Three

SUNDAY AFTERNOON

Midafternoon, still snowing hard. By now Jean was bored to death cooped up in the condo rattling around with nothing good to read, no good movies on television, too much snow to go anywhere, visit anyone. She prepared Christmas cards in the kitchen. Norman might be home within the next hour or two.

After Norman left she tried for nearly three hours to discover what else Norman had hidden around. There were no clues in the briefcase. She thought the designs were for some kind of medicine, or something having to do with drugs, but she was not sure because they were so hard to understand.

What she couldn't miss were the big "confidential" stamps all over the documents or the numbers in the upper right-hand corner: 1-B. Was there a 1-A also? These were obviously partial plans for some new product. Other memos in the briefcase outlined a schedule for something called Choice to be "rolled out" in the spring. Discussion of stock issues, finances to be raised, some handwritten notes on a separate pad she could not decipher. Nothing she could see, nothing in the briefcase or elsewhere in the condo that would explain the bankbook and its sum of money.

Along the way she found an earring lost almost a year, a misplaced packet of birth control pills, Norman's secret shoe box of treasures from the past including three love letters from junior-high sweethearts and a third-place ribbon for a track event, which must have been when he weighed one-forty, a long time before they met. She also found an extremely interesting, obviously well-used collection of erotic magazines, carefully stored in a drawer in the old bureau stuffed in the bedroom closet. She was shocked to find them. Her Norman? Undersexed Norman? Looking at the pictures, she got pissed. Here the bastard was so fucking squeamish with her, rubbers all the time, no tongue stuff, lights off mostly—the bastard collected pictures of threesomes, four-somes doing everything. Even one big color magazine, noth-ing but cum shots. He probably masturbated looking at these pictures, Jean thought. She was a little shook, to be truthful. He found her unattractive somehow, was that it?

Later on, end of the day, bored, bored, bored, she pulled out the collection again, looked through it, and found herself getting aroused. Plenty aroused, come to think of it.

She went upstairs, took care of that, came downstairs, went back to the Christmas cards.

The telephone rang. She let it go a few times. Let the creep suffer, maybe even make him walk home through the snow—although by now the plows were keeping up and she knew she could drive all right—let the bastard suffer.

"Hello."

It wasn't Norman.

"Jean Newman, please."

This was a strange voice.

"Speaking." For some reason Jean sat down.

"Are you alone, Jean?"

Jean had a way of dealing with guys like this, she used to get calls like this all the time living in the city.

"Listen, you creep, I'm not alone, and if you call again you'll have to answer to the cops!" She slammed down the phone.

It rang again.

"Listen, lady, I am not a nut caller."

Jean began to feel nervous. What was this?

"I know you are alone. Your husband, Norman Newman, is in New York, right?"

"Who is this?"

"Relax, Jean." This was the last thing Jean was about to do, relax, her hands were sweating, she was sitting down, edge of the seat, waiting. For what? "Last week you arranged a flower show in Baltimore, right?"

"Baltimore," she said. Perhaps this guy was in the trade-show business.

"Yeah, Baltimore. Lovely show, I understand. Well attended. Nice setup, I hear."

"Thank you." What the hell was this about? Alarm bells, serious alarm bells, were starting to ring.

"And you were booked out by the airport, right?"

Uh-oh. That was what this was about.

"Go on."

"Is that necessary? How about room five-one-eight, Holiday Inn, a Tuesday night? Franklin Benson?"

Jean remembered the flash that night. She was blinded, interrupted in her ecstasy. She saw it all again and shuddered.

"What do you want?"

Even in her shock she saw this was no divorce thing, this was something else. Blackmail.

"Would you like to receive the photo? And the negative? To insure neither the negative nor the photo falls into the wrong hands? Norman's hands, for example? Your employer's hands? The hands of a magazine featuring an amateur photo section?"

"What do you want?"

"Good. Got your attention now, right? Norman should be returning home soon. He left his briefcase on the way to work today, right? You have to photocopy what's in that case before you pick him up at the station tonight."

"He's due home anytime now!"

"Better get moving, then. Think of this as a dry run, Jean. A test." Bullshit, whoever he was, he wanted those plans, or the bankbook, an idiot could see that. Jean suddenly remembered the library was open until six Sundays.

"And if I do? Copy them?"

The line was dead. Jean looked over at the unlocked briefcase. She put the phone down, punched her thighs with her fists, rapidly, lightly, shaking her hair.

"Jesus. Jesus. Jesus."

The picture! It was her all along! Not Frank! Jesus! This was all to do with those plans! How did the caller know Norman was in New York anyway? Was he watching the house? She moved away from the window. This was pressure on her to get some plans from Norman. He couldn't be in on it, could he?

The idea of Norman seeing the picture made her cringe. He sure wouldn't put it in there with his collection, no, sir. The idea of that picture ending up with her boss, or, even worse, far worse, published! That made her skin crawl, just thinking of it.

She made herself a cup of coffee. While it was brewing she drank a beer, then another.

Maybe that guy Frank set this up, had it planned. But he was in the picture, too. And why? The guy was married. He had nothing on Jean. As soon as she had seen him enter the dining room that night she'd known right off, here was a possible, a likely one. Dressed nice, big but kind looking, decent body but no ego-driven bodybuilder, the sort who got off only watching themselves, not the women they were with. Soon as he sat down, ordered a drink, then another, and she came on to him, she knew then this guy might take some work but the drinks would make him loose for the night, like she was loose. Nothing else. No hidden agendas about ungrateful spouses or bullshit lies like saying, in response to the are-you-married question, yes, but separated. None of that. This had been straightforward nice sex: We're both loose for the night, let's have a good time, laugh together while talking and then get into it.

It couldn't be Frank, Jean figured. It couldn't be Norman.

She knew Norman, or thought she did until she'd found his stash of porno books today. They had a shared vision, she thought, to move out horse country way, Bernards Mountain, out with the mansions and farms. Jean would be the pretty wife to accompany him. It was her dream, too. She'd give him pretty babies and good sex. She did give him good sex, damnit; what'd he need those pictures for?

She didn't honestly know anymore. Today she'd discovered Norman had two secrets she now knew of—one not so big, the sex books, and the other much bigger, the twenty-four thousand. Maybe there were others.

"Well." She spoke aloud, for the comfort of hearing her own voice. "Well." She laughed, a hollow chuckle, not funny at all.

Chances are whoever's after me with that picture is also after Frank for whatever he's hiding. He's probably hiding something. A man like that, he'd probably been around the block a few times. Jean had found, in her experience with men, most had something to hide, and a lot of such secrets had more to do with money than sex. I wonder if Frank's been approached yet? He said he lived just outside Philadelphia. I wonder, is he being called, too?

Shit, there was no one, absolutely no one, she could call for advice on this.

"Frank." She could call Frank. Oh, boy, would he love to hear from her! Most likely, he was as disgusted by the end of that evening as she had been, probably cringed even thinking of it like she did. But she could call him. He might understand.

Assuming he wasn't in on it.

In on what? *What?*

Getting a little drunk here, she thought, feeling the warm beer buzz and the need to use the toilet. The phone rang; it was Norman.

"Jean, I'm at the station. Can you pick me up?" Like nothing was going on.

"I'll be there soon."

The station was not far from the library, which had a copy

machine. Which library was open, weather permitting, until six, Sundays.

Jean rushed from the house with the case and drove as fast as she dared to the library. With nightfall the air had chilled and the roads were icy, although by now the snow had virtually stopped. Jean rushed into the library, open only fifteen more minutes. She gathered a pile of quarters from her pocketbook and began to run the briefcase material through the photocopy machine. The blueprints, or plans, too big to fit all at once, had to be copied several times, each copy a different section. The typed notes on the stock offering were easy.

She also made copies of Norman's bankbook.

When she finished the librarian had closed off all the lights and was ready to leave, get home this snowy Sunday night.

"I'm amazed you were open today," Jean said, gathering the papers, replacing the originals in the case exactly as she remembered finding them, thrusting the copies she had made into her coat pockets.

"So am I." The librarian was a friendly woman Jean's age. "I came in here at two. I had filing to do. Actually a lot of people came by. Sort of like one of those stops as they bushwhacked around town."

Jean smiled.

"I know, this morning I took my husband to the train, it was a real challenge. I'm sorry to keep you here, I had this last minute copying to do."

"No hurry," the librarian said.

"Thanks."

They left together. Jean offered Joan, whose name she'd seen on the desk at the main counter, a ride, but Joan preferred to walk, striding off across the parking lot in high boots, a book bag over her shoulder. Joan seemed to think life was still a college campus, her face clear, open, totally free of guile. Jean watched her cross the lot.

On to Norman, standing on the platform, stamping his feet. Jean had left the briefcase on the front seat, his seat, sending him a message. Norman had to place it on his lap in order to sit down. He got it, she could see, understood her message. He avoided her eyes, staring straight ahead.

"I called over thirty minutes ago."

"Why not wait in the coffee shop across the street? I'd have looked for you over there."

"It was closed, Jean. Long time to wait in the cold." Norman glanced furtively at Jean. She caught it. He was worried. Had she opened the case? What would he say?

They drove over freezing pavement, the temperature plummeting. The car skidded as they turned up the hill.

"You have something to explain?" Jean asked ominously.

"What? This is easy to explain," Norman said. Jean smiled. It was impossible to explain. How could he explain it? She waited for his explanations, expecting:

The bankbook is my Christmas present to you and to us, a fund for trips. We'll take a lot of trips this year, go to the Caribbean for a Club Med vacation; or—

The bankbook is a company fund, in our name for the moment in my capacity in the finance department. It is registered in our name for corporate tax reasons, and in fact will be returned to the general fund within a few days; or—

The bankbook? Just funds established for an end-of-the-year bonus to me, structured this way to reduce my tax liability; or—

What? That book? None of your business!

"So explain," Jean said once they were back in the kitchen.

"Explain what?"

Jean wasn't surprised. Norman had taken the "What? What bankbook?" approach. Enough already. But when Jean started in he was surprised, although not as surprised as she was. She had meant to start with the briefcase, then maybe work up to Norman's secret collection and what that meant with respect to the two of them.

But instead of the briefcase, she began, "You bastard! You hypocritical shit! For almost five years I've lived with all this stuff about how you don't like the messiness of sex. Oh, you deny it, but I can tell! For Christ's sake, you lying creep! All this time you, you bastard, you treat me like some kind of china doll, must be afraid I'm some kind of evil whorelike person, I don't know. All this time instead of being with your wife you're looking at stuff like this!''

She threw his most dog-eared magazine on the table. She had stored it under a paper.

"You're just like a little boy, afraid of women, afraid of everything, probably one of those who has to have the lights off even alone, for God's sake!''

Jean surprised herself. She hadn't planned to get into this, not until after the briefcase. She had taken one of Norman's magazines from the collection, stored it under a paper on the table, with vague ideas of perhaps showing it to Beth or another friend in the coming week. she had not, consciously anyway, intended to confront Norman with it, although she knew she was pissed about the sex thing. But still, she surprised herself, the words just came pouring out.

Norman was mentally primed for some fast talking on the briefcase issue, a strong series of outright denials because he could think of no ready explanation. He had been working on a manufactured counterrage to offset Jean's and was entirely unprepared for this sudden, and, in his developing black anger, totally unjustified invasion of privacy.

"You prying, sneaking bitch!'' Never before in all their years together had he yelled at her. This was unique. Jean took a step back, almost as if she were blown back by the gust of reaction. "Get off your high horse! I know all about you, Jean, all about what you do on your road trips. Don't play this game with me! Hypocrite! I'm a hypocrite? It's you, not me! I at least stay faithful to you. But you, I know what you do. Your fucking friends hint broadly enough about that subject, for Christ's sake!''

Jean was silent before this angry, unfamiliar Norman.

"You think you're such a precious commodity, like it's a gift for us to be together. Be honest here. You claim it's me who's all prissy but it's you who makes the remarks about showers, cleanliness. It's you, not me, never fails to talk about the 'messiness of sex,' and it's you, not me, who doesn't want kids. Don't deny it, get honest here!''

Norman was shaking, he was so angry.

Jean backed away as Norman yelled. He looked formidable just now, nothing like the potato she usually thought he was; more like a granite boulder, eyes snapping behind his glasses, shoulders rolled forward aggressively, even in his anger speaking and shouting clearly to make sure she heard every word.

''Which friends, Norman?'' she rallied. Wrong rally.

''Huh. You'd like to know, huh? Who do you think? Who is it you brag all your exploits to, all the details? Who is it you have lunch with every Friday? Who, by the way, can't keep her mouth shut when she calls you on the phone and you're away on a trip. The time you were in Baltimore she called. I said you're at a hotel by the airport, I think. She says, you don't know which hotel? I say you haven't called yet. She says, of course. What am I to think of that?''

Beth, Jean thought. Beth?

She, Jean, didn't want kids? She, the one wanted him prissy? He thought that?

''So, yes,'' he continued, picking up his magazine. ''Big deal. You find my magazines. So what? Tell you something, Jean—think about this—what kind of wife, sexual partner are you? I have to resort to magazines like this for variety, think about that.'' He took the magazine, shoved it in his briefcase. ''Tell you what, you think you're such a hot little number, doing me favors in bed, well, tell you the truth, lately the less good magazines are interesting enough. You're slipping, not what you were a couple of years ago. No indeed!''

He was putting his coat on. Where was he going?

''Jean, you're such a hard-ass on things. You don't even know me! Maybe I'm trying to help us. You ever think of that? Huh?''

Norman shook his head, blinked, stopped for a moment, stared at his wife.

"Look at some reality here, Jean. Accept what you have, and I'm what you have. Believe it or not I care for you, really do, but I won't be patient forever."

"Where are you going?" Jean couldn't believe it. Everything was turned around. Here she thought she had him on the ropes over the briefcase and the bankbook and somehow it was all turned around. This was definitely not the potato she thought she was married to. He was going somewhere. Now who could she talk to about this voice blackmailing her?

"Norman—"

The door slammed.

Oh, I blew it, she thought, staring at the closed door. Instead of finding out about the money and why someone wanted those plans, I went and blew it, just unloaded about the sex thing.

Three big lessons today, not two. This made it a big day, perhaps as big as any she'd ever had. Blackmailed, that was new, too, making it a terrible day as well. But being blackmailed taught nothing. I learned my husband is somehow involved in something delicate enough for me to be blackmailed to get information from him. Then I learned Norman needs to look at pictures because he doesn't find me attractive enough. Third, now I see he isn't the wimp I thought he was. He isn't the person I've been so ruthlessly putting down these past two years.

I'll kill Beth, next time I see her.

I'm all set for that voice who called me earlier today. At least I got Norman's work copied in the library.

The idea of the picture appearing in one of the magazines terrified Jean. As she prepared a Swanson's dinner and mixed a small salad she pictured what would happen: Early summer, six months from now, she's practically forgotten the whole thing, just about convinced herself it never happened to begin with, when the phone rings and it's Beth saying, "Jean, my boyfriend, he brought me this magazine, he thinks it's you in it, in color, no less. No mistaking what moment is captured there. My, but he was big..."

Or, worse, her boss calling her into his office to tell her that her services and skills are no longer "appropriate" for the firm . . .

Or, an old boyfriend or lover passes her on the street sometime in the future and says, "Never thought you'd be so photogenic, dear."

Oh, God, her face and breasts and sex displayed for the entire community to see. She could not imagine what they'd say out here in suburbia. Wouldn't do Norman any good either, not in his work, might harm him, in fact, make his career path a little rocky. To say the least.

On the other hand, picture of her in a magazine, that's what Norman likes these days. It might brighten up their own life a little, think about that.

"Come on, Jean," she muttered aloud.

Without even realizing it, she had consumed the microwave dinner, a dish of ice cream, and made fresh coffee. Somehow she was by the phone, lifting it, calling information asking for a listing for a Frank Benson in Philadelphia, then nearby communities. She received his listing on the fourth try.

He made a little error, Jean thought, my blackmailer, he confirmed that Frank Benson is his real name. If he wasn't lying to me that night, the guy's been around, done some hard time in the army. Maybe he won't get pushed around like I can get pushed around. If I call him and he hasn't been pressured yet by this guy, I'll ruin Frank's day. He'll probably laugh at me if he doesn't hang right up.

But if he, too, is being pressured, he's the person can maybe help me, help us, get that picture back, keep each of our lives in some kind of order. Not that mine, right now, is doing so well in any case.

Oh boy, Frank, this should be a surprise.

She started to dial.

Frank arrived back home just about dark. In the kitchen he mixed himself a double vodka gimlet, plenty of ice, a nice piece of lemon, a good stiff drink.

Michelle wasn't there. Neither was Suzie nor Brad. Frank remembered the piano recital scheduled for that afternoon. He and Suzie were sure it had been canceled, but not Michelle. She wouldn't agree, and he pictured Michelle forcing Brad into a button-down shirt and tie (Suzie was entirely capable of dressing herself properly) all the while working her jaw with anger that he, Frank, had stayed too long at the hospital. In her mind, anything over an hour was too long. So there she would be, left alone again, forced to manage everything again, all the work and worry of making sure Suzie's outfit was on correctly, Brad's fussing under control, his tie on properly. Frank knew she didn't know how to tie a Windsor knot. He could picture it all, saw the station wagon tracks leaving the driveway, imagined Michelle furious, Suzie nervous, and Brad disgusted, lurching through the snow to the closed church hall.

Michelle was so stubborn sometimes. You couldn't tell her anything she didn't want to hear. She was sure to be in a rage if the recital was canceled, yet everything was canceled today. He knew Michelle and the kids would return shortly, the trip futile; that is, assuming she hadn't been hit by another driver this day—the driving conditions were terrible still, and he knew her anger would likely be at a high pitch. Somehow, too, it would be his fault it had all happened.

Jesus, here I am working myself into a state over what I don't know for sure has happened yet. They could arrive this minute and report that Suzie played great. I must be nervous because of what I have to talk about with Michelle tonight: bringing my dad home, missing the family trip to Atlantic City. He was nervous, for he knew his news would come as an unwelcome and distasteful shock.

Taking the shovel, he dropped his coat inside the back door and reshoveled the drive and walks.

Back inside the house, he mixed another stiff drink, flipped on the television to get the West Coast NFL game. Raiding the refrigerator he noticed a fresh lasagna, covered with foil, probably tonight's dinner. He placed the lasagna in the microwave and set the timer for fifteen minutes. Dinner would be ready any time.

On television was the announcer, John Madden. The guy never flew in planes, took the train everywhere, wouldn't fly at all. Frank wished he had the guts or the money to do that. Madden was talking about the "amazing last-minute Giants collapse," all Frank needed to hear.

I'll set a bed up for my dad in here, in the den next to the kitchen and the downstairs bathroom. This will be his area. He can watch television, be close to the food, the action. I won't have to carry him up any stairs. It oughta work all right here. I'll rent one of those hospital beds, line up good professional nursing. The doctor told me he'll give me some names tomorrow, should work good.

Fifteen minutes later the station wagon pulled in the driveway. Frank turned on the light over the back steps, finished making a salad, and placed glasses on the table. He threw another dash of vodka in his drink before the kids came through the back door.

"Warpath, Dad," Brad said.

"The recital was canceled, Dad, just like I told Mom it would be," Suzie said. "Driveway looks nice. What smells so good?"

"Lasagna."

Suzie cringed.

"Lasagna?"

"What's the problem?" Through the window Frank saw Michelle jerk down the garage door.

"That was for tomorrow, for Brad's class trip."

"Oh. Well, chances are that trip'll be canceled. There won't be school tomorrow."

Brad came back into the kitchen after hanging up his coat.

"What smells so good?"

"Don't ask." Frank and the two kids watched the back door.

Michelle was, as Frank knew she would be, absolutely ripped. She would think he had shoveled the driveway too early, long before the snow stopped, before running off to visit his father, all afternoon. Frank knew she couldn't understand it, a whole afternoon in the room with Death itself. She couldn't imagine how he stood it. Frank suspected, though, she was angriest with herself, though she would never tell Frank that, for she had been too stubborn again, had not listened to either Frank or Suzie, and just gone off and hazarded herself and the kids on a long, dangerous drive to nowhere. Frank knew, too, she would be desperate for a little helper. Usually she had her second of the day just before supper. But her doctor had stopped her prescription, and now she had to deal with everything on her own all the time.

When she came in the kitchen she smelled the lasagna right away. Frank was waiting for her to say something. They all were.

"That lasagna, if that is what I smell, is for Brad's class trip tomorrow!"

"Michelle, don't you think that will be canceled?"

Frank was pleading.

Michelle started to retort, then paused, finally nodding, sitting at the table, defeated, tired, depressed.

"I suppose so."

Frank knew there would never be a good time for this. As he started to lay out the dinner, helped by Brad and Suzie, he started in.

"After I saw my dad today I ran into his doctor. He says that dad may live awhile like this, not any better, not much worse. The doctor suggested when I asked him that it would now be possible for me to bring him home—"

As he said this Frank stood by Michelle's chair, looking down at her intently.

"—which I want to do, and plan to do."

There was a silence. Brad and Suzie had nothing to say. Michelle stared back at Frank.

"This means that I will set up the den for him. I can arrange my work to be here most of the time and I plan to hire professional nursing help so you, Michelle, won't have to care for him, and this way he can have a homelike atmosphere until the very end, like one of those hospices. Um, because I will get my father here later in the week I will have to remain here over Christmas while the rest of you go down to visit with the family in Atlantic City."

There. It was all out.

Michelle began to gasp. Suzie and Brad stood transfixed.

"You mean, bring him here, Dad?" Suzie asked.

Michelle caught her breath.

"I can understand bringing him here, Frank, but not come to Atlantic City? You must come to Atlantic City, you know how much I depend on you there, how important it is to my parents to have you there. This is terrible!"

She was recovering fast and Frank did not know how to defuse things. The lasagna sat steaming on the table while his family stared at him, ignoring the food, shocked and stunned by his news. Frank thought of his dad, alone there in that room, still all there upstairs, and he said, "I know this is sudden but—"

The doorbell rang.

"Answer the door, Brad, will you?" Frank spoke without taking his eyes off Michelle. He placed his hand on her shoulder, trying to calm her. She shrugged his hand off, reaching for some food.

"Dad. Some guy here with a delivery letter. You got to sign for it."

Frank said, "Be right back," and went to the front door.

He couldn't believe it. Some guy in a messenger hat working for a delivery company was standing there, hard to see him in the dark, handing over a big envelope, asking if he was Franklin Benson, Holland Drive, Wilton residence. Something familiar about the guy. You don't see a gold tooth too often, not like this guy had. Something about him like he'd seen him before. Frank took the envelope just as the phone rang. Frank grabbed the extension in the front hall.

"I got it, Suzie," he said when Suzie picked up in the

kitchen, and he said to the guy on the front step, "I gotta sign for it, right?" Then, into the telephone, "Hello?"

Paul came into the front hall, doing his best to hide in the shadows. The guy was at least as big as he remembered, bigger even. He had a nice house, nothing too fancy. It sounded like someone crying in the other room. He could hear forks and knives clicking against plates. The rest of his family must be eating. Jesus, he was a strong-looking son of a bitch.

"Hello?" Frank said into the phone, looking at the delivery guy but not really paying attention to him, trying to listen to the phone instead.

"Uh, Frank? Frank, er, Benson?"

"Yes, who is this, please?"

"Er, Frank, ah—"

"Listen, can you hold on a second, please?" Frank held the phone to his chest and scrawled a signature on a sheet handed him by the delivery man. "Thanks, fellah, you got a helluva job, working Sundays in the snow." What was it about this guy that looked familiar? Why was he almost acting as if he wanted to hide? What was it about that gold tooth? Jesus, it flashes when he smiles. As the front door closed on the delivery man Frank said into the phone, "Sorry, what can I do for you?"

"Look, I'm sorry to call you at home, or even to call you at all. I'm the last person in the world I know you want to hear from. But . . . I'm Jean. From Baltimore?"

Frank took a moment for it to register. When it did, he gripped the phone tight and ducked his head away from the door to the kitchen. In the kitchen Michelle, Brad, and Suzie were loudly discussing the issue of his sick father. On the other end of the phone, Jean waited for Frank to hang up, which is what she would have done.

"What are you calling for?" Herpes, she's calling to tell me that. Or she's calling to tell me . . . pregnant. She's pregnant. I got crabs. There's a chance I have AIDS.

"Can you talk?" He thinks I'm calling to tell him I gave

him a social disease, or that he gave me one. Huh. I wish. She chuckled despite herself.

"What's funny?" Frank's family was paying him no attention. They could not hear him from the kitchen. "Yes, I can talk."

"This isn't what you think, Frank, which, if I were you, I would think concerned sex."

"That's a good guess. Does it?"

"Not the way you think."

"In what way does it?"

Frank couldn't help it, even here, in his own house, he remembered how attractive Jean was. At the same time, here, in his own home, talking to this woman made him uncomfortable. It was a contradiction in terms. Without the drinks in him he felt wrong to be doing this.

"I don't have a disease, I am not pregnant . . . I am not calling because I have thought only of you since we met or because I must see you again." Frank was relieved but at the same time a little disappointed. He thought he'd really rung her bell. He had sure thought of her. "But today, just now, I got a call, some guy who is trying to blackmail me about that picture that was taken. I wanted to warn you, tell you you might hear something. I think he's going to chase you, too. Have you heard anything?"

"I haven't." Not yet, anyway. That gold tooth! Only other person I ever saw with a tooth like that, except the movies, was that snake I hit with the beer when I was with Jean! At that moment it struck him who had just been standing in his front hall, in his house. It chilled him. He stared at the envelope he had just signed. "Jesus! Listen, give me a number. I can't talk now!"

He took her number on a card in his wallet, wrote it carefully. "I'll call you later." Hanging up, he raced to the door, looked out. The street was empty, the bogus delivery man long gone. Frank stared at the envelope. In the kitchen the kids and Michelle were arguing. Hands trembling, Frank tore open the flap. Inside were a note—"I'll call"—and a photograph.

Even before turning the picture over Frank knew what it was.

Outside, leaving Frank's neighborhood, Paul headed straight back to Baltimore. He needed the sleep, he was damn lucky to get out of there in one piece.

In Maplewood, Jean placed the phone back on the wall and shook her head, feeling foolish, tiny, and exposed. Not a good feeling.

Chapter Four

MONDAY MORNING

Wentworth Randall, Junior, administrative assistant to the CEO, Bonnell Corporation, rested and prepared for the week ahead, arrived forty-five minutes early for the nine o'clock special projects team meeting. He nodded hello to Stella, Ironjaw's personal secretary, and entered the conference room. Stella, naturally, had arranged everything in its proper order. The chairs around the long table were pulled back. A black pad of paper rested on the table in front of each chair. Each place had its own glass of water, with fresh ice cubes still gently clinking. The red knitted seat cushions were a nice contrast to the dark walnut chairs and shining table. Yellow pads, a thin pencil beside each, were precisely arranged. Coffee, already brewed, waited on the credenza.

Stella had been Ironjaw's secretary for thirteen years, starting with him back when he was deputy chief financial officer, before he earned his nickname. She, in fact, greatly resented the way Ironjaw's new administrative assistant, Wentworth Randall, Junior, assumed that because he was Ironjaw's main boy he had the right, the duty, to lord over Stella's work.

When she arrived at seven o'clock this morning the conference room was a shambles, the table gummed with bits of pizza, pizza cartons scattered over the credenza, wastebaskets overflowing with soda cans and crusts of Italian bread, hundreds of sheets of paper crumpled all over the floor. Apparently there had been a weekend meeting. Stella knew Ironjaw had not attended. He had been at Killington for early skiing with his two sons. Even Stella, who never skied, knew the snowstorm must have provided great conditions. He was due in at nine, late for him. Stella had slaved to prepare the room, not for the new administrative assistant, the Perfect Yuppie whom she hated and mistrusted; not for the other executives and staff due to arrive any minute; but for Mannie Maroules, also known as Ironjaw, chief executive officer, the billion-dollar Bonnell Corporation.

"Looks very nice, Stella. I know we left it a bit of a mess yesterday. Everyone had to catch the last train home last night."

"It was nothing, really, Wentworth."

"Well, thanks, anyway. Mannie coming in soon?"

"Nine o'clock."

"I'll be in here, making some last minute notes."

Wentworth always sat in the chair at Mannie's immediate left. A professor he'd had at Wharton once launched into a long monologue about the politics of placement at meetings, where to sit. Among the points he'd stressed were, at meetings, the main people sat at the table, the flunkies in chairs along the wall. Wentworth always made sure he sat at that table. He also knew, whoever controls the agenda controls the meeting, and he now sat alone drafting up an agenda for Mannie. Especially now, the last few weeks, his control of the agenda was critical. It had been, in fact, since he started his own personal agenda and The Event, last June.

Wentworth considered The Event. When he had started at Bonnell two years ago, his career path was clear, had been since he could remember. A Randall has an obligation, his father would tell him, an obligation to serve. And while some families served the nation or various causes, Randalls served the national wealth, for as we grow, so too shall all those we touch. This precept was the bedrock upon which Wentworth viewed the world. And in order to serve best, one must remain smart in business organizations; good grades and an outstanding academic record are only the start. Once in an organization, one must know how and when to move, and as soon as Wentworth heard the whispers about the "special project" he knew where he must aim. His father had taught him, if you stick to it, do well, you will inevitably rise to executive status with your hands firmly on the tiller of one of the *Fortune* 500. So his father had taught, as his grandfather had taught his father.

Actually his father never rose to such a height. Not tough enough, Wentworth now believed. He was certain that those who reached true power had style, his father had that in plenty. But the man had lacked a killer instinct. Another obligation the Randalls had, he said, had to do with principals, law, and ethics. Junior believed those lessons were for a kinder, gentler time. Then, some years after it was clear to all that his father would never pass beyond the title of vice president, he dropped dead, heart attack, collapsed at his desk, precisely when Wentworth Junior was playing in a tennis match for Princeton.

Arterial blockage, the doctors said. Heredity, as well. Hadn't the first Randall died of heart failure at fifty-six himself?

Wentworth merely continued his diet, his vigorous walks in the morning, his moderate alcohol consumption, his certain knowledge that when he reached thirty, now less than two years away, he would cease smoking cigarettes. He remained moderate, in control of all areas of his life. And he found, both at Wharton and later with Bonnell Corporation, that such moderation, such carefulness, stood him in good stead. It allowed him to steer a straight and narrow course while his peers rose like rockets only to crash, or never rose at all, so sodden with confusion, or drink, or fatigue in the face of the pressures.

Be careful, his father had said. Recognize that you will make mistakes, he said. Keep a clear goal in mind. Do your work well and never, never attend a meeting unless you are better prepared than anyone else. And, what his father never said, a lesson Wentworth learned himself in school in the face of academic requirements that were in his view excessive, cut corners, take risks, depend on no allies.

The Event. Wentworth rose and poured himself a cup of coffee, added a dash of cream, sipped, and considered.

Bonnell had, shortly before Wentworth joined, vastly expanded its research and development budget at the same time that it purchased a new small company in the field of genetic engineering. The race was on all over the world to develop, test, and bring to market medicines produced by genetically engineered bacteria. Insulin was a major focus for much of the battle, but other firms were well ahead in that area. Bonnell was after something else, something bigger. The biggest of all. In Wentworth's view, Bonnell's search was the Holy Grail of the late twentieth century, promising vast rewards to Bonnell and Bonnell's stockholders (of which Wentworth was a small but growing member). More relevant to Wentworth's personal agenda, vast rewards to Wentworth himself if he managed, as he planned, to sell the secret to Bonnell's competitor, Boothbay Chemicals, in exchange for a vice presidency.

What felled his father, and grandfather before him, and more Americans every year than any other five diseases combined, was heart disease. For literally hundreds of thousands of men and women each year, death arrived from veins and arteries clogged with plaque from heavy, rich diets, high cholesterol counts, and consumption of animal fats. The small company purchased by Bonnell, really a garage-size operation run by three disorganized biochemists who were nevertheless brilliant, had been in the process of engineering a bug for use with lab animals. The bug they were trying to grow would have vastly reduced the number of animals required to produce statistically valid results, in addition to vastly shortening the time needed for testing. Such a bug would have saved hundreds of medicine and chemical companies billions of dollars in testing costs.

Something went wrong, however, aside from running out of the start-up venture capital money that had been raised. The bug they developed mutated, failed to meet the laboratory criteria, and was a total loss in terms of the original objectives. However, during the testing procedures that followed, to determine what went wrong, it was found that the bug produced a substance that, by chance, appeared to have the capability of dissolving arterial plaque without any negative side effects.

Wentworth had been at Bonnell one year, and aware for three months of a special project, when after substantial manipulation he was tapped to serve as Ironjaw's personal administrative assistant. Six months later Ironjaw called Wentworth into his office and handed him a thick document, saying, "I have a project for you to oversee. Secret. Top, top secret. Word gets out, you're fired. Never work around this city again. Got it?"

This was it! The payoff for all those months of toadying to this blustering asshole! Fighting for calm, Wentworth managed to nod sagely. "Yes sir."

"Report directly to me. Read this. Only copy. Read it here."

With that he gestured Wentworth to an armchair. For the rest of the morning Wentworth read the report, his excitement growing with each page until he could hardly sit still.

An artery unclogger! What a beautiful concept! Eat what you want, whenever, whatever. Meat. Whipped cream. Eggs. Milk. Pies. Fudge. Ice cream. The works. Take a pill once a week! One pill! Wentworth knew millions of women learned to take a pill every day so they could fuck free of fear. This was even better! One pill a week, that was all that was needed to release a substance into the bloodstream which dissolved plaque and fatty buildups. Which totally cleaned out the vascular system, eliminated blockages, opened constrictions, prevented strokes, prevented heart attacks, assured plenty of oxygen to all tissues...

No more need for cholesterol checks, stress tests, draconian diets to keep the blood free of fats!

No more need for coronary bypass operations.

The ultimate end of the bypass industry!

A virtual death knell for coronary care units and heart surgeons!

With people able to eat whatever they wanted, people would start to get fat! Need diet help! Exercise workouts!

Really, Wentworth thought, I better buy some stock in diet books, exercise centers, there'll be a lot of people getting heavy once this appears!

It was beautiful. Beautiful!

According to the report, the substance had been tested in the lab, was virtually inert. It had also been tested in a few prisons. The stuff worked perfectly. Wentworth read that there were documented cases on over four hundred people, all with serious blockages, who with treatment were virtually cleared out within four months.

Two hurdles remained. One involved FDA approval of the substance itself, and the other involved packaging the substance in a pill for proper release into the system. Currently only injections were possible, and they required extensive laboratory controls. The trick was to bind the stuff with a good solid or liquid-capsule vector so it could be ingested orally.

"What do you think?" Ironjaw asked Wentworth when he finished reading.

"Brilliant. This will be brilliant."

"So you're impressed. Ought to be. Now here's what we do. Use only this conference room here, first off. Work with technical staff, financial and legal staff, the scientists. Keep the group small, no more than ten people tops. We ought to get FDA approval for the substance and the binder in a year or less. Can't keep it secret after that. My techies say the pill problem's a few months off, too. We've got to get finance to figure how we go into production, budget for rollout, the whole works. Here's the names for the group."

He handed Wentworth the names.

"You remember a couple of years ago they came out with evidence aspirin reduces heart attacks? What happened?"

Wentworth thought.

"If I remember, the very same day the medical results were reported by the National Institute of Health, or whoever, all the aspirin companies hit the media, radio, television, papers, everything with a huge orchestrated campaign. Must have cost a hundred million dollars. They must have had those ads in the can, ready to go, long before the results were published."

"Exactly. And that's what we're gonna do, but bigger. Bigger! A hundred times bigger! Buy stock, boy!"

I'd rather buy your company, Wentworth thought, and it was at that moment his private agenda began. Right then.

That had been many months ago.

Wentworth opened his briefcase, pulled out some papers, made a few notes, drafted a simple agenda. Every Monday the team met in this room. Ironjaw chaired, of course. Drexell Aspin, the attorney assigned the project, managed the process of gaining proper approvals. He sat to Ironjaw's right. His assistant, Karen Frucci, also attended. Wentworth thought he hated her. She was already deputy counsel, New Business, and at twenty-seven a year younger than Wentworth. Wentworth had asked her out months ago. She was attractive. He thought they would make an imposing couple, two tall, slender young professionals on the way up. She had laughed at him.

William Doane always sat opposite Ironjaw, at the table's other end. Forty-seven, a runner, former Rhodes scholar, captain of the Harvard lightweight crew when in college, he was Bonnell's chief financial officer. Ironjaw relied on Doane heavily. With Doane, always, were two others, brought in once the team felt the project might be a real go. Arthur Stein handled the marketing and promotion program. He was so thin Wentworth thought him anorexic. Norman Newman, who was the number cruncher, the guy who plugged into the terminal in the corner and ran the numbers based on various estimates made by the group, was a virtual genius with the computer. The day before, he had left his briefcase at home. The briefcase contained all the sensitive material on this project, as Wentworth intended—in fact his leaving the case home presented a rare opportunity that Wentworth tried to exploit—but even without the materials it only took him five minutes to get the information up on the screen during their meeting yesterday.

Sitting next to Wentworth across from the lawyers were Horace Taylor and Emily Mott, the techies. Taylor, one of the three biochemists Bonnell had bought out, absolutely fit the mold of mad scientist. Bald on top, a wild fringe of gray hair over the ears, thick glasses, Adam's apple the size of a lemon, he always wore a spotted lab coat and spoke a million words a minute. Emily's only function appeared to be interpreting what Horace said to the rest of the group. Wentworth thought they might be fucking each other.

The agenda Wentworth prepared was simple—reports from each of the sectors, legal, technical, financial, to be made by the respective leaders, a report from him on the outcome of the meeting yesterday, attended by himself, Karen, Emily, Arthur, and Norman, and then a discussion whether any developments had occurred in their tracing of rumors since The Event. Six months before, The Event occurred, the distressing disappearance, for a few hours, of one-half the necessary schematics for producing the plaque-dissolving substance. A final schematic, for FDA review, had since been prepared, but when one of the copies of the earlier two-part design had turned up missing the previous May, the shit had hit the fan.

Horace Taylor had reported the loss at the regular Monday meeting, the last week in May when the heat was intense and humidity unbelievable. For once Emily was not needed to interpret what he said. They were all seated, with coffee, about to begin when Horace blurted, "Part One-A is gone."

"Gone?" Ironjaw asked. "What, exactly, do you mean, Horace, by 'gone'?"

"Er, missing. I took the copy home with me over the weekend. I needed it to prepare the next phase of binding estimates . . ."

"Jesus!" Karen glared across the table. Next to her Drexell's mouth hung open.

"Lost? Stolen? What!" Ironjaw thrust his chin forward.

"I am sure I misplaced it. Maybe I never took it home. But it is not in the lab safe, I looked this morning. As you know I live by myself and always keep my briefcase locked. No one visited me over the weekend. I was there most of the time working, except for a shopping excursion Sunday, and of course my bowling league Saturday night." Horace looked around the table. Everyone stared at him as if he had crawled from beneath a rock. "No one had been in my place, I am sure. I triple-lock it."

"Horace, we know that." William Doane graced the table with a smile. "Your paranoia is legion."

Ironjaw lowered his head, shook it.

"Horace, are you sure you didn't misplace it in your house?" Everyone dared a smile. Horace's clutter was famous.

"Perhaps, but . . . I looked carefully . . ."

"Look again. Now. Go home this minute and look now. I won't panic until you have looked again." It was obvious Ironjaw was a long way from panic, if not from rage.

Horace left. The meeting that Monday droned on, without focus, direction, adjourning early.

Later that same afternoon Emily Mott telephoned Wentworth.

"Wentworth, Horace just called from his home out on Long Island. He says not to worry, he found the plans after all." Wentworth suddenly found her voice over the phone sexy, very sexy, an amazing feature of this otherwise plain, nondescript woman. "He says," she rushed on, "he found it lying on his desk under some papers, almost in plain sight, he doesn't understand how he missed it before."

Two minutes later Horace telephoned Wentworth himself

with the news, but by then Wentworth was already reporting to Ironjaw in his office.

"Stupid idiot," Ironjaw said. "Typical genius. What do you think?"

Wentworth waited. He had learned such a question really meant, here's what I think. Ironjaw went on, "Horace Taylor's a genius. A genius and a slob, totally disorganized, totally unmanageable, he knows I don't want such stuff brought home, or if so only in locked cases, it's like only myself, Bill Doane, and Drexell really understand the danger of industrial espionage. The rest of you young comers are too fucking self-absorbed to give it a thought, but I consider it a real fucking risk! Now Horace very likely forgets to lock his briefcase, and for that matter his house, because he's the type of person who'll leave his keys inside, lock himself out, so over time to save the trouble he'll just not lock the house, know what I mean?" Ironjaw was nearly shouting. "You know what I think?"

Now it was Wentworth's turn.

"I believe the odds, sir, while very high that Horace in fact is totally capable of overlooking something right before his nose, nevertheless may indicate the design was stolen, removed, copied, and then replaced." What else could Wentworth say? Ironjaw was no dummy. He had to offer this idea, if only to divert attention from himself. Where it belonged—Wentworth had, in May, arranged for Horace to take the plans home with him over the weekend, then called his man with directions and instructions.

"And? And!"

"If so, Mr. Maroules, the holder of that copy now has one-half the necessary information to replicate the bug."

"And the fucking substance! Without having invested three million in a crazed off-the-wall company, going broke fast, or the over four million since to perfect the material! Which means?"

"I would suggest this event indicates one of our competitors either is now, or is now being offered, for a price, half the necessary plans needed to be in the market.'' What else could Wentworth say?

"At the same time as us, or before us!"

They stared at each other.

That had been late May, months earlier. Since then the project team all hoped and prayed that Horace had merely fumbled, misplaced the document, and in fact as time passed they came partly to believe that had been the case. Partly. But Ironjaw tightened security. Accelerated the program. Prohibited removal of any written plans or memos from the company building unless absolutely necessary.

Despite Ironjaw's prohibition, Wentworth had in fact allowed portions of the plans to go home, twice with Drexell and Karen, to assist them in their filing needs for the FDA, once with Arthur, who needed details for the promotion program. Most recently, the plans had left the office—three days ago—with the idiot savant Norman Newman, who was structuring a new stock offering to raise necessary funds for the marketing program. Wentworth arranged this for two basic reasons—first, regarding his own agenda, suddenly half the plans were not enough, and he needed to arrange for copies of the other half to be available so his man could steal them. The only way to do that was to send them home with the others. Secondly, in the event the word got out someone was stealing the information, Wentworth was covering his tracks by involving the others, never himself, in having the copies beyond the company site.

Wentworth began his third cup of coffee.

Karen Frucci walked in, dressed, as always, to kill.

"Randall."

"Karen."

"I suppose you left Stella to clean up this morning."

"I didn't see you offering to help last night, Karen."

"I had tickets for the Vienna Choir, you knew that."

"Of course." I hate her, Wentworth thought. "Where's Drexell?"

"Here he is."

Drexell Aspin appeared, followed by William Doane, Arthur Stein, and Norman Newman. As soon as Drexell sat down and lit his pipe, Wentworth pulled out a cigarette, his one permitted personal vice. As always, Karen flinched as Wentworth's smoke passed over her head. Wentworth never saw her flinch when surrounded by Drexell's Turkish haze. Arthur Stein also lit up. He would have a cigarette hanging from his mouth for the next hour at least.

Wentworth had learned this about the politics of smoking in big organizations. First of all, smokers were a dying breed, increasingly on the outs. If the boss smoked a pipe, everyone else could freely smoke cigarettes, leaving the rabid non-smokers or even more rabid ex-smokers gagging but silent. If the boss smoked cigars, no one else smoked. Wentworth believed this had something to do with a collective cultural attitude where everyone jointly agreed that cigar smoke, alone, was too noxious to permit other smoke. Underlings never smoked cigars. If the boss was a nonsmoker, no one else ever smoked.

Ironjaw was a smoker, and it warmed Wentworth's heart to see Karen squirm. William Doane, never a smoker, he was too aerobic for that, paid such politics no attention whatsoever.

Yesterday, when Wentworth, Karen, Arthur, Norman, and Emily met here, Karen tried to keep a smoke-free environment, weakly supported by Emily. She had failed and Wentworth could tell she still resented it. She also wanted something other than pizza, Chinese, or some health concoction, and, overruled again, had refused to eat anything.

Norman Newman looked exhausted. He sat somewhat slumped in the corner, opening his briefcase furtively, as he always did. Wentworth could tell he was remembering leaving it at home the day before.

Horace, always last to these meetings, for once appeared at 9:00, exactly, rushing in with his usual huff, somehow casting pencils, pens, and even little scraps of paper—punch-outs for a ring binder fluttering from his pockets—around his place at the table within two minutes. Emily, next to him, tried to keep some order.

Wentworth placed the carefully penciled agenda atop Ironjaw's notepad. In the corner Newman's terminal hummed.

"Have a nice weekend, Drex?" Doane asked.

"Just fine. Except for the snow, of course." Aspin knocked his pipe in the ashtray. Ashes and pieces of tobacco scattered over the table. Wentworth was pleased to see pipe dottle fall off the table into Karen's lap. "Did you see the game?" Drexell Aspin was a season ticket holder at the Meadowlands. He went to every Giants game.

"Afraid not, Drex." Doane smiled. "But I heard your crowd lost."

"They did indeed." Aspin appeared untroubled. To Wentworth he always appeared untroubled, never showed emotion, yet he was not a cold person. Like William Doane, one of the elect, born in the certainty of high responsibility and proper rewards. Wentworth believed he was one of the elect, too. Wentworth shopped for his suits where Doane shopped, had even managed to run into him there once. He firmly believed the chance encounter cemented a shared, private moment between a lion and a rising cub, unaware that Doane never registered the encounter to begin with, let alone remembered it.

"Sorry!" Ironjaw barked, not sorry at all, just late. He threw off his coat, caught by Stella as she trailed him into the conference room, and marched to his chair, glanced before him at Wentworth's agenda.

"Reports. Drex."

Karen handed papers around the table as Aspin began to report.

"The filing and approvals are virtually complete. My sources at FDA"—everyone knew his source was his former college roommate and brother-in-law, now deputy administrator—"indicate the formal review and reserve period following final testing will be complete February fifteenth. Final approval should then follow April first. This date also coincides well with Bill's campaign regarding the stock issue, scheduled for January tenth, and the marketing program. I will allow Bill to brief you on those matters. Legally, we are in excellent shape."

As always, short, to the point, and sweet. Wentworth did his best to imitate the style when he spoke.

"Potential problems!" Ironjaw demanded.

"Not of a legal nature, Mannie. However." Aspin was refilling his pipe, a complex ritual involving a small knife, a pipe cleaner, frequent knocks against the ashtray, and tobacco pulled and spilled from a well-worn leather pouch. "Our copyright schedule is now growing critical, and although we have most necessary materials and documents submitted, and certain verbal assurances regarding propriety, until we formally submit the master composite design and blueprint we cannot enter the sixty-day final review period. This requires us to finalize all systems"—here he glanced over his glasses toward Horace—"by the end of January to be registered by the start of April. And, as you know, our confidentiality risk rises exponentially once filing is complete."

"And of course our other issue—" Karen interjected, immediately falling silent when Aspin slammed his pipe against the ashtray.

"Sorry, Karen, clumsy of me."

Wentworth loved it. Aspin hated to be interrupted, especially by his aide. Karen sat there crimson. Arthur Stein smiled through cigarette smoke.

"We'll get to that, Karen," Wentworth offered, calm, smooth.

Karen glared.

"Horace! Technical report! Keep it short!" Ironjaw slapped the table for emphasis.

"Re-regarding the c-copyright," Horace began, "the composite design material is nearly complete. Of course the biochemical data information and cad-scan cross sections and data points require additional coding, printing, and review, but—"

"Horace."

"Oh, sorry, uh, Mannie. The plan will—will be ready after Christmas." Even as he spoke it was clear Horace had his own doubts. "We have now combined both earlier sections and are well on the way to a proper vector choice—"

"Well on the way! Well on the way means not there yet!"

"Well, uh, sir, the solid binder we tried in October has shown adequate stability, adequate solubility, adequate resistance to humidity. The only remaining issue concerns shelf life. A minor matter."

"A minor matter!" Stein declared. They had all agreed that the pills required at least six months shelf life. Ironjaw raised his hand.

"Well," Horace said, "our difficulty is that to hold the material in a form easily absorbed by the circulation system requires us to bind it such that shelf life is somewhat limited." As he spoke Horace ducked his head, awaiting a barrage.

"How limited is somewhat limited, Horace?" Ironjaw's eyes were rifle barrels aimed toward Horace. "Five months? Three months? Six weeks?"

There was a pause while Horace squirmed.

"Ten days," Emily Mott said, sitting straight and placing her hand on Horace's forearm, facing Ironjaw, jaw set.

Ironjaw laughed. The laugh echoed.

"About enough time to ship from here to a warehouse in San Francisco. Great."

Horace flinched.

"Mr. Maroules." Emily spoke quietly but with force. "A month ago we had no shelf stability whatsoever. Horace has increased the factor four thousand percent, mostly in the last several days."

"At this rate," Karen began. She stopped, as if waiting for permission to continue. Ironjaw nodded. "At this rate do you believe you can assure us that by March we will have the necessary three-month minimum we projected as necessary to begin sales?"

78

Horace nodded eagerly.

"Yes," he said. "We will continue to experiment with the mixture. Now we know the ranges of proper balance, we have begun a strict program to isolate the specific balance allowing proper shelf life and proper integral release."

"What, Horace, do you mean by 'integral release'?" As always, Doane's query was polite, gracious.

"Um—"

"What he means is," Emily said, interpreting, "the substance in pure form acts as a dissolving agent. However, when added to a vector, its ability to function appears impaired. Horace has identified a molecular bonding that takes place in the vector we now use which, if not properly balanced, renders the substance insoluble. He is now working with tolerances at the ten to the minus seven sensitivity. Parts per billion. The change from one hour shelf life one month ago to ten days, the last batch we monitored, is incredibly slight from a molecular perspective. We have another run in the system now, entered Thursday afternoon, which we believe is the answer. When he says 'integral release' he means allowing us to bind the substance in a pill which when ingested can be digested without harming the passage of the substance into the bloodstream."

"What she means," Ironjaw declared, "is we proceed toward a projected April first rollout, with a review in January. Now. William. Report."

"Yes." Doane smiled at the group. "We have been working on two fronts, both on schedule. Arthur here has good news to report on the promotion and rollout program. Much of the media material is not only in final draft form but we have managed to virtually complete the film material absent final voice-overs. Arthur?"

Arthur Stein stubbed out his cigarette.

"Winston Advertising handles our account, each year almost a hundred million dollars. All they know to date about Choice is we have in the pipeline a new pill, like aspirin, they think, something about the heart. They only have the name,

Choice, and that very general concept. They know we need a last-minute push at the end for certain report results, which only we know at this time are the FDA test results. They have all the film material in the can awaiting the text for voice-overs. They have recommended—and I believe this will be a very powerful medium—that we buy substantial airtime on New England television, Boston Channel Five, which this year is filming the Boston Marathon in its entirety. We can make a major, major regional play before and all during the race, perfect audience. All the health nuts or even better, the slobs who dream of being health nuts." Arthur paused to light another cigarette. "It'd be an excellent chance to kick off the regional effort up there. I'm notifying them after this meeting here, if we're still on schedule as it sounds like, to lock in a major portion of airtime, approximately one-half million on Channel Five alone. That race is April eighteenth this year, which will allow us to kick off the national campaign and then hit that region heavily after seeing what the early sales results are."

"Thank you, Arthur." Doane leaned forward in his chair. Wentworth could observe even through Doane's suit coat and shirt the lean muscle definition, the spare, fit frame. The man had the body of a twenty-year-old. Which he ought to, Wentworth reflected. The man still raced competitively with the New York AC crew, had even stroked the winning four-with-cox in this fall's around–Manhattan Island, twenty-four-mile crew race, where each of the thirteen boats had to be followed by its own powered skiff in case of collision or sinking. Wentworth, a tennis player, who reached number four one year on the Princeton team, thought crew jocks were crazy. Once Doane, in a rare personal query, asked Wentworth if he had ever considered "rowing sweeps," as Doane put it. When Wentworth had shaken his head, announcing he'd played tennis, Doane merely shook his head, said, "Pity, you've the build for it." Now Doane steepled his hands and cracked his knuckles.

"Concerning the stock issue, we are prepared for sale

January tenth. This will raise sufficient capital to support the rollout program and pay off what we have drawn against our line of credit to capitalize our manufacturing operation in Iowa. Which, incidentally, is ahead of schedule. Norman Newman here has done a terrific job on this effort. Great independent thinking.''

Norman flushed, apparently embarrassed by the unexpected compliment. Actually he was furious; while Doane praised him to the group, he nailed him on his fitness reports.

"Problems?" Ironjaw asked.

"None to report, Mannie. None to report."

The table took a breath, everyone shifting and inhaling, some more than others, and for other reasons; they would now get to the meat of it, yesterday's meeting, the subteam chaired by Wentworth informally titled Damage Control. As coffee cups were refilled, papers moved, and chairs scraped back Wentworth reviewed his summary, what he would say.

"Wentworth. Short, keep it short. I have another meeting in ten minutes." Ironjaw leaned back, closed his eyes, his *listening carefully* position.

"Yesterday, Mannie, we met here for several hours to discuss our strategies and options available based on certain assumptions about The Event." Wentworth paused. "While everyone agreed that there was a chance, perhaps a slight chance, that Horace's plans had been stolen, copied, and replaced, and that we must now act, from a strategic perspective, as if they have in fact been copied, I emphasize that we all feel the risk of copies having been made is slight.''

"Reason." Ironjaw kept his eyes closed.

"No evidence as yet, sir." Wentworth would have stared earnestly into Ironjaw's eyes had they been open, with a clear, untroubled gaze. He was excellent at lying through his teeth, and even better when he was making statements that, while in a narrow sense true, were in fact known to him, personally, to be false. "Drex has received no indication from his sources in the other companies that anything is up, anything major about to break. There has been no evidence of sudden new promotions for new products. Emily reports similar results from her lab contacts. Norman reports no financial irregularities. Perhaps most significant, Karen has found no evidence of new filings by any other major firm in this area, and although we all know specific product testing is confidential, there are usually rumors, and here there are none." Wentworth continued to project earnestness, truth. "We consider that, were any other of the major firms in on this matter, we have developed sufficient networks at our level within the industry to isolate any rumors." Wentworth smiled. "We found none."

"We still tight here?"

"No rumors about us, either, Mannie."

"Don't like it. Never have." Ironjaw now stared at the ceiling. "Drex? Bill?"

Aspin was cleaning his pipe again.

"I hear very little on this matter from my brother-in-law, although he did say once that many new biochemical products are now being reviewed. I am led to believe, however, they are not products in the plaque area."

"What about medical journals?" Doane asked. "I myself have heard nothing, although there are rumors that the *New England Journal of Medicine* is about to report on a new heart medicine, but this seems tied to the aspirin issue, which many firms are after, and not cholesterol. As you know they are very closemouthed about upcoming articles in the pipeline. They have better security than Fort Knox. But, have there been any whiffs there?"

"When is the next issue due out?" Doane asked.

"This Wednesday, actually," Arthur said. "Day after tomorrow."

Horace coughed.

"I don't know why they weren't interested in my outline," he muttered. Six months earlier, in an effort to have results reported in this most prestigious of medical journals, he had tried to offer an outline for review, but he had been refused. Wentworth felt the reasons had more to do with his turgid style and his inability to be very specific, on Ironjaw's orders, than with the actual content. Nevertheless it had been a disappointment. They now were forced to rely on FDA approval to kick off the program.

"His summary correct?" Ironjaw asked of the others who attended the Sunday meeting. "Wentworth miss anything?"

"I have a concern." Karen spoke softly, smiling toward Wentworth, not a nice smile.

"Yes." Ironjaw leaned forward, gazed toward Karen.

"Over a month ago Wentworth reported a high likelihood the plan in Horace's apartment was not copied. This was based on his retaining one Henry Fallon, ex-policeman turned investigator, who I have since learned was cashiered from the Newark force for having his hand in the till, and although we all approved hiring this man at the time—"

"I objected," Drexell said. "I considered it dangerous to bring in an outsider, even before we had developed the cover story we were looking for stolen plans for an aspirin substitute."

"But you agreed in the end," Wentworth pointed out.

"Wentworth, at the time we agreed with your suggestion to hire this person, we stressed the need for regular, written reports, to better assess Mr. Fallon's efforts. None of the rest of us have even met him." Karen continued to speak softly.

"And I felt that committing anything to paper would be highly risky. If any of that material got out we would be compounding our original error!" Wentworth was emphatic.

"But, Wentworth," Karen went on, "throughout this entire exercise we have been forced to rely on your word that you have been briefed by Mr. Fallon, we have cut checks to this mysterious H. Fallon. Not once have any of us had it confirmed that he did any work at all! We only have your word that his research failed to identify evidence a copy was made!"

Wentworth knew he had to go on the attack, divert this.

"I deeply resent your implication, Karen! Are you accusing me of being somehow involved in The Event? Are you?" Technically, of course, Wentworth was not involved in The

Event itself. Henry had stolen and copied the plans, not him. Because he was, in a narrow sense, speaking honestly, Wentworth was able to inject a full measure of outrage in his tone.

"Wentworth, I merely wished to draw everyone's attention to the fact that our major source for agreeing that copies were probably not made is you, only you!"

"Are you! Is that what you are doing?" Wentworth leapt to his feet, dramatic, incensed. "I have busted my ass to resolve this thing to our mutual benefit. Didn't I just say that despite our feeling the copies were safe we were treating this as if they were stolen? And you! You sit over there throwing darts!"

"Wentworth—"

Wentworth swung to face Ironjaw.

"I must protest!"

Ironjaw said, "Shut up, Wentworth. You shut up, too, Karen." Karen lowered her eyes, face red. "Last fucking thing we need is two ambitious aides shooting back and forth. I could give a shit about this Henry Fallon. He was just insurance. The fact is the rumor mill is quiet about anything like our bug plans being possibly stolen. Fallon or no Fallon, it looks pretty clean. So you, Wentworth, you let him go, settle with him, that's it. Karen, this ain't the time to start shooting inside the tent." Ironjaw paused, looked around the table. Even Norman had turned away from his terminal, was giving the table his undivided attention. "It ain't time to be shooting inside the tent," he repeated. "This is it, folks, we have everything riding on this one. We are still on schedule for a March or April rollout, so let's stay calm, keep the peace."

Across the table Wentworth and Karen glared.

"Now at the board meeting Wednesday I plan to make an announcement about Choice. They've been asking questions. So we better all meet here, seven-thirty, Wednesday morning, breakfast, final review." Ironjaw grimaced for a smile. He strode from the room.

Wentworth, taking charge, to deflect Karen's remarks, raised his hands. "I'll take care of it, you'll hear from me later today. We'll just parcel out the work."

Aspin nodded, and left, followed by Doane, Stein, Horace, and Emily. In the corner Norman assembled his papers, discs, shut off the terminal, left.

Wentworth leaned toward Karen.

"Don't ever do that again, Karen."

"What? Ask the proper questions? I don't know what your magic is with Mannie or the others, but you don't fool me for a minute. You are a totally unprincipled, nakedly opportunistic person driven by greed and ambition only!"

Wentworth smiled. She was so angry spit flew.

"Just the qualities I thought you found most attractive in men."

Karen blinked.

"I don't know what you're up to, Wentworth, but it's something, I'm sure, and when I find you out I'm going to nail your hide to the wall!"

"Up there with your ball collection?" Wentworth smiled. Karen was actually sputtering. He finished replacing papers in his briefcase. For a moment there, the way she was starting in with the others, he thought she was on to him, knew something specific about Henry and his deal, but she was just firing in the dark, hoping for a hit. She knew nothing, nothing important, anyway.

Wentworth kept his smile and left the room. When he got back to his office there was a call for him. He closed the door.

"Wentworth Randall," said the voice.

Wentworth jumped, gripped the phone.

"What are you calling me here for?"

He and Fallon had an agreement: no calls direct to the office unless absolutely necessary.

"Relax, boyo." Wentworth hated being called boyo. "Thought you'd be interested. Turns out Newman for once failed to lock his case when he left it home yesterday. So you got a few brains, anyway. His little lady has the copies. I reached her, like you suggested. She's like peanut butter, real easy to spread around smoothly.''

The day before, after Norman left his case at home, an unexpected opportunity, Wentworth ducked back to his office after the pizza arrived, called Henry, told him to try to leverage Jean for some copies on the bet she could get into Norman's case. Maybe the whole thing could be taken care of fast, without softening her up for a period of time.

"She do it?''

"Believe so. Just called her. I'm arranging for their pickup tomorrow. Tuesday morning, eleven o'clock. How about we meet late afternoon? What's that place in the city, by your apartment, we meet there sometime, settle up then?''

Wentworth smiled. Done, he thought. Almost done. Now to get rid of Henry, pay him off, let him go.

"Henry, at our meeting today Mannie recommended very strongly that your services will not be required any longer, so if you would prepare a final invoice for our records I will settle with you tomorrow.''

There was a pause, then Fallon said, "Sure, for the company, but our little arrangement, you and me and Sammie, we settle that tomorrow also.''

"Get me Jean's copies and yes, twenty thousand, as agreed.'' Wentworth thought, I get the copies from this crude person, pay him off. Would twenty thousand be enough?

"Hey.'' Even over the phone there was menace in Henry's tone. "You're a smart young kid. You and your partner there, Sammy, are real smart. Got a big future before you, play your cards right. Maybe even if you don't play them at all, you got a lot of style. But I hear rumblings here that sound to me like you'd like to set up a cross, know what I mean?''

"Henry! Absolutely not!'' Wentworth said, thinking: absolutely.

"You think about this. Who's working for who here? Think about that.''

"Henry—''

"Don't go and get squirrelly with me now, and don't even

think what you've been thinking. Nothing you can think of I haven't done before or planned for. We have an agreement! I also have a file, all we did. Period. And we got a few other terms, besides the cash, we gotta discuss. Like stock. So I'll call you later, set up a time for us to meet end of tomorrow. Got it?''

It had grown complicated. Something else his father never told him: You cut corners, you triple your work, quadruple your risk, it gets a lot more complex.

Sam and I, we can handle Henry, he's just a big greedy ex-cop.

Wentworth adjusted his tie.

Chapter Five

MONDAY AFTERNOON

Monday. Jesus, trying to work feeling like this. I'm getting too old for this, Paul thought. Making pickups in the van, everything in slow motion, operating on about zero hours' sleep. Today was just like most Mondays except worse, a lot of pickups before eleven, then racing all over the place in the afternoon making deliveries.

Paul had returned to his apartment just before two in the morning, then had to shovel a space to park the van where the plow had piled snow from the street. On three hours' sleep he had risen to be in the van by seven, get the radio assignments, no breakfast, no coffee, a lukewarm shower, no sleep.

Just one of those days to get through.

Today his route included the firm in south Baltimore he used to run private envelopes for. Lately there had been no side action. The girl at the desk was different, and he had lost touch with Cheryl, the first one, the lady who'd been moved up to the big private office.

Arriving just at the end of the day, his final delivery, he was surprised to see Cheryl when he came in the door.

"You look terrible," she said. She didn't look much better.

"Thought you had left all this grunt work behind, moved up." He placed the packages he was delivering on the desk, looked down at her. She looked beat, wrung out somehow, but she was still a nice woman to look at.

"It's a long story," she said, with a tired smile. "Long." She glanced toward the clock on the wall. Paul stood there feeling dreadful—he had to beat it for home, shop for the week's food. It was a thirty-mile trip back to his place; he needed a shower. "Buy me a drink, Paul, I'll tell you about it."

"You'll have some grubby company," Paul said. "Yesterday I had to go up to Philly, didn't get back until after three. Grubby."

"No worse than the company I've been keeping upstairs," she said.

Paul drove Cheryl down the road to the fern bar they'd used the previous spring, the place catering to the younger help from the company she worked for. The place served strong drinks and at five on weekdays was packed for happy hour. They wedged into a small booth at the back.

"What've you been up to?" Cheryl asked.

"Same old thing. Driving."

"It's hard to keep up your ambition sometimes, isn't it?" She spoke quietly.

"Uh, I suppose. So how come you're back at the reception desk? I thought you hated it there."

"I did. I do. But it's a job." She twirled her drink with a finger. She looked up at Paul, smiled. Paul thought she had nice eyes. Right now, wounded eyes.

"When I did you that favor, last spring? You were really loving it, then."

"Shit! Errand girl! Fetch-it!"

Paul, tired as he was, knew this was a chance to learn some stuff. He was curious. Just what was that package he had picked up? Not coke, Henry said, industrial espionage. Secrets? He could tell—the message was clear—Henry had him down as a gopher, employee, trying right now to derail him on horse-face. Paul nodded at Cheryl sympathetically, vowing to himself not to take advantage here, just have a drink, leave.

"What was that I delivered, anyway? Coke, maybe?"

"Oh, no!" A bitter laugh. "At least then I could have had a couple of toots!" Cheryl bit her lower lip, frowned. "I thought I had been moved upstairs because of merit! I tried so hard down here! But that wasn't it! One day I get a call, come upstairs, we have a sudden vacancy, need a good girl, work with Sam Dworskin. All of us know who he was, the new guy hired to set up a new division, special project. All the girls noticed him, the clothes, the Porsche 924. A real comer, you know. Rumor had it he went through secretaries like water, hard to work with . . . I jumped at it, anything to get away from the front desk. I've been going to school nights for two years, two years! Got my B.A. last spring, and now I want to get into an MBA program. Enough of this shlepping for the bosses! So I took the vacancy, even with the bad reputation. I thought I could handle that, you know? When I interviewed with him he seemed all right, wanted a special assistant for this project, gave me a ten percent raise."

Paul remembered Cheryl had a small boy at home. The one time he went back to her place the boy must have been with his father, but there'd been toys all over the place, a tiny townhouse apartment down by the river, probably built over some toxic waste dump. Paul had trouble imagining the life: single mother with a small child, working forty or forty-five hours a week, having to get up, dressed, the kid ready for school. All the hassles arranging proper care for when the kid's out of school, rides, all the logistical details, then coming home from a full day of work to prepare dinner, do all the things a parent does to give the kid a desperately normal semblance of a life, almost but never too busy to have those awful cold moments of reflection: Is this what it is, worrying about the child support, are there any men there willing to take me and this huge seven-year-old overhead? It was a hard place to be, Paul was certain. He respected her for it. He remembered after they made love, just that one time, she cried a little. He liked her. She was nice. He remained friendly with her, but he was secretly relieved when she moved away from the front desk. He had no interest in getting into anything heavy with her.

She was still talking.

"Time I called about that package, I'd been up there less than a month. Sam said he had a job for me. Real secret." She stared into the distance, remembering, shook her head. "Day after I'm up there it's let's have dinner. Against all the rules, but Sam's sorta cute, I wanted to date a Porsche anyway once in my life. We go to dinner, he's smooth, a little oily, you know, but smooth."

Paul sat quietly, let her talk.

"He lays this big line on me, how he's seen me at the desk for months, coming in to work, liked my looks, found me very attractive, tried to arrange to have me work for him. Oh, he laid it on thick. Thick! I ate it right up. Stupid me."

"Not so," Paul said. She was not stupid. Just alone and in a bad position.

"Oh, it was real hot and heavy, then. I was warned, the girls warned me, but did I listen? He started to tell me things, I was seeing stuff across the desk, hearing things. Sam must have thought I was stupid, I see now, stupid!" Paul lit her cigarette. "I guess he set me up, told me his new division had been designing a new medicine, something to do with cleaning blood. I think it must of been for a kidney machine, that's all I could think. He says his competitors are after him hot and heavy, stole something of his. We were in bed, at his place, you know? He comes on all worried, needing my help, he says, how if he's caught for letting the plans out he'll be fired, how he's arranged with this private eye up in Jersey to get the plans back. But he needs someone, not him, to get the material. I ate it all up. For all I know, even to this day, maybe it was the truth! Anyway, Sam suggests I use my 'envelope' connection. At first I didn't get it, but then it turns out that this guy, big young executive, knows all about the little envelope system you and I had. I think he was behind it, maybe even the big dealer for the company, that's what I think now. Jesus, listen to me go on here, finished one drink already and halfway through another. . . ."

Paul started. This Dworskin guy had been watching him?

"So he pressures me to use you, Ryan Express, if I can, and just by coincidence, I guess, when I call you you're going up there already!"

"The coke, I thought."

"The stolen plans!" She smiled, finished her drink. "That time you came in, dropped the package off, I felt bad then, wanted to say something. Maybe this was a big crime. I didn't want you to get involved, but at the time Sam had me going real good." She paused, remembering. Paul saw she had really gone for this guy. He'd really done a job on her. "Soon as he got the package, things changed. Suddenly too busy for me. No time. Complete switch. Door closed all the time, saying nothing, all these secret important meetings and him even yelling at me. I was suddenly shut out of his life, of his project, a gopher sitting up there in this nice office waiting for the phone to ring, for something to do." Paul sipped his beer. Cheryl paused and had to smile. "No more dates with a Porsche. Then I was returned down to the desk, just like that. I think Sam was afraid I'd sick the company security on him for the coke deal, except because I was involved months ago I couldn't blow the whistle! At least down at the desk I get to see people!"

"You think all that was just to recover that package?"

"Hard to believe, huh?" Cheryl said.

Paul thought Dworskin just wanted to get rid of her now he'd stolen the plans. They must have been stolen from someone else, not stolen from him. Also, Paul suspected Cheryl was just another in a long line of women the guy used his Porsche, his job, probably his supplies of coke, to play with. Paul could tell, looking across the booth, that's what she thought. She was probably right.

"You ever find out what those plans were for?"

"No. Not really. Something with blood. But I know this:

After I gave him the package, he called in some scientist types. They had this very long meeting, and when they came out Sam was like a cat with cream. Excited, you know? Like he'd found what he wanted.''

Paul listened to Cheryl. He felt invaded, manipulated. *I was being used and set up as a delivery boy by this Sam guy and it never even crossed my mind. Some PI I'm turning out to be. Using those envelopes to test me as a mule to deliver hot goods, then those plans . . . Those plans, going to all those lengths on those plans, must be something big.*

And he thought, *where does Henry fit in? Sam, he and Henry must be working together. Or, Fallon's working for this Sam and wants more of the action?*

Am I being used by Henry, too? Stupid question, Paul.

"You still trying to become an investigator?"

"Funny you should ask that, I was just thinking that maybe it's not the field for me after all." Paul felt the two drinks in his system, the illusion of energy, the quick buzz erasing his fatigue. "Yeah, maybe. But I wanted to be working for the good guys, I guess. Not as an industrial spy. Surprises me these big companies do this."

"Not me. Uh-uh." Cheryl was emphatic. "Sam Dworskin, he's a prince of the realm here, the new hero. They've been spending a fortune here on something new for months!"

Paul smiled, unaware his gold tooth glinted in the smoky barroom.

"Then something happened. Last week, week before? Suddenly Sam's moving his office. Special projects is moving to a new area in the plant. I overhear him on the phone just before I'm sent back downstairs to the desk talking to some high muck-a-muck, the boss of the bosses, maybe, something about 'erasing the corporate memory.' Made no sense to me, but the next day, Friday before last, I get the message, you're returning to the desk. Period! So I'm being erased, I guess."

Paul watched her talking, twisting her napkin, then tearing little sections off, trying to make sense of it, unable to.

"Just like that."

"Just like that. Sam's disappeared, can't see him. Then Roberta my friend goes to work for him. Suddenly, it's like I'm on the other side, warning her, you know? Makes me sick!"

Paul ordered another round of drinks, some nachos to chew on. The barroom was now packed, mostly people who worked in the company, Paul was sure. In the corner a small band was tuning up.

Drink this one slow, Paul thought. They're hitting hard tonight—no sleep, bad combination. He noticed most of the crowd were in their twenties, younger than he was. This must be the watering hole for the up-and-comers, the junior yuppies. He saw a lot of young executive types working the ladies.

One, in particular, he saw at once was a real charmer, dressed to kill, ready for success, a thin, smooth, hard-eyed guy paying serious attention to a nice-looking young woman. Then Cheryl said, "Oh, shit, there's Roberta. And Sam." She ducked her head. She did not want to be seen, talk to these people. She was still in raw pain, confusion.

Paul covered her hand, said gently, "Come on, Cheryl, I'll drive you home. It's on my way. You don't have to take the bus tonight." After paying for the drinks, he led her from the barroom.

As Cheryl was putting on her coat Paul turned back, looked again at Sam Dworskin and Roberta. He could tell this guy was very aware he was slumming in this joint, awing them with his corporate presence. There he was, a guy about their age operating on an entirely different level, one of the predators mingling with the prey. Paul could tell he would do to Roberta what he'd just done to Cheryl. He liked Cheryl, but tonight, because he was tired, he would not come in when he took her home, however much she wanted the company, a warm body to be with. No need to complicate her life. Or his, to be truthful.

But Paul would very much enjoy complicating Sam Dworskin's life.

I got enough problems. Now I want to go on a revenge

mission on account of some woman I hardly know? I must be real tired tonight after all, to be as crazy as that.

But the thought warmed him, kept him awake during the ride home. It was still with him for some time thereafter.

That Monday afternoon, after Ironjaw's meeting ended and lunch hour had passed, Wentworth Randall managed administrative matters. Norman waited impatiently for the workday to end. Horace and Emily monitored the stability of the latest binder test, which continued to hold. Ironjaw occupied himself with the upcoming board of director's meeting, scheduled for Wednesday morning, when he planned to announce the final schedule for the rollout of Choice. Drexell Aspin took a long lunch with his broker. William Doane played a handball match at the Vista Executive Fitness Center, easily defeating his opponent despite their age difference.

Karen Frucci completed her work before three. She then told Millie, her secretary, she did not wish to be disturbed. She closed her door, sat behind her desk, and made a few calls.

"Brendan! How are you! . . . Been a long time, I know. Got a minute? . . . In between cases, Brendan? Don't you have pretty legal aides to do that for you? . . . Why, thank you, Bren, for the thought, but my legal secretary days are somewhat behind me. As you know. You are one of the few men who actually knows my true age, did you know that? . . . Listen, Bren, something has come up, and while I won't bore you with the tawdry details of corporate intrigue . . . What? . . . You mean your work as a junior, almost-partner lacks such gossip? . . . What? When! . . . Oh, Bren, congratulations! So you're in the bonus money this year, are you? Bastard . . . Whaddya mean, whaddya mean? . . . I know, but somehow it's different, here. I'm with a company, not a legal firm, it's not the same. Anyway, listen, Bren, I have a slight problem here, and as you have always been excellent at keeping confidences I need to burden you with my concerns, ask you to help me think this through. Also you were—at least before you stuffed your shirt at Crump, Crump, and Fudge, or whatever your firm is called—a darned good thinker. So here goes.''

Karen leaned back, glanced toward the door to make sure it was closed, lowered her voice.

''Bonnell has been working like mad to bring a new product to market. This product, it's big. The biggest. You know I can't say any more, and certainly not advise you to buy stock. I'm not doing that, of course. Wentworth Randall, the guy I'm about to mention, he calls this thing the Holy Grail of the late twentieth century, at least for Western civilization. He may be right. Well. A few months ago, last spring or summer, our chief scientist, who is truly weird, took home half the plans for this product. He reported those plans lost, and they were, for half a day. Our boss sent him right home to look again and he apparently called in, said he found them right on his desk, couldn't understand how he'd missed them. He is nutty, like I said. He is truly absentminded sometimes, so the idea of him doing something like that is not unexpected. But I really think those plans may have been stolen for a few hours, copied, and then returned. But I seem to be the only person here who thinks that! The AA, that's administrative assistant, for your clarification . . . what? . . . Why, yes, amazing asshole does apply! He's been asked by Ironjaw, the boss, to investigate this so-called event, or possible disappearance and theft. He's murky, you know? I don't trust him. He's too quick to argue the plans were never lost at all. We've been meeting, a small team, every week since this event, and as time has passed this guy has convinced everyone we are on safe ground. He even says he hired a private eye. I've seen the bills, an ex-cop who after I did a little digging I find was involved in some scandal a few years ago, had to leave the Newark force. Anyway, this AA, Wentworth Randall—do you believe that name?—he says the private eye says no evidence has been found that copies were made.''

Karen sat forward, still speaking.

''I don't know, Bren, that's what I wonder about. We've

never even met this guy. We have to take the AA's word for it. I don't trust him, Bren. He's funny about all this, shifty, you know? . . . What? . . . Bren! No, not at all, not my type. Asked me out once, right after we met, late last spring. I laughed at him, he never tried again, but him? He's such a sycophant! Ambitious. Anyway, Bren, I have the feeling this guy may be involved in some pretty strange stuff, like maybe even he is behind this whole thing with the disappearing plans. How can I get the goods on him?''

Karen then listened, made notes. Brendan Dugger had been the fiancé of her roommate in law school. That relationship collapsed early on, but along the way Karen had found one of her few male friends, now a partner at a Boston law firm. They saw one another once or twice a year. When they got together they asked each other why they couldn't find nice dates, boyfriends or girlfriends. They even both believed that eventually, for lack of an alternative, they might be forced to marry each other. When they reached that point, usually at the end of a long meandering talk about their respective lonely lives, they would size each other up, stare at each other and then, more often than not, burst out laughing. They didn't ring bells together, that was obvious. They were much happier as friends. As Bren would say, "Nice to have someone in the other camp."

Brendan talked for a long time, frequently asking questions. By the time the call ended, it was growing dark and Karen felt much better.

She then made three more calls, to her three best professional female friends, colleagues elsewhere in New York. All still single, all professional lawyers or MBA's, their advice on the matter was certainly not Bren's.

They all said, her professional female friends, that she should rifle Wentworth's files, schmooze his secretary, get the goods that way.

Brendan Dugger said she should rifle Wentworth's pants.

The guy who called her in the morning, asked if she had made the copies, had said he would arrange to pick them up and would call again at three-thirty that afternoon. Jean panicked. She immediately called in sick to the office.

Throughout the morning she compulsively cleaned. She even shoveled the back walk, which led nowhere. The night before, after Norman left and after she called Frank, she was so embarrassed and humiliated that she drank most of a bottle of wine, forcing herself to be ready to make peace with Norman when he returned, have a serious adult discussion with him. The wine, on top of the beers during the afternoon, made her sleepy. She never heard Norman come in and didn't hear him leave this morning, either. She knew he had been back because the couch cushions were on the floor, a blanket thrown over them.

This is terrible, she thought, I'll give the copies to this guy and then he'll be back for more. He'll keep working me for all he can get, play on my fear of that picture appearing in public. Then she thought of Frank. He won't call me. Why should he? This blackmail has nothing to do with him. It's these plans that are important.

In the morning after the blackmailer called she studied the copies she had made. They made very little sense to her, formulas, even diagrams of molecules, she thought. The only decipherable mark was in the lower right-hand corner where a box indicated a date just two weeks earlier in November, a name, Horace Taylor, and the inscription "Arterial Flushing Schematic/Binding Schedule."

What was an arterial flushing schematic? Something to do with arteries, but what? Was this something that flushed arteries somehow? Of what? She tried to remember her high-school chemistry; she had been good at that. It looked to her as if the plan outlined a part of a method to culture something in a lab. Was this a plan for one of those new magic drugs the companies were developing bugs to grow?

Lately, despite his usual tendency to avoid speaking of work, Norman had let slip what sounded to her like a name, a product name. Rejoice? Was that it? Hoist? Something.

Whatever was in the plans, could they be traced back to Norman leaving his briefcase at home? If so, in addition to her being humiliated, Norman might get in real trouble, might get fired.

How would she feel then? It was one thing to be mad at him, even think about leaving him, quite another to face the thought that by giving over these copies Norman might get fired. He might be humiliated if that picture appeared in public. He might become virtually unemployable, not to mention that the picture would almost certainly precipitate their divorce. Really, this was not a good situation.

Jean drank most of a pot of coffee after finishing the house. Her wine headache went away. She hated it when she had too much wine. But last night, after the phone call to Frank Benson, after the fight with Norman, she had been humiliated enough. What had Frank thought?

How could she get out of delivering the copies?

She had some shopping to do. That would keep her busy. She picked up the phone to call in an order to the meat counter, have it ready when she arrived. When she picked up the receiver, instead of a dial tone a voice said, "Hello?"

It took Jean a moment to understand that the phone had been just about to ring. Someone was calling.

"Yes?" The voice was unfamiliar. It's him, the blackmailer, to tell me he wants the copies now.

"This is Frank."

Frank? Frank! The voice sounded close. What's he doing calling me at home? I was right after all. The blackmailer must have tried him last night.

"Uh, listen, I'm, ah, sorry I bothered you last night, Frank, I had a big scare yesterday . . . You're lucky to catch me at home. Usually I am at work this time but I called in sick and—" She was babbling, making words.

"You were right last night. I'm in this, too."

"I can talk now."

"You really sick? I'm, um, I'm here, in Maplewood. At the coffee shop down by the station?"

"Here? In Maplewood?"

"Yes."

"The coffee shop across from the station?"

"Yes." Frank was chuckling as she repeated herself. "You well enough to meet me here or are you really sick?"

"I can be there in two minutes."

Before leaving the house she reapplied lipstick, changed to a newer pair of designer jeans, checked herself in the mirror. She looked fine. Who cares how I look, for Christ's sake?

This would be strange, a first, in fact. To see again in the cold sober light of day someone she had taken as a lover during the night. On those occasions when she had taken such a lover, she had never stayed the night. Consequently, she never saw the guy again. The next day she always felt guilty anyway.

At the coffee shop she spotted him right away, in the back corner facing the door. It was him all right. As she approached, wondering, do I shake his hand, how do I do this, he rose and nodded, gestured.

"I ordered you coffee. You drink coffee, don't you?"

"This is strange," Jean sat across from him.

Frank smiled. He looked as uncomfortable as she felt. At least he met her eyes.

"That was some storm yesterday. Roads are clear now, though."

"You drove up here?" What a stupid question.

"It's not that far. I have some business this afternoon in New Brunswick, a security system I upgraded for a client there. Just a follow-up call. Actually, that was the excuse. I came up here on the chance you'd be around. If you were really sick, I don't know . . ."

He was an odd-looking man. Big, heavy bones, sort of knobby. Not handsome. Not even very nice looking, except for the eyes, he had nice eyes. He was much quieter and calmer with coffee instead of Scotch in him. He was being very nice, actually, now patiently waiting for her to say something, not hurrying her along. As she stirred some sugar in her coffee she thought, I bet this man doesn't ever panic. Perhaps I was right to call him, and she said, "You first or me first?"

"I don't have much to say, Jean. Just I got a message last night."

"A telephone call, right?"

Frank shook his head, reddening.

"Is it all right to talk here? I mean, uh—"

Jean knew what he meant, he was asking if people here in this shop would see them, make something of it. It was nice he was concerned for her.

"Not to worry. I know hardly anyone here, even though I've been in this town for four years. My work keeps me busy." Nevertheless, she lowered her voice.

"Well." Frank sipped his coffee. "Last night was the end of this big storm. Seems like I spent the whole day shoveling my driveway. End of the day, just when you called, matter of fact, the doorbell rings. Here it is after six on a Sunday night and it's some delivery man with an envelope for me. I was on the phone to you, actually, when I let the guy in."

"I remember, you asked me to wait. I'd have hung up, myself."

"Well, anyway. I take the envelope, sign for it. Then he smiles, thanks me. I should have got it then, but I had my attention on you right then, if you know what I mean, and it wasn't until after I hung up that I remembered where I'd seen the guy before. It was the gold tooth. When he smiled, it flashed. Just like it did after I got him with the beer in Baltimore. That's right, that guy. Then I open the envelope." Frank paused and his face grew redder. "It was the, ah, picture. With a note: I'll call you, it said." Frank paused. "Matter of fact, for a moment there I thought the whole thing was a plot, you calling me just as he arrived. But how could you be in on it? You're in the, ah, picture also."

Jean blushed, thinking of her position the moment the picture had been taken.

"That's what I thought at first, too," she said. "That somehow you were in on it."

"Way I interpret what happened last night, whoever's on you is sending me the message he's on me, too. Now it's just a matter of time before I get the phone call."

"The guy delivering the envelope was the lounge lizard?" Jean asked.

"Yup."

"I thought he was cute," Jean said. She looked at Frank. "I wasn't interested in cute that night."

"Huh. So, what did your caller say to you?"

"Look." Jean reached in her coat, spread the copies of the plans over the small table. Frank moved the coffee cups aside, stared at the material. He was no engineer, that's for sure, but in all his work with computers and electronics, he had developed an eye for this stuff. These were plans for something. As he studied the plans, he figured they were formulas and programs to bind together two different materials.

"What's this?"

Jean took a deep breath.

"Sunday. Yesterday? My husband had to go to the office in New York. Norman works for a big drug company—Bonnell. Have you heard of it?"

"That some sort of holding company? Drugs?"

"Norman is in the finance department, although his area is really computers. He's been involved in some special project, very hush-hush, some new product they are developing. Matter of fact this morning I was trying to remember the name of it. Oh! It's Choice, that's it, Choice! Yesterday all of a sudden Norman gets a call and has to go into New York. I took him to the train, but he left his briefcase behind. I was angry at Norman. We're not getting along. At all."

Frank nodded uncomfortably.

"So when I got home I looked through the case, which he'd left unlocked. Usually he locks it even at home. I found these plans or whatever they are. Then, later on, Norman's still in the city, the telephone rings. It's this voice, says,

'Jean, are you alone?' At first I thought it was a nut caller and hung up. He calls back, starts asking me how I liked Baltimore. Then he asks how I liked the Holiday Inn. I got it then. He asks me, do I need to go on, about Frank Benson and room five-one-eight . . .''

"The guy who took the picture. Or arranged it, right?"

"He says if I want the picture back, I must copy the stuff in Norman's briefcase. If I do that, I'll get the picture and the negative, too. Otherwise, he'll get the picture published, or give it to my boss." Jean fumbled in her purse, pulled out a Life Savers mint, offered one to Frank. "Norman's about due back at the station here, so on the way to pick him up I stop at the library and make these copies. Then I pick up Norman. I can tell he wants to know, did I look in his case, and he knew I had because I needed to talk to him. There was other stuff in there, too." Jean paused. She wasn't ready to tell Frank everything, not yet. It got all into her relationship with Norman, too complicated.

Frank watched her talk, listened. This must be hard for her. She was edgy as she spoke. There was obviously some connection now between the picture and her husband's work. Jean took a breath.

"After I picked up Norman last night we had a huge fight and he left, went off to a movie or a bar. I couldn't think of anyone to call but you. And, after all, the blackmailer gave me your name."

"You had my name. I gave you my name."

"I know. Not that it matters, but I gave you my real name, too."

They looked at each other. Jean said, "You always give your real name?"

"*Always* sounds like I do it a lot. I don't."

"Me, neither," Jean lied, leaning back against the booth. "Then the blackmailer calls this morning, asks, did I make the copies. He surprised me, I wasn't ready for him, so instead of saying no I hesitated. He said he'll arrange to make the trade tomorrow: the copies for the picture.'' Jean looked at Frank and smiled a thin smile.

''Well.'' Frank paused. ''Here's what I think. I think it can be no coincidence the same guy I had my little run-in in Baltimore appears at my door with an envelope for me containing a print of the photograph—I tore it right up, by the way. With it was a note saying he will call. So you and me have the same problem. Which means that while this person is after you, now he'll try me out, too, even if only to raise hell with my marriage, except somehow I don't think that's it. At first I thought, after that picture was taken, it's my wife's father. He and I don't get along and he's looking for a good excuse to drive us apart. He's down in Atlantic City and he's uncomfortably close to some of those goombahs who run the casinos. I thought he had me followed, try to get me in a compromising position, get the goods on me.'' Frank paused, thinking, as he had thought the whole drive up to New Jersey, if it's not Michelle's father, then it's got to be the scam. That's the only thing I'd pay off for. If I pay off at all. He stirred cream into a fresh cup of coffee. ''I'd say that was a compromising position, anyway. Jesus.'' He reddened, thinking about it, remembering, then remembering the moments before, living his fantasy with this woman, Jean Newman, who now sat across the booth from him, dressed nice in jeans and a collared shirt, pretty band of narrow gold around her throat, gazing back at him, now calm as they talked, very nice indeed. She was even blushing a little. She must be remembering, too. ''I figure it this way—they had me marked even though they seemed after you, get the goods on you, but why not try and see what we can do about squeezing Frankie, too?''

''Frankie?'' Jean laughed. ''Frankie?''

''Uh, yeah, all my life, my old man, I was Frankie to him. Still am in my head, I guess. Anyway, it was a message, they're already planning to squeeze me and I'm being softened up.'' Frank paused. ''Either way.''

''Either way, what?''

"I mean, let's say it is a straight divorce thing..."

"I thought that, too."

"If that's the case I still don't want to play. Michelle's father makes me very nervous, tell the truth. In your case this looks like a scheme to get copies of these plans here. Could be big trouble for you legally, not to mention your husband. So. Either way I figure each of us has got to get that negative first."

"This person, Frank, he's going to arrange to trade these copies for the picture tomorrow. He said he'll call again at three-thirty this afternoon to confirm it."

"You think he'll give the picture back?" Frank asked.

Jean frowned. "Probably not."

"So." Frank paused, studied the plans again. Jean watched him. He carefully arranged the copies in order, traced the designs and carefully read whatever was written. He pulled a tiny calculator from his wallet and made some estimates. He had nice hands, she'd noticed that down in Baltimore. After a few moments, he said, "Jean, I can't figure these plans, except they must be part of a design for some sort of medicine or product—"

"Choice."

"Yeah, whatever, but whatever they are, way you tell it to me, the guy knew you were alone in the house when he called. Maybe even knew Norman left his briefcase home. Means either Norman or some other guy in that company is in on this. An inside job, as they say."

"Someone from the special team, maybe!"

"Norman?"

"Norman?" Jean asked. Norman? "No, too elaborate. If he wanted to make trouble, he'd just leave me! Why would he blackmail me? Why not just sell the copies himself?" She thought of the twenty-four thousand dollars contained in the bankbook. But that was a joint account, in her name, too.

"I see what you mean. Doesn't make sense, does it? How about the others on this special group, you know who they are?"

"Not really. Norman reports to a William Doane, I know that. And then there's Mr. Maroules, the big boss. Ironjaw, they call him, I think. Other than those two—wait, Norman mentions someone, Wentworth, I think, he hates him, I think this Wentworth is in charge of the group."

"We don't know enough. Don't know anything, matter of fact. It's got to be an inside job. Someone in that group is trying to sell off this Choice plan to another company, using some outside party to give himself deniability."

"Using me to get Norman's material!"

"That's right."

"You know what? This ticks me off. I don't like this at all!" Jean leaned forward. "So what's he got on you? Aside from us, I mean. Unless that's enough?" Jean raised an eyebrow. Frank flushed.

"Ah . . ."

"Come on, Frank. You wouldn't be here if there wasn't some damn good reason."

Frank shifted in his seat.

"Let's just say I know a lot about a bunch of banks' security systems. Last six years, all I've been doing is going around to banks and big companies, troubleshooting their security systems, their computer systems."

Jean was listening. The coffee shop was beginning to fill with the lunch crowd.

"You see, what with computers, everything being set up now with terminals, interconnected phone lines, things have changed. Used to be if a bank wanted to be safe, they'd build a huge steel vault in a concrete basement. Now, it's totally different. Billions of dollars are floating around in phone lines as electronic bits of information, what with all these wire transfers and so on. All a good thief needs is a terminal, a password, and balls. Excuse me. So these banks, they spend one, two, twenty, even thirty million for a total hardware-software system. How do they know, really, how safe it is?"

"I have no idea."

"They hire a guy like me, ask me to find for them the

106

chinks, the weak spots. I'm asked, really, to break into banks for a living, except the banks know it and it's all controlled. Still . . . someone puts pressure on me, like that picture, gets me to work for them, they could make a lot of money. Me, I'd be in Danbury prison but quick."

Frank was certain it was his scam that was the pressure point. Somehow it had been discovered, and not by the feds. But as he spoke to Jean, he realized that the reasons he gave her were uncomfortably valid.

"So if our mutual blackmailer does any simple research on you he'll know that?"

"Afraid so." Frank reflected. "That picture of me with you gets out, it's no more marriage, no more reputation in the security business. What bank's going to hire a guy been caught in a 'delicate' position?" He grinned. "My experience, most bankers mix poorly with good sex."

"Your experience?" Jean started laughing. "You run into a lot of female bankers?"

"Never. Just an expression."

"All right. So you stand to lose plenty if this picture isn't recovered." Jean reached over, placed her hand on his. "So what do we do?"

Frank knew all along it would come to this, this question, what would they do? All the way, driving up, knowing he had left a client pissed off near his home, he'd provided a sorry excuse on that one, he had wondered, how to stop this guy? How even to find him? He knew, somehow, they had to move fast, once the first exchange was made it would get tougher. The trail would go cold. Here he had a job to do in Philly and a family situation with his dad, due to come home in three days. It would take that long to get the room set up for him. He also had to deal with Michelle's ironclad resistance to the whole idea to begin with. Last night what they got into after the kids went to their rooms had been something. He had enough to do already, and now this thing as well.

"You said this guy will call you today?"

"He said three-thirty to set up the exchange for tomorrow."

"Huh." Frank gestured for more coffee. "So we got to find out who it is, that's for sure. Maybe he gives you the picture, the negative like he said, you give him the plans."

"Maybe." Jean doubted it.

"Huh. You hungry? It's almost lunchtime."

Jean looked around. The coffee shop was crowded. She shook her head.

"Not right now. Go ahead, order something."

Frank ordered the tuna plate, diet version, whole wheat toast, diet soda, and a small tossed salad. Jean blinked.

"Why is it, a big strong man like you, eats like a bird?"

Frank frowned. "It's a bitch. Doctor tells me, your cholesterol's too high, over two hundred. Two years ago, when I went, my count of two-forty was below the danger line. Now all of a sudden it's got to be below two hundred. So I eat like this when I'm on the road. It's being on the road, that's what kills me, when I get into the bad habits, the ice creams, the red meats. I gotta confess, I sort of like this type of food now." He rubbed his chin. "Now and then I go on an ice-cream binge, though."

Jean was watching him.

"So what do we do, Frank?"

"I really do have an appointment later today, or tomorrow morning. Tell you what. I'm gonna have to be around tomorrow. We'll stay in touch. Once the guy calls and picks a place, I can check it out, watch maybe from nearby, follow him, even. It'll be a chance to determine who it is. That's a start."

"What, you drive up early in the morning?"

Frank gazed at her with a slow smile.

"Maybe not, better I take a room up here, someplace out around Newark Airport. . . . I'll check in on the way down to New Brunswick, let you know."

He was watching her closely now. Jean was silent. He saw a red flush start up her throat.

"That's real close to here, less than ten minutes," she said, staring at his hands.

"Tell you what," he said, as if he were getting an idea. "You got some time, why don't you accompany me over while I check in. That way I'll get a fix on the area, how to get here from there, be better for tomorrow."

"I have a map of the area in my purse, as a matter of fact," Jean said, "and that way I'll know where you are, be able to call, maybe even leave a message."

They looked at each other. Frank was startled when the waitress brought his food.

"We can do some more talking on the way over," she said.

"Sure," he said. Talk? Who wants to talk?

"You really hungry?" Jean asked.

Ten minutes later, when the waitress came by the booth, a ten-dollar bill lay across an untouched tuna plate and salad. She was young, this was her first job waitressing, she knew the customer was always right, but she couldn't understand why those two people had up and left without eating.

They must have been having a fight.

Chapter Six

MONDAY EVENING

Karen Frucci knew that Wentworth was a corporate hero, the type who always stayed later than the boss even if it meant twiddling his thumbs in his office. She assumed he would still be in the building after five o'clock. She waited for everyone to leave. She thought: He's Mannie's right-hand man. What happens to right-hand men? They wait. They go down if their mentor goes down. They're treated by other executives for what they truly are—pale reflections of the true power held by the mentor. One route, he could move from where he is, move laterally to an assistant something, but that's it. No matter what, to go far here at Bonnell, starting as Mannie's boy, would take time. Patience. Wentworth is impatient to get in the driver's seat. He's in a hurry. I think he's more concerned with turning the big three-oh than most women are.

Karen smiled to herself. Now and then she thought about turning thirty herself. Hard not to with every magazine you picked up these days trumpeting articles about professional women and clocks ticking, articles about the shortage of available men. It would be scary if you thought about it too much. But she was only twenty-eight, three years out of law school, already deputy general counsel, Bonnell, life was great. Thirty was over six hundred days off. Karen still thought two years was a long time.

God, but this would be hard, humiliating. The jerk would only see it as his due. But he was up to something, Karen was sure of it. What could it be? What was the worst-case scenario?

He's a closet homosexual. But that's a secret, not being up to something.

He's pulling off some maneuver internally. He's after someone's job, maybe William Doane's. Maybe he's setting someone up for a fall and Bill Doane's the only candidate. Drexell's a lawyer, and Wentworth isn't. Wentworth's virtually unknown to the other managers since this project started last spring. Doane? So what, anyway, he sets up Doane and Doane gets fired, so what? Wentworth probably wouldn't get his job anyway. Being chief financial officer for a big firm like this one takes time, dues.

What else? Of course, what I said at the meeting, maybe that's it. We all assume Wentworth bends over, does tricks to keep Mannie happy. Mannie says, find a good PI, check out the chance the plans have been copied. We all think Wentworth runs right out and does it. Anything to please the boss. But what if he's running his own program?

Karen turned on the lamp over her desk. Night was falling. It was ten minutes after six.

Think. Mannie put Wentworth in charge of damage control. None of us think Horace's plans were copied that time. But thinking about it, who has led the charge on that theory? Wentworth. He says the PI Fallon found nothing. So no one is really worried now. But what if that's not true?

Could Wentworth be running his own deal? Him? That shallow person? What sort of deal? Only thing makes sense, he's stealing the design for somebody else. He would make a lot of money.

He could write his own ticket anywhere, doing that.

"Jesus." Karen sat up straight. Other thoughts tumbled through her head. Mannie prohibited anyone taking plans from the building. Yet she had done it. So had Arthur, even Norman. And Horace. All under Wentworth's direction.

"Am I being set up?" Her voice echoed in the office.

The way I'd do it, if it was me, I'd get copies, sell them, make a deal, highest bidder, but I'd make damn sure the trail went to a bunch of others. I'd make damn sure someone else could be blamed. I'd make certain others had, therefore, plenty of opportunity.

Was Wentworth doing that, setting it up so she, Arthur, Norman, even Horace could look like the culprit?

And how much money in this? What's his cut, assuming that's what he's doing? Karen was annoyed, thinking of the twenty-one thousand she still owed for law school loans, the additional thirty she wished she had to buy the nice studio she was now renting. This deal, if it was the deal, was worth millions, in stock anyway.

If I find out which other company Wentworth's buying stock in, I'd know who it was, wouldn't I?

"Stop it." Karen sometimes hated her mind. She would go off on these mental excursions, like this one. They were fine when thinking through points of law but hell on her personal life. She always ended up, in these journeys, either alone and middle-aged or a bag lady.

It troubled her that her fantasies rarely included men, or children. She even went to a therapist, Catherine, to work this out. Catherine said, at your time of life, career is all, make it all, you have a rich life now.

Therapy. Seventy dollars twice a week with a chain-smoking, anorexic counselor who drank coffee from a cup that said, if they can put one man on the moon, why not all men? Nevertheless, Karen felt better if she went to Catherine, talked.

She wondered what Catherine would say about her plan now, to get Wentworth's secrets the oldest way of all.

She wondered, rising from her chair and grabbing her coat, if she could really go through with this. She wanted to believe, Wentworth was such a self-absorbed shit, he'd unload everything after a few drinks without her having to perform her part of the unspoken deal, but she had her doubts.

Career is all, this time of my life. I hope Catherine is right.

Was Wentworth right, that crack of his, that she found people like him attractive? Bad question to ask right now, she told herself, and she marched to the elevator, took it one floor above, fifty-one, the boss's, and therefore Wentworth's, floor.

Wentworth was still at his desk, jacket thrown over an armchair, digesting the legal reports provided by Karen at the morning meeting. The closer he was to closing his deal, the harder it was to concentrate on day-to-day matters, to keep up his standard of output and behave as usual. He planned to play several pickup games of squash this evening at his health club, burn off the tension, flush the smoke from his lungs.

He planned to get the copied plans from Henry, then close his deal with Sam and Boothbay. It was all going as planned.

Except for Fallon, who had become hard to manage. Wentworth knew he'd better call Sam down at Boothbay, get him thinking about what they'd do about Henry Fallon when Sam came up to New York to pick up the last shipment of plans. Now that it was coming down to it, paying Henry Fallon ten thousand of his money, ten thousand of Sam's, maybe there was some way to get around it.

Wentworth was considering Fallon when he heard the elevator stop outside in the corridor, the doors open.

When he saw Karen Frucci stop just outside his door, he thought, what do you know? Months and months of the cold shoulder, the disdainful glance, and here she was, standing hesitantly, just over the threshold. Wentworth was not surprised. He knew his remark after the meeting had scored, she must have reassessed him in that context. And here she was. Finally. Well, well.

"May I come in, Wentworth?" she asked. It was easy to ask the question haltingly, as if she were uncertain. She was uncertain.

Wentworth gestured to a chair, smiled.

"Karen! Of course! What can I do for you?" It was his office, his domain, no No Smoking Unless All Occupants Agree signs, and while it would have given him the greatest of pleasure to light up, let her have it, he granted her the unspoken plea to keep the air clear. He could be magnanimous. He knew, sitting as he was, the light low on the desk, between him and Karen, he was in the most favorable light, or shadow. His faint adolescent acne pits could not be seen.

Karen noticed his cigarettes on the desk, noticed he did not light up. At least he was perhaps trying.

Here goes, she thought, sitting up straight, shoulders back, leaning forward slightly. Let him see the figure.

"I, uh, owe you an apology." God, this was hard to say, that is, hard to say keeping an apologetic expression, she had to work at it. "I was out of line this morning, it was unfair of me to make those accusations, totally out of line. I hope you can forgive me." She said this last sentence wistfully, arching her back just at the end. Wentworth's eyes were riveted on her chest.

"That's, ah, not necessary, Karen." Of course it was necessary. She just needed a good shot in the ass to come around, to see him as a possible ally, not an enemy, or, worse, a nonperson. Wentworth waved his hands. "We're all under tremendous pressure here right now. Everyone gets a little bent out of shape, especially lately. Not to worry." He was comfortable in his speaking-for-Mannie mode, lecturing without realizing it.

Karen watched him. Jesus, what an egomaniac. This is easy. What a weapon I have here. The guy's practically drooling. Where's the decisive, moderate, organized, tight-lipped yuppie now? The bastard is so goddamn self-absorbed I truly believe he expects me to be here, apologizing. I bet it never crossed his mind I might be here to continue our discussion, let alone try to seduce the story out of him. I honestly think he thinks I'm actually attracted to him.

She finally saw the light, thought Wentworth. Like all the other professional women he had known, Karen Frucci was seen by Wentworth as at heart a husband-hunter, someone who really wanted to settle into married bliss in the suburbs with children and give up her work. He was less threatened believing this. It gave him comfort to feel that while she was a corporate star right now, her time was short. All professional women's time in the workplace was short. To Wentworth, when he bothered to think about it, women fell in two categories, fuckable and unfuckable. Karen was definitely the former now she had climbed down off the high horse. And now, probably awash in guilt and remorse over her own quick tongue, not to mention sexual uncertainty, she would need reassurance and the comfort of a strong and impressive man like himself.

"Karen, if you have no plans for this evening I would like to take you to dinner, bury the hatchet." Among other things.

It's this easy? Karen thought.

"Wentworth, what a pleasant idea. We can get to know each other." Hopefully not too well.

"Let me just tie up a few loose ends, make a reservation down at Windows on the World. You ever been there? I just have one more phone call I should make. Can I meet you in fifteen minutes?"

"Of course. Why don't I meet you down in the concourse?"

"Fine, Karen. I am very pleased you dropped by."

He watched her leave. Nice figure. It was all coming together. He just had to get the other copies from Fallon and get them down to Sam. They were urgently needed as a final reality check, the final hoop to go through. It was coming together nicely.

Buoyed by Karen's visit, the evening squash game forgotten in the face of much more exciting activity, Wentworth carefully neatened his desk, filed the papers before him. He telephoned Windows. They could fit him in in forty minutes.

Then he called Sam in Baltimore. Every Monday, at five-thirty, either he would call Sam or Sam would call him. Wentworth felt some need to mention to Sam one of the staff might be somewhat suspicious but it was not an urgent call, especially given who was waiting downstairs. Sam and he had, Wentworth believed, a firm agreement. Wentworth would bring the Choice design to Sam and Boothbay. In exchange, Sam would install Wentworth as assistant vice president, Business Development, reporting to Sam, who was a full vice president, Business Development.

It bothered Wentworth, matter of fact, that he would be reporting to someone just about his age, but the promised title and salary were too good to pass over. This was his move and he had to make it now, cut the corner at the proper time. Moving to Baltimore was much more of a problem. Wentworth felt he would be relocating to a cultural wasteland, but he also knew and expected that he would be forced to move in his career to the wastelands once or twice. Baltimore was better than Chicago, Denver, not to mention Texas or Kansas City.

When Wentworth had first met Sam Dworskin at a squash tournament, months earlier, he already had the idea for his own project. He was in the market for a buyer. That had been delicate, difficult. There were only four or five other companies capable of handling this new substance and he needed to find the person in each he could safely approach. Asking around among his acquaintances who worked down on Wall Street, those associates of his close to the megadeals and the big corner cutters, the name Sam Dworskin, Boothbay, came up. When Wentworth heard the man was a squash player, he made some calls and arranged to be in a tournament with him.

Wentworth reflected. He knew immediately on seeing Dworskin that here was a person entirely lacking any of the necessary social graces to move smoothly upward in a large firm like Boothbay. Here was someone driven to be in charge at once, to hell with the consequences. He was someone, also, who appeared to measure his success partly by a body count of women. Even at that first tournament it was obvious he was after one of the usherettes, though a fair-looking consort already watched Dworskin from the balcony. Wentworth thought, I have the social skills and I will cut the necessary corners. This Sam Dworskin is all cut corners. He has

116

minimal social skills. I am a man of the boardroom, he a man of the street.

I will outlast this guy. I can use this guy. And, with that thought, one tournament later, in the second preliminary round, played in fact at Princeton one Thursday evening, he and Dworskin were opponents.

It was an early round, no spectators, just two opponents slamming the small black hard balls relentlessly against the front, side, rear walls. Nobody talked, except calling the score, now and then saying "nice shot." It was an early round without drama or very much excitement. But when Wentworth, the former number four Princeton player, smooth, elegant, who thought himself ruthless, played against Dworskin, the self-taught, vicious street fighter to whom *ruthless* was a preppy word for reality, their match was no "preliminary" round. By the third game, second set, blood flew.

Wentworth elected to believe he lost by intention, to soften Sam for the after-match proposition he intended. This night, with no languid lady hovering outside the dressing room, Sam agreed to have a beer in town. He could tell at once this character Randall wanted to talk about something. Before the first beer was finished Wentworth made his approach.

"So you're engaged in Boothbay special projects?" Wentworth asked.

"That's right."

"My boss, Mannie Maroules, Bonnell CEO, just assigned me to a special project. It's in an interesting area."

"What area is that?"

"Biogenetics."

"Everything's that these days. What are you working on?"

"Confidential. That's a nice car you drive, by the way. Those Porsches as fast as they say?"

"Gets there. Sounds like your special project is like some of mine. I'm in charge of organizing projects to identify and develop new products for the medical market. Lots of interesting things happening."

"Like what?"

"You know. Insulin. AIDS, of course. Mood changers that aren't addictive."

"You, ah, in the market for something already developed?" Wentworth was watching Sam carefully.

Sam's eyes widened. This guy was trying to make a sale, just like that. Maybe he had balls after all.

"You mean?" he asked, purposely vague. When Wentworth nodded, he smiled. "What do you want, Wentworth, for this 'something'?"

"Stock options. A vice presidency."

"Cash?"

"With this material, if I have stock in the company that brings it to market, cash will not be necessary."

"Good. Stock options I should be able to deliver. My division is new, business development and special projects, and we will be looking for an assistant vice president in a few months. That can be put on the table." Dworskin leaned forward. "What's the deal?"

Wentworth smiled.

"I'll need the commitment in writing. From the head, personnel division, first."

"You don't ask for much, do you?"

"This is the Holy Grail, Sam. The Holy Fucking Grail." He wanted to sound manly around Dworskin. "Let me ask you something. In the fifties, sixties, what was the Holy Grail then?"

"What's a Holy Grail?"

Oh my God.

"Back after Christ there was a relic, a grail, or a cup, that caught Jesus' blood when He was on the Cross. This Grail was the subject of a tremendous search all through the Middle Ages. King Arthur and his knights and all that. By Holy Grail, I mean, what thing are people most searching for? For example, back in the fifties, sixties?"

"You a religious nut?"

"Bear with me, please."

"I wasn't even around in the fifties. Well, barely. Just a kid in the sixties. I don't know, what did people want? Ah, my history isn't so great, but, something maybe to put in the air, make it impossible for atom bombs to go off?''

Wentworth tried to maintain his poise facing Sam's lack of basic facts. The guy may be ignorant, but he was a good corporate fighter.

"Sure, that's possible. What about in medicine, the business our companies are in?''

"Oh, shit, a pill to cure cancer?''

"All right. Now what would you say is the Holy Grail for the eighties, nineties?'' Wentworth turned around the placard on their small table, a promotion for a low-cholesterol sandwich platter, so Sam could see it.

Sam looked at it, thought. Wentworth waited.

"Right now, I guess something to take, help the heart. Something to reduce cholesterol? Something, to, say, prevent the hardening of the arteries?''

"Bingo, Sam.''

Sam Dworskin stared at Wentworth, eyes probing. Wentworth nodded.

"Holy shit, Randall.''

"Can we deal?''

That had been May, their start, the beginning. First, the arranging of the theft from Horace's apartment, and now, close to the end, the need for the plans for the binder. Sam's engineers needed those plans so when they developed a binder of their own it was different enough, chemically, that there would be no patent or copyright hassles. Wentworth had gotten his promises from the head of the personnel division: a position as assistant vice president at a time to be arranged shortly in the future. Wentworth was buying Boothbay stock with every penny he had. He had even taken a second mortgage on his condo apartment in New York.

Early on, back in June, one weekend he had driven to Baltimore and met Sam. He looked over the area and saw where his office would be. It was not fifty-one floors up, but it was three times the size of his present office at Bonnell. As he now began to dial Sam's number for the five-thirty call, Wentworth remembered that later on that weekend he and Sam went to someplace in Baltimore, walking distance from his hotel, for drinks, dinner. The whole evening was paid for by Boothbay, Sam said. Wentworth knew Sam was an operator, but that night, he found, so was he. The next day, driving home, again picturing the lovely skin, flanks, lips he had shared his bed with, his estimation of Baltimore rose considerably. The women in Baltimore were more, well, approachable than these here in New York. Most New York women were like the old Karen, the hostile Karen. Not like the new Karen now waiting downstairs. Now dialing, Wentworth, the subtle operator himself, dismissed the tiny red alarm bell ringing somewhere in his head. He was, after all, as Sam had shown him, a mover in all ways. . . . It never occurred to him his Baltimore visit was a total schmooze set up by Sam, including the Evening Frolic Escort Service, All Major Credit Cards Accepted.

The five-thirty call was picked up by Sam, first ring.

"Sam. Checking in here."

"Wentworth. Listen, I, ah, got a lovely lass waiting outside, taking her for drinks. What do you hear about the plans?"

"Fallon called, he'll pick them up at eleven tomorrow. Then he wants to meet us, tomorrow afternoon in New York, a place called Kearney's, up a block or so from my place, to make the exchange." Wentworth paused. "It'll be good timing. Today this snooty lawyer, Karen Frucci, almost accused me of theft! She's suspicious! And Fallon, I know you recommended him, but today he told me we're working for him!"

"Shit." Sam lit a cigarette, Wentworth heard his lighter click. "Listen, Wentworth, I'll arrange it. I'll come up there tomorrow and meet him with you. I want to get the plans myself first. I don't want to use that delivery mule again like the first shipment."

Wentworth said, "Fallon's acting like a loose cannon!"

"I think we've got to head Fallon off," Sam spoke slowly.

"You think our agreement for twenty will be enough to satisfy him?"

"You just get your share and I'll bring mine. But if we play this right, we'll get the money back." Sam chuckled. "The way I intend it, Fallon won't have those funds for long. I'll explain to you tomorrow when I see you. Oh, also. The business reason I'm coming up tomorrow is to make a big stock offering and I'll have your options for the five thousand shares. I'll have them with me."

"Fine." He replaced the receiver. Wentworth stretched after making the call. It appealed to him, a rising young executive about to be holding clandestine meetings, carrying thousands in cash. This was what corporate challenge was all about. You needed brass balls and a gambler's iron stomach. Wentworth rose and grabbed his coat, picturing Karen's breasts as they moved beneath her dress.

Awash in the potential of the evening ahead, he headed downstairs.

Down in the concourse Karen waited against the wall opposite the elevators, in a shadow, not wanting to be seen by her late-leaving colleagues. Karen would have been mortified to be seen leaving with Wentworth, however noble the cause.

Fortunately, Wentworth Randall was a handsome animal, a nice specimen, one of those tall angular frames that could wear anything and have it hang just right. Karen was well aware that she, too, was a nice specimen. Six one-hour aerobics classes every week attested to that; those plus week-end runs in the park, swimming at her club. She was lucky, her club had not yet become a pick-up joint, probably because of the cost—almost two thousand–a-year dues. It disgusted her when some sculpted, dim-brained Adonis attempted to engage her in conversation as she sweated on the treadmill.

Yet she worried, too. For instead of the social life she once imagined for herself, she spent time at the office or at the club, almost as if she were filling the day. And for all her judgment about the club as a pick-up place, there were a few men who used the facilities she wished would engage her in conversation. What was it about her, anyway, that seemed to scare them away? Could it be her own attitude? Here she had just turned Wentworth, mister supercorporate ball-less cerebral conniver, into a six-foot-two-inch hard-on just by arching her back and fluttering her eyelashes. She couldn't believe she, honors Law Review, had stooped to that. And she was, really, unpleasantly surprised at how well it worked. Her trouble was, the type of men those moves worked with, limp ego-driven yuppies, didn't appeal to her. Sometimes she wondered if there was any man out there with enough self-confidence not to need her opinion to be happy.

He was handsome, she admitted, now seeing him depart the elevator, head swiveling to find her. She looked at his coat, his charcoal gray scarf. She wondered what endangered species his shoes came from.

She was smiling when Wentworth saw her. He assumed she was smiling for him. Both of them pleased with themselves and each other, for entirely different reasons, they headed off to dinner.

As Wentworth expected, they made an impressive couple. Heads turned when they entered Windows on the World, one hundred seven stories above Manhattan, at the top of the World Trade Center, Tower Number One, thirteen hundred feet above the city. This evening, the city, covered by the blanket of chill air that had followed the snowstorm, was a dazzling carpet of lights stretching away for miles below them.

They were seated by a window facing east. To the north aircraft rose, one after another, from LaGuardia. Further east, out past Brooklyn, the big jumbos came in from the Atlantic to touch down at JFK.

"Very nice, Wentworth. I have never been here before," Karen said, lying.

"Thank you. It is a lovely night; I thought you would enjoy the view."

They settled in, ordered drinks.

They talked shop. Karen steered away from the project.

She would leave that for later. Wentworth, once he had a drink or two in him, loosened up and even told one or two mildly amusing tennis stories. Karen, matching Wentworth drink for drink, boldly suggested they order an entire bottle of wine for dinner. Once she took the occasion to lightly graze his hand with her own. She even let her leg lean against his under the table. She told Wentworth a few amusing law school stories of her own. The meal arrived.

Wentworth was pleased to see he had selected the proper restaurant. Karen had been impressed. Upon arriving at the top of the express elevator he had been struck by the horrible thought she was after something, finally acknowledging the alarms ringing in his head all the way downtown in the cab. But after two cocktails, and most of a bottle of wine, the alarms fell silent, replaced by such thoughts as: Will I ask her back to my place? It's a mess, but— Does she practice safe sex?— What was I worried about? She finds me practically irresistible.

Blissfully unaware of Karen's intentions, Wentworth swallowed thickly when she offered him cognac at her apartment on the way back uptown. He was a made man, he thought, fingers now entwined in hers, already having forgotten the shock when a dinner check for two hundred eleven dollars had been presented. Swaying with the cab heading up Broadway, his thigh pressed warmly against one of hers, Wentworth was relaxed, expansive, all powerful.

"You know," he said, brushing her ear with his lips, "New York is a lovely town."

"Yes. I love it." Karen was wishing she had drunk more wine at dinner. This was somewhat unpleasant, now that she was getting down to it.

"I'll be sorry to leave," Wentworth said, full of hope, promise, wine. Karen felt an electric thrill of excitement.

Leave? Leave where? A new job, perhaps? Part of the deal he made? Here it is.

"Here we are," she said. The cab pulled up in front of her building. "Let me get it, Wen." Still holding onto his hand as she paid the fare, she then lead him steadily—he was not walking too well—up to her studio apartment. Karen opened the door. Before he could grab her, she tossed her coat on a chair, waved toward the couch. "Sit. Let me get the coffee started. Do you want cognac now or later?"

Wentworth sat on the couch. "Whenever, Karen, whichever you choose. This is a lovely place." Actually, he thought: This place is tiny. "Is it yours?"

Karen was in the kitchen. "No, I still rent, although there are rumbles that it will go condo. I am trying to get my finances together for it, but it's tough. For all they told us at law school, the money we lawyers make isn't that good. I sure could use more."

There. Drop him the hint I can be bribed.

Wentworth barely registered what Karen had said. He was listening to a growing buzz in his head. Suddenly his eyes were not in focus.

"I think I'd better have just coffee for now, Karen."

"That was a lovely meal, Wen."

Wen. He liked it. Informal, crisp, neat. Affectionate.

"Your first time there?"

"Yes, first time. The view was amazing! Amazing. So, ah, romantic." In the kitchen Karen started the coffee machine and returned to the living room. Wentworth sprawled on the couch, looking a little vague. She turned on the radio. Soft music filled the room.

"Wen." Karen sat next to him, placing one hand gently on his knee, "I'm really so sorry about this morning. I was being a jerk, and unfair to you." Pile it on as heavy as you can. "We all have so much riding on Choice. Are you assembling a good stock package?"

Wentworth grinned. "Indeed I am." He leaned back, draped an arm behind her. "I must confess, Karen, for a moment there I thought you were accusing me of being behind The Event—"

"Oh, no! Not at all!" She leaned forward and kissed him.

"Which, to be honest, was a little flattering. It assumes I am capable of some pretty devious corporate infighting..."

Karen kissed him again, quickly.

"Well, Wen, your career has been so impressive! I mean, to be Ironjaw's AA and in charge of the Choice project team—what a burden! I may have a big title, deputy counsel, but what am I really? A glorified executive secretary for Drexell, that's all, truly! It's your position that carries the weight here. You're obviously picked for great things once Choice is introduced. And you know?" Karen, pressing forward, stared into his eyes. "I must confess my attitude toward you, at least until tonight, was motivated by jealousy. Isn't that ridiculous?"

Wentworth wished the buzzing in his head would stop.

"But now I can see you had to act that way with Mr. Fallon, keep it close to just you. That was best. Would you like some cognac now?"

As she rose to pour she let her hand trail lightly up his thigh. Handing him a full snifter, Karen again pressed close on the couch.

"What did you mean in the cab, that you'll be sorry to leave New York? Is Mannie going to assign you to the plant out in Iowa?"

"Iowa!" Wentworth spluttered. "My God, no! I'd never go there. No, Karen." Wentworth placed his cognac on the coffee table, turned to face her, reached up to stroke her neck. "Not Iowa."

Where? Karen placed her hand again on his knee. "You're taking a position elsewhere?" she ventured.

"Not at the moment." Wentworth, drunk, wanted to impress her. She was so interested in him! "Well, perhaps yes. In a manner of speaking. Perhaps as assistant vice president, Business Development, another firm down in the Washington area. It may be in the cards. It's all very preliminary right now." The buzz in his head was now a low roar. He looked down at Karen's hand on his knee, at her satin lower thighs where her dress had risen as she sat. He began stroking Karen's shoulder. Here it is. *Closure*. Lay it on thick with the big title, the big job. Then lay it on Karen.

"Where?" Karen said, thinking, the Washington area?

"Well..." God she had smooth skin. "With all the networking we did after The Event, we met a lot of people. One of the companies was impressed with me and has been chasing me. After we roll out Choice I may consider a change."

Keep talking, please, Wentworth. If you keep talking, I will happily suffer your sloppy, clumsy caresses. She moved closer and kissed him.

When he started mumbling again in her ear, she knew the evening was going fine.

Back in Maplewood at three-thirty Monday afternoon, Jean was waiting by her telephone, not nervous, not scared, almost hopeful. She knew that Frank was close by waiting near the airport to hear from her. Now she had an ally.

She picked up the phone on the first ring.

"Hello."

"Jean. The picture lady."

Jesus Christ.

"Yes?"

"You have the materials?"

"Yes."

"You know the Short Hills Mall?"

"Yes." We're going to make the exchange at the Short Hills Mall?

"Eleven o'clock tomorrow. There's a stairway and a waiting area just outside Bloomingdale's. On the north end, the eastern end, you know it?"

"Yes." Once she and Norman had had a huge fight there.

"Wear a blue outfit, yellow scarf."

"Yes. How will I know you?"

"I will say, 'Is this the east end?'"

"I see. And you have the picture, the negative?"

"Please. Be professional here. Of course."

"Eleven?"

"Yeah, that's correct. Alone."

Jean immediately called Frank's motel.

"Room five-one-eight," she said, grinning. When they had arrived at the airport and selected a motel to check in, Frank asked if room five-one-eight was free. It was, and they both stood in front of the receptionist, laughing. The receptionist took a look and immediately guessed, these two are here to fuck. So what was so funny?

Waiting for Frank to answer the phone, Jean thought, at least this five-one-eight had no balcony, no sudden surprises this time.

" 'Lo."

"Frank. Hi."

"You okay? He call?"

"Just now, like he said."

"What's the deal?"

"I'm to wear a blue outfit, a yellow scarf, and meet him at eleven o'clock tomorrow morning at the Short Hills Mall." Jean wanted to giggle, the Short Hills Mall was so, well, so unblackmail-like.

"A mall?"

"That's right. You're from Philadelphia. You don't know. This is a mall to end all malls: three stories selling just furs, just furs, for Christ's sake! There's a Bloomingdale's, Abercrombie and Fitch, Brooks Brothers, that sort of place."

"When's it open?"

"Ten o'clock during the week."

"Where're you meeting?"

"Supposed to be at the north, or east end, by the stairs to the second level, just outside Bloomingdale's. There's a sort of waiting area on the ground floor where I'm to meet him."

"Smart."

"What?"

"At one hour after opening there will be just a few people there. It will be easy for this guy to make sure you're alone, yet not stick out all by himself. He's got to make sure you haven't called the cops—"

"The cops!" Jean imagined Short Hills' finest in her

house, listening as she said, please, come with me to the Short Hills Mall, these plans, I stole them, but never mind, I need to trade them for a picture that shows me and this man at the very moment of our mutual sexual crisis, please come with me. "What do we do to prepare?"

"Is there a place we can meet tomorrow beforehand? Close by? I don't know this area."

"There's a Friendly's in Chatham on the main street off Route Twenty-four. It's close but far enough away so he won't see us. How about there?"

"I'll check it out right now, after I hang up. If the mall's open now I'll also take a look at it. How do I get there?"

"Simple, you leave the airport, take Route Seventy-eight west to Route Twenty-four, follow that north to the signs. Easy."

"One thing we do know, Jean."

"What's that?"

"This guy meeting us isn't Gold Tooth. He wouldn't need you to wear something special to know you. He had two hours to memorize your face that night."

"Frank. We didn't talk about whether or not I give him the plans."

"What do you think?"

"How about, no?"

"Attagirl."

Chapter Seven

MONDAY LATE

Paul made it back to his place just after six-thirty. No food. No beer. No cigarettes. He'd have to go down to Pathmark.

The phone rang.

"Paul. Fallon here."

"Where's my pay, Henry?"

"You deliver the envelope?"

"I got there. Where's my four hundred bucks? Plus the hundred you originally promised?"

"Was that guy Benson home? Did he have a lot of expensive toys in his yard?"

Paul frowned. Benson was just another working slob like him, trying to do the best he can however he can. When he was in that guy's house he could tell, here was a home, a place this family's been in for years, some kind of argument going on. Nothing special here. If this guy's robbing banks, well, more power to him. No Porsche in the garage, either, just a beat-up station wagon and a little shitbox Honda.

"Where's my pay? We agreed I go to Philly, I get the four hundred I was due in Baltimore, plus the hundred to take the picture, remember? It cost me, going up there in the snow. Gas."

"To get the four hundred, just one other thing."

"Bullshit. It's five hundred, first of all. That's it, what I want. Period."

Fallon was silent. The phone hummed.

"Paul. Your attitude sucks. I have information on you, distribution of a controlled substance. You keep pushing me, that information goes to your parole officer!"

"Fuck! Five hundred dollars!"

"No! You fuck! Nobody gets away threatening me! You can forget the money, how's that? Huh? I got a commitment next day or so. I'll be busy, but then, just then maybe I'll give that information to your parole officer! For a laugh! Haw, haw!"

The dial tone buzzed in Paul's ear. Fallon had cut the connection. Paul stared out the window, then looked in his cabinet. One can of vegetable soup, one can of beef and lentil soup. Paul opened both, mixed them together, turned on the stove.

Paul had never opened or checked any of the packages he carried for Ryan, and, afraid to know, he had also never looked in the envelopes he moved for Cheryl. Now, alone in his cold, barren apartment, fearing that in the near future Fallon might nail him, he wished he had stopped in at Cheryl's. He could use a warm body to lie next to. Cheryl had been so hurt by that Sam. Sam was working with Henry. When I came up here for Cheryl that time, I was working for Sam even then, except I didn't know it, he thought. I met Henry with the stuff for Sam, so they had to be working together.

Stirring the soup—soup and macaroni were his staples— Paul thought, Henry will never give me that evidence. Why would he? I'm just another gopher for him. A mule. He doesn't even have to pay me. He owns me the same as he's using that guy Frank, that woman Jean, even Cheryl. We're all the same: suckers.

How do I get clear of Henry? Who do I do it with? I'll need

help, for sure. What was his name? Frank Benson? Start with him, maybe.

I'm sure he thinks I'm one of the bad guys. Sees me down in Baltimore, then up at his home. Shit, he probably thinks I'm behind it all.

Who else is there I can call, though?

When Paul called Benson's house, Frank Benson was not there.

"Frank Benson? You must mean my father." Paul could tell this was a young kid, probably a boy, about ten, twelve years old. "He's not here right now."

In the background Paul thought he heard voices. Crying?

"Will he be in later on?"

"Uh, I think so, he was up in New Jersey today. That's what he said when he called. He was going to spend the night there but . . . He should be here in an hour, maybe less. Can I take a message?"

This kid had better phone manners than most adults.

"Please. Tell him a Paul Johnson called. Paul Johnson, okay? Tell him I made the delivery to his house last night."

"Oh, I remember that! I answered the door. Kind of silly, driving in so much snow. On a Sunday."

Kid was honest, too.

"It sure was, kid. Tell your dad I'll call him later on tonight. It's important. But tell him it's not what he thinks, all right?"

"Tell him it's important but not what he thinks."

"Thanks."

"You all right, mister? I mean . . . never mind."

"I'm not nuts, kid, that's what you're thinking. Your dad and I, we have some business together. I'll talk to him later."

" 'Bye."

Later on, as Paul went out the door for more beer and cigarettes, he decided he would stop at Pathmark, cash a check, fill the van with gas, and drive again up to Philly. He had to handle this face-to-face.

Norman returned home just after seven. Jean had worked hard preparing dinner. Curried chicken, rice, Caesar salad, fresh chutney, melon for dessert, a real nice dinner, which they shared in the kitchen silently.

"Norman." The meal was over. Dessert was finished with not a word said. "Norman, what is going on?"

"What do you mean?" Norman knew exactly what she meant.

"You can accuse me of invading your privacy, I don't care. Yesterday when you left your briefcase I opened it! You left it unlocked. I never got around to this last night but when I opened your case I found a bankbook with a joint account totaling twenty-four thousand dollars!" She leaned forward. "That's a lot of money, Norman. What did you do for that money? Are we in trouble? What's going on?"

"What do you mean?"

"Norman! I'm not stupid, you know. Someone has been paying you off for something! The bankbook is the proof! Now what are you doing?"

Norman rose from the table and started some coffee.

"Jean. Yesterday? Are we so bad together? Sex-wise?"

"That's not the point but, yes, we are. Bad, I mean."

"Am I so unattractive?"

"No!" Actually he was not unattractive to Jean. A little heavy, maybe, but still nice in a huggable sort of way. "It's your attitude!"

"My mind has been on work, Jean."

"Fine! Let's talk about work! Leave sex for now. That, we can deal with another time. What are you into? Is it illegal? Is it dangerous?"

"All right!" Norman slammed his hands on the counter. "All right! Is it legal? I think so!"

"What is it?"

Norman poured himself fresh coffee and added milk. He

faced Jean. "All right. One question for you, Jean. Did you see anything else in the case?"

Jean was not yet ready to discuss what was happening to her, but she nodded. "Norman, I saw some plans, or part of some plans. Designs?"

"They mean anything to you?"

"Not really."

"Well, they are designs for a vector, or binder, something to add to a very sensitive substance to create a pill. Bonnell's bringing out a new medicine this spring. It will be very big. It's one of those biologically engineered substances."

"What medicine?"

"It's called Choice. It's to do with cholesterol, plaque in the arteries." Norman smiled and scratched his neck. "This medicine will dissolve the buildup in blood vessels."

So, we pretty well figured it out, then, Frank and I.

"I'm on this special Choice project team. Been on it since last winter."

"You mentioned something about it." Jean poured herself coffee.

Norman nodded.

"Things have not been going well at work, Jean. I didn't tell you, but in the spring I received an unfavorable appraisal. I tried to move over to MIS, the computer department. I thought they wanted computer nerds like me, but they refused me." Norman frowned. "I'm stalled at Bonnell, Jean." He shifted, glanced away from her. "Then, ah, after I was assigned this project, Wentworth Randall, the AA, gave some of us these designs to take home if we needed them to do work. And I thought..."

As he was talking his eyes took on a steely glint as he remembered whatever he had been thinking.

"So at a conference I went to—one of those job fairs—I met this guy, he and I started talking. He represents a company also in drugs, small firm, wants to set up a new MIS department. He was very interested in me, and, well, one thing led to another..."

Norman? Her Norman? Every day a new surprise with this man. She was facing a stranger, gaze firm, lips tight, jaw thrust forward, a man who had made a decision, one he was comfortable with.

"What did you do?" Jean was fascinated. It was such a contrast to the potato she thought she had married. "Norman! *What?*"

"I, uh, told this guy what Bonnell was doing, the project. He wanted to see the plans, but . . . listen!" Norman raised his hand. "This other firm, they are trying to design a similar medicine. It's made totally differently, not with bacteria. So all my information was just a reality check for them. It let them see how the competition was doing. They paid me for what I told them, Jean. I didn't ask for it. They just paid me and asked me to keep them informed. They promised me if I keep quiet, I'll have a job. There is no way I can be liable for anything! That's what this money's for!" Norman reached across the table and touched her hand. "Wednesday I'm going to take a personal day from Bonnell and I'm going over there to register, fill out forms. Starting next week I'm slated to start as director, MIS Division."

"Where?" Jean thought, what company? Will we have to move? What a thing to spring on me now, his own wife.

"Look, Jean, after Wednesday, all right? I want to be sure. I won't have to go to New York. It's over in Elizabeth, closer, less of a commute."

"But, Norman, if you informed on Bonnell, what's to keep you from getting in trouble?"

"I won't get in trouble. What I did is irrelevant because the medicines are different. And I did it after something else. Last May, our scientist, Horace Taylor, took the plans home, lost them for a while. We all figured Horace just misplaced them, but they could have been copied! I thought, why not?"

Her Norman? Thinking, why not?

"Jesus, Norman." Jean stared at her husband, the stranger seated across from her. "So what happens now?"

"Once things are tied up Wednesday, I give notice to Bonnell. That's it. Over to a new job."

"Will it mean moving?"

"I told you, Nauset's, er...this company's in Elizabeth. Ten-minute drive. New small firm, went public a year ago. When they get this new medicine out, they'll be a major firm. Just like that! If I start with them now, I can grow with them."

Jean thought, Nauset? Hadn't there been a story about Nauset some time ago in one of the magazines, the best-managed new firm on the block? Didn't he just say that they're chasing this cholesterol thing, too?

Norman sat back, smiled.

"Staff of just three, to start. Manager, MIS. Company's going to do their entire personnel, production, inventory on a new system, the one I trained in for two years. They're getting a big new mainframe. When I start, I'll be in charge of setting it up."

"How much?"

Norman flushed.

"Sixty-two five."

"Sixty-two thousand dollars?"

"With that income, and your pay, and the cash I have here, we can start looking for property out in the horse country." Norman was playing with a spoon, tapping the table. Jean watched him, incredulous. Their income would jump by over fifty percent.

"Wow." The horse country? Really? Sixty-two five? For Norman?

"I wanted this to be a surprise, Jean—your—our, Christmas present. I was planning to take you out this coming weekend, to dinner, tell you all about it then, have it be a nice big surprise." He grinned. "Next week, I'm going to turn over a new leaf. With the shorter commute, I'll have more time, and I'm registering at the health club to get back in shape." He reached down, grabbed the roll of flesh over his belt. "Get rid of this."

Jean sat silent, staring.

"I was going to say all this next week, but now the story's out, I'll tell you. I know it's been real shitty the last couple of years. I know you've been very unhappy. We've had a terrible marriage. For all I know, you want to be out of it for good, but hear me out first. I still think we might have a future if we both want it and I want that chance. I change jobs, we get a nice house, maybe even start a family, let's let bygones be bygones, me, my shitty attitude in the bedroom, I'll try to take you off the pedestal. You, finding what you need elsewhere—no, let me finish!—please, let it ride a little, let's see. Please."

This is what guilty feels like, to have your husband plead with you only hours after a roll in the sack with someone else.

This Norman, this one here, I like him a lot better than the old one.

How can I tell him now what's going on with me? That unless me and Frank neutralize this blackmailer it may all be for nothing in any case?

And she started to cry.

"Jean—"

"No, Norman, it's all right. I'm touched is all. Let me be. Let me cry. I have a lot to absorb here, a lot to think about." And a lot I can't tell you, not yet. "Will you just hug me now, please?"

Norman, huggable Norman, hugged her.

Frank spent an hour at the Short Hills Mall studying the terrain. The Short Hills Mall was the perfect upscale emporium, a big long aisle of classy high-priced shops located on two levels, with huge stores at the ends. In the open middle were fountains, a ridiculous glass elevator rising all of ten feet from the ground level to the balcony on the second level. At the east end was the stairway Jean had mentioned, rising to the second level, with the waiting area beneath. Pure glitz.

One exit to the parking lot lay about forty feet from the waiting area, just outside the entrance to Bloomingdale's.

Frank then swung by the Friendly's in Chatham, to place it, and returned to his motel.

Frank had planned to do some work in his motel room, a security installation plan he had brought with him, but when he called home just after he got in those plans changed.

"Hi, Brad, it's Dad. Mom there?"

"Uh, Dad, she's asleep."

Frankie felt the stirrings of alarm. Asleep? At five o'clock? "What do you mean?"

"Well, ah, she's been asleep for a couple of hours."

"Now?"

"Listen, Dad, something strange is going on."

Over the phone Frankie heard the catch in his son's voice. Brad was terrified.

"What's going on there, Brad?"

"Aw, Dad, I don't know. You better talk to Suzie."

"Dad?" Suzie's voice was too high, she spoke fast. "Mom's been acting real strange, Dad, since this morning. After you left today she called my school, demanded I come home. It was weird. Like she was afraid to be alone? I got a ride home with Mr. Bretton, the guidance counselor. When I got home Mom was running around crying and yelling."

Crying? Yelling?

"What happened?"

"That's just it, Dad, nothing, not really. She was all upset about everything. Gramps coming home, that was a lot of it. But all sorts of stuff. I didn't know what to do. Mom was tearing the house apart looking for her little helpers." Everyone in the family knew what the little helpers were. "Dad, I didn't know what to do." Suzie started crying. Frank listened, holding the receiver to his ear in the motel room, the bed in disarray from earlier with Jean, a hollow, lost feeling growing in his chest.

"She's asleep now?"

"Dad, I didn't know what to do. Mom refused to see a

doctor, refused to leave the house. She was tearing the house apart. You know how Dr. Schwartz stopped her prescription a few weeks ago? Well, Brad and I had already, even then, hidden away some bottles. We thought Mom was taking too much then. In fact the bottles Brad and I hid were ones we saw Mom hide earlier. She was stashing them, Dad! Remember when Mom was looking for those bottles in her bureau? Those were the ones!'' Frank remembered, Michelle said she was looking for all the pills to throw out, only it wasn't that at all. "I gave her three pills, Dad! The yellow ones?" Ten milligrams. Enough to put someone to sleep, Frank knew. He'd taken some of them himself when he flew in commercial airplanes. He hated flying, had ever since the service.

"Suzie, you did fine. Mom will be fine. She'll sleep. It isn't dangerous to take three pills. I've done it myself when I fly—"

"You're such a chicken. Really, Dad." Suzie sniffed.

"Listen, I'm coming right home. Be there in less than three hours. We'll get Mom fixed up tonight. Get her in a place for help."

"What's wrong, Dad? Mom's been acting so strange!"

"She must be addicted to these so-called helpers Schwartz prescribes her every time she goes to see him. She needs professional help."

"Dad, what about Gramps, Christmas, what . . . ?"

"Calm down, honey. It's all right. Put the leftover lasagna in the oven. That will get dinner started. I'm leaving now."

Before leaving Frank called, left a message for Dr. Andros, his father's doctor, and explained to the answering service he had a problem at home, his father's room was not yet ready, how was he doing, please call him at home after eight this evening. Then he telephoned the treatment center, recently opened, in the new hospital wing adjacent to the wing his father was in. He'd seen the signs when going to visit his father, an alcohol and drug rehabilitation center. In fact Michelle had lately insisted that he consider the place to resolve his own drinking behavior. She had even left little pamphlets around the house for him to read. He now wondered if those messages had actually been a cry for help from her?

He did not call Jean. The way they had left it, if he was not there, at the Friendly's, she would not go to the mall. Right now Jean did not cross his mind, except to make him feel guilty. Here he had been gamboling away the afternoon while his kids tried to deal with their mother, his wife, having some sort of breakdown.

When he left Newark Airport the rush hour traffic was heavy. On the New Jersey Turnpike, he stopped at the first service area for a coffee to go.

Sipping the coffee through one of those tear-off lids, he tuned in a classical station on the radio, a change from the usual rock and roll. He drove on. The snow from the previous day lay in huge piles along the side of the road. Here and there a car was still buried. The storm had been a big one. On the radio the announcer said it was the heaviest snowfall for early December since 1964, twenty-six years earlier.

More than a quarter century ago. Jesus. Frank thought, in December 1964 it was just after the Tokyo Olympics and I was nowhere near New Jersey, Philadelphia, or even North America. Matter of fact, I was just about two months in-country overseas. Learning firsthand why my dad used to say, said to me just before I shipped out, it ain't no fun, boy, not at all, not in the jungle. Only my war was a little east of his, which had been Burma. How I used to wait for mail call, his letters, about his hunting trips, his dogs, his projects around home. I have those letters still, somewhere up in the attic, probably in the trunk with my other military stuff. His letters kept me sane sometimes. Now look at him, all shriveled there in a bed.

Jesus, things have gotten complicated. Bad enough, this picture thing. I had thought the scam was perfect, only it wasn't. Look at what's happening now. He wondered how he could bring his dad home now that Michelle was ill.

Michelle. Frank finished his coffee and threw the empty cup on the floor of the car. As usual the engine was overheating.

When had Michelle started with the pills? It had been a long time ago, right after Brad was born. Back then, the late seventies, doctors prescribed those pills for everything—anxiety, muscle pain, insomnia—and Michelle started with the fives. Five milligrams, once a day, to help her sleep. Then it became a regular thing, no big deal. One little pill a night, until after a while they were her "little helpers."

When Brad had a lot of trouble in the third grade and had to change teachers in the middle of the year—a true personality conflict if ever there was one—Michelle began with pills morning and night. Somewhere in there she moved from the blue fives to the yellow tens.

And I never paid it any attention, Frank thought. None at all. We had already drifted pretty far apart. It was like she wasn't really there, spaced out all the time. I couldn't reach her.

Of course I couldn't reach her. She was spaced out all the time.

Three years ago, Frank had saved and hidden money away. He took Michelle to Saint Martin on a surprise winter four-day getaway. The trip was hell. Fighting, yelling, tears, all for no reason that Frank could see. He suddenly remembered that on that trip she had left her pills at home. She even tried to get Schwartz to transfer a prescription to the island while she was there.

What was happening now made sense. She was addicted even then. He was too stupid to see it, too stupid or preoccupied. Now he was driving back to his home to take his wife to treatment and he felt responsible for all of it.

Guilty. This is what guilty feels like.

He and Michelle had been happy the first few years. What happened? Maybe addiction happened.

It seemed a long drive to Philadelphia. When Frank arrived home just after seven, Michelle was awake, slumped at the kitchen table, facing a plate of cold, untouched lasagna. She stared ahead blankly, hair tangled, eyes puffy and red. Brad and Suzie hovered in the living room, frightened.

Frank glanced at Michelle in the kitchen and spoke quietly to his children.

"Suzie. Go pack a case for your mother. Underwear, casual slacks, two shirts, sweater, her toilet kit. A comb." He squatted before his children. "Mom's become dependent on those little helpers. I'm checking her into the hospital tonight for treatment. She will be there a few weeks. I think her strange behavior these past weeks happened because her prescription was stopped by Dr. Schwartz. She have any in her now?"

Suzie nodded.

"Fine, that will keep her calm. We'll get her checked in with no fuss." He was speaking quietly. He did not want Michelle overhearing him. "I've made arrangements to keep Dad in the hospital a few more days, too."

"Will Mom get better?" Brad's lower lip trembled.

"Yes, she will." Frank was uncertain.

"Dad, what about us? Here? School?" Suzie was asking. "With Mom away and your traveling, who will take care of us?"

"Listen, honey, I've rearranged my schedule so the next few weeks I'll be home most nights. I did it so I could watch over Gramps. Now, he'll stay where he is, for a few days anyway. I'll still be here. Except maybe tomorrow, tomorrow night, I may be in real late. I still got a job to do up by Newark." Recovering blackmail photos. What a job. How could he explain that? "So I've arranged with Sue Kitchner—Becky and Tim's mother—to put you two up for a couple of days while I get things sorted out here."

"What about Christmas?" The kids liked going to Atlantic City for Christmas. Michelle's father made Frank uneasy but Brad and Suzie found him intriguing.

"That's still ten days away. We'll work it out. Now, Suzie, you go pack for Mom, then yourself. Brad. You pack for yourself." Brad nodded. "All right. Start working on it. Sue will be by to get you pretty soon." Frank knew to get people doing mundane tasks in strange, scary situations like this. Keep their focus on the simple, immediate things. With all this worry and uncertainty, if someone wasn't busy then they'd think, which led to obsessing. And when that happened, being in your own head was like being in enemy territory.

Frank went into the kitchen, sat down across from Michelle, took her hand.

"Michelle. Honey?"

Michelle's gaze slowly turned on Frank.

"What's happening?"

"Look, Michelle, what's happening is Dr. Schwartz removed your little helpers about a month ago, right?"

Slowly, Michelle nodded. At least she could respond to questions.

"You haven't liked that, have you?"

Michelle barely nodded.

"I feel fine now, Frank."

"You have a helper or two in you now, Michelle."

"Oh. I see. I acted pretty crazy this morning, Frank. I scared myself."

"Listen, Michelle, I am going to take you to the hospital and have you looked at. Dr. Schwartz suggested it."

"He did?"

"Yes," Frank lied. "To check you out. Something's not right, honey, I think even you know that. . . . We'll go right now. You'll have a good series of tests."

Michelle allowed Frank to lift her to her feet, help her into a coat. Frank wanted to get her to the hospital fast, while she was agreeable. If she started to fight, she'd never go.

Suzie returned with a small bag, handed it to Frank. The kids hugged their mother.

"I'll be back in about an hour, maybe two. Sue's coming by to pick you up about seven. I'll shop for some food on the way home. Then I'll clean the house. It's a mess, don't you worry about that."

Before he left with Michelle he hugged his kids.

Michelle sat quietly in the car.

"Is this a nervous breakdown?" she asked.

"No, Michelle!" Actually Frank had no idea.

"Is it the pills?"

"I think so, honey."

When they arrived at the hospital Frank walked Michelle to the treatment center, carrying her bag. A nurse on duty welcomed Michelle warmly. Frank put his hands on Michelle's shoulders and looked her in the eye, smiling.

"You'll be fine here, honey."

"Oh, Frank." Michelle huddled in Frank's embrace, shoulders moving. The nurse gently disengaged her. Michelle, smiling weakly through her tears back at Frank, let the nurse lead her away. A few minutes later another nurse joined him, carrying a handful of forms.

"Mr. Benson, your wife will be fine. She's in the right place. You will be able to call her in two days to say hello, but we ask that there be no visiting for two weeks. At first, for most new patients, there is a great deal of denial. They do not want to be here. First we must get the substances out of their systems. I have some literature for you to take home and read and a lot of forms for you to fill out."

It took Frank fifteen minutes to complete all necessary forms. In the box marked method of payment, he wrote, cash. With my dad in one wing and Michelle in another the scam fund won't stay large for long, he thought.

Before he left the hospital complex he looked in on his father. Sleeping on the narrow bed, his dad looked like a starvation victim, twisted in a fetal position. Frank did not wake him. He sat quietly listening to the hoarse, infrequent breaths, wondering what would Dad say about all this: him in one wing, Michelle across the parking lot in another, the house a wreck, my profession at risk because of a picture taken on the road, my freedom itself perhaps in jeopardy because of the scam. What would he say?

Sounds like you've bitten off a little too much, Frankie. That's what happens when you get confused. You sound confused to me right now. All I can say, do the best you can, take care of your family, cover your flanks. Keep it as simple as you can.

"Thanks, Dad," Frank whispered. He kissed the pale, wrinkled forehead and returned home, first stopping at the local supermarket.

Back home, he packed away the groceries, rinsed the dishes, and started the dishwasher. He was wiping the counter when he noticed a note on the table: "Dad. Somebody called named Paul Johnson. He said he will call you later. Important. But not what you think. Brad. P.S.: Sue is here to get us. P.S.S.: Send our love to Mom. Brad again."

Who was Paul Johnson?

In the living room he started at one end and began. Michelle had emptied every drawer in the room. She must have been in a frenzy, looking for pills. Frank knew she must have terrified the kids. She must have terrified herself.

The telephone rang.

Thinking it was Sue Kitchner, Frank said, "Hello?"

"Frank Benson?"

"Speaking."

"Good. You got my message? Last night."

So here it was. Just like Jean predicted. Jean's blackmailer. Now, his blackmailer, too. I'll see what you look like tomorrow, you bastard.

"Excuse me?"

"We have some business to discuss. You will want a negative from me. I need something from you."

"Photographs do not threaten me."

"Jail should. This has to do with a large and growing sum of money not originally your own, and the elegant little system you must have designed to so deftly relieve certain banks of the funds."

"Go on."

"You're working a nice little system, Benson. Has to do with taking funds from several banks you evaluated for security. Losses not yet noticed, by the way."

"Not yet, you mean, but soon, notified by you, I suspect, unless—?"

"You're quick, Benson. I want both the funds and the system. After I have those, I will lose my urge to go public."

"What do you want?"

"All of it, Benson. There is a public bus locker at your local Greyhound station, number three-hundred-sixty. There's a key in your mail. You will withdraw the funds, all of them, seventy-eight thousand dollars, and place them in the locker. I want this done by tomorrow night before ten."

This son of a bitch is going for the double play, two of us in one day. Seventy-eight thousand is just one of the three accounts I have. Maybe he hasn't figured it all out yet.

"And then?"

"I will contact you again."

Frank started some coffee. The empty house felt hollow. No muted heavy metal rock music from Brad's room, no distant sound of Suzie chattering on her phone upstairs. Not even Michelle's recent fussing. Just him, the house, the mess, and silence.

So if this guy found out, who else will? *Shit.* I get caught at this, I'm done. I'll never get more work, that's for sure. Jail, also, for sure. Too damn easy. It always was too easy.

Frank's father used to say if you make a mistake and you know it, don't sit around waiting, rectify it fast. Ever since Jean called him the night before, he had wondered how safe his little system was. Now he knew—not safe at all. Time to get clear.

Walking quickly to his small study, the guest room, Frank turned on his computer. It didn't take long, a few keystrokes after figuring some reprogramming. He hooked up the modem and sent out the commands. And, just like that, the scam was history, no more hundredths of cents shaved, dumped in his own account. No more funds to be added to the over two hundred thousand he had already salted away.

Just like that.

Frank had to cover his dad's illness and Michelle's stay in

the hospital. Maybe a few thousand would be left over by the time all this hospital, rehab, home care work ended. Not much more than that, but that, at least.

Just enough to pay the bills with a little left over.

He'd get the house cleaned, before facing a short night and an early start back up to Jersey. Checking the mail, he found the locker key, no return address.

Another phone call.

"Frank Benson?"

"Yeah."

"This is, ah, Paul Johnson."

"Oh yeah. You're the guy talked to my son earlier. Do I know you?"

"Listen, I, ah, have to meet with you. I'm the guy, ah, oh, shit, I'm the delivery man. From last night."

Frank stood utterly still. Gold tooth. What had Jean called him—lounge lizard?

"You the character was here with the delivery last night?"

"Uh, er—"

"Gold tooth?"

"Listen, mister, we got to talk. It isn't what you think. I got a problem with Henry, too . . ."

"Henry?"

"Henry Fallon. He's the guy who hired me to find a Jean Newman, dance with her so a picture could be taken by the bartender. He set her up to pressure her to get something from her husband. Only, ah, you were there already, and, uh, ah . . ."

"I'm listening."

"Mister, can we meet? Tonight?"

"I just got off the phone with your partner, fellah. Fallon, if that's his name, he's already laid out the deal. What's your angle?"

"That's just it. My angle has nothing to do with him."

"Where are you calling from?"

"Citgo station. About four miles from you."

146

Jesus, this guy was serious. He'd come up here from somewhere. What harm could it do to listen to him?

"Remember how to get here?"

"There! Your house?"

"No one is here tonight."

"Uh, ten minutes?"

"I'll be here." Frank hung up.

He went back to the living room, climbed the stairs, went to the closet in the master bedroom. Michelle had strewn clothing from the closets and bureaus all over the floor.

At the back of the closet, a tiny stairway led to the attic. Frank pulled the light switch and climbed up under the eaves. Under a lot of other stuff—boxes of Christmas ornaments, photos, old books, a box of toys—Frank saw the battered metal military trunk. He pulled it free.

His old marine locker, stowed back when they'd bought the house and forgotten until now.

Opening the top, Frank reached past the carefully stored dress uniform, the mothballs, and the stacked, carefully bound letters from his father and pulled out a worn canvas bag. He closed the locker and returned downstairs carrying the canvas bag. In the kitchen, he emptied the bag on the table. One knife, marine issue, two clips of ammunition, and one pistol kept from his MP days after he came out of the jungle. The pistol was clean. No rust, the barrel shiny.

Frank wondered what the hell he was doing as he quickly stripped and cleaned the pistol. He had been the fastest man in his battalion, cleaning his weapons. Then he snapped an ammunition clip into the pistol. It had been about seventeen years since he had fired a gun, and then on a target range. He had once been excellent with a rifle. But his pistol skills had never been very good. He was likely to shoot off his own foot now, if he had to fire the thing.

The doorbell rang.

When Frank opened the door the first thing Paul saw was the big cannon in Frank's right hand. My God, this guy is going to shoot me right here on his front step and claim self-defense, protecting his home and family. Paul nearly wet his pants and jumped back, eyes wide with fright. Frank reached out, grabbed Paul by the arm, pulled him inside, saying, "What's wrong?" Then he realized he was still holding the pistol. He laughed. "Relax. I'm not going to shoot you."

Paul wasn't sure. His heart had been jumping all the way up here from home. The closer he came to this guy's house the faster his heart jumped. Making the call a few minutes ago had been one of the hardest things he'd ever done. Seeing the gun terrified him.

Frank took a hard look at this guy. About six feet, one-sixty. Not too strong, out of shape. Obviously very nervous right now. Whatever this guy wanted, it didn't have to do with putting pressure on Frank.

"I got some coffee in the kitchen." Frank removed the clip from the pistol. He placed the gun on the mantelpiece over the living room fireplace before leading Paul back to the kitchen. Paul's relief was intense when the pistol left Frank's hand.

"What do you take?" Frank held milk in one hand, a packet of sugar in the other.

"Uh, lotta milk. Sugar." Paul liked his coffee light and sweet.

"Sit." Frank poured two cups, prepared them, placed one cup in front of Paul. "Take off your coat. Relax. I won't kill you." He smiled. I was right in that bar last week, this guy is one of those the women just head for. He probably thinks all us men are approached like that. Little does he know.

"Talk. Why are you here?"

"What was it, with the gun, for God's sake?"

"Scared you, huh? Didn't mean to. I was just upstairs, rummaging around, found it, brought it downstairs, just cleaned it. I'd just loaded it when you knocked."

Sure, Paul was thinking.

"Hang on a minute, I gotta make a call. Not the police. Relax, all right?"

Frank called over to Sue Kitchner's.

"Sue. Frank here. I see by a note Brad left you got the kids a little while ago."

Paul waited, listening to Frank's half of the conversation.

"That's right, a couple of days? Is that all right? I have a project to finish up in New Jersey. Then I'll hold the fort here . . . I checked her in an hour and a half ago . . . Four to six weeks, they said . . . Yeah, little helpers, that's what we all called them . . . No visitors, they said, not for a few days, couple of weeks at least . . . He's still there. Not too good, Sue. Couple of days, I'll bring him home . . . Yeah, in the guest room, downstairs here . . . I know. No one said it would be easy . . . Sure. Let me speak to them."

While Frank talked to his kids Paul finished his coffee, poured himself more. He was starting to relax. This guy did not appear that threatening, not face-to-face talking. As long as that cannon stayed in the other room.

After Frank finished, he turned back to Paul.

"All right."

"Yeah." Paul took a breath. "I'm a driver for Ryan Express, van deliveries around Baltimore? It's a job, just a job. Reason I was here last night—"

"Hold it." Frank raised his hand. "Start at the start. Before last night I ran across you in Baltimore. At the Holiday Inn last Tuesday."

Paul swallowed.

"I thought you didn't recognize me from that night."

"Didn't, not until after you left. Wouldn't have, either, except you smiled. Your gold tooth."

"Shit. Well. Recently I've been trying to do some investigation work for a few people, thought it might turn into a business. I ran into this guy, Henry Fallon, when I was picking a van up in Newark for the company. Actually, one of my stops around Baltimore, Boothbay Chemicals, the receptionist was cute. She asked me to carry some envelopes to other Boothbay divisions on my route, private carries, her to other secretaries, the pay for that was pretty good. I thought it might be money I was carrying. Maybe coke. I didn't ask about it much, just did the deliveries. Then she offers me a lotta money to pick up something from this Henry guy. Which I did. When we meet, he gets heavy with me, you know? Tells me he knows about the earlier envelope deliveries, that he has evidence I was distributing and selling. He said he'd go back to his former bosses, the Newark Police Department, and have them call the Baltimore Police. I'm, ah, *shit*, I'm on parole. I did eighteen to twenty-four for passing bad checks, Mitchell Medium Security. Got out ten months ago."

"This guy, Fallon, used to be a cop?" Jesus, you get the goods on an active parolee, that's tighter than slavery, he'd do anything.

"Yeah. After that first pickup he called me a few times just to needle me, but he had no work for me. Then last week he offered me a hundred bucks to drive out by the airport to the Holiday Inn, dance with a Jean Newman. He told me his client wanted a picture of her dancing with some guy."

Frank raised his eyebrows.

"So that whole thing at the bar, it was about that?"

Paul nodded. "I get there, you were with her, no dancing by the time *I* arrived. You were all done dancing by then. So after a while I came over, had to, to ask her to dance, not that she wasn't a nice-looking lady. She was, very. But this time, anyway, I was on business." Paul chuckled. "That was quite a move you pulled, throwing beer at me."

Frank laughed. "All that time I was sure you were about to make a move. You sure looked like a snake to me—"

"Anyway. When I got dried off, came back out, you were gone. The bartender said Henry upped the fee to four hundred if I go up, use a passkey he had—the bartender had, that is—come in your balcony door, get your picture." Paul leaned forward, speaking slowly, carefully. "I, uh, took your picture, you and, ah, Jean, then took off, down the stairs, dropped the camera off in the bar. You never looked there when you came downstairs. That's where I was."

"Jesus!" So this guy took that picture? Jean would kill him.

Paul sat back, raised his hands.

"I needed the money! Then I ended up staying over there. Some woman thought I was a big photographer, said she wanted her picture taken, so I went to her room. You'd never think I'd stay in the hotel, was I right?"

"You were. I figured you'd run out to a car in the parking lot. Froze my ass off on the balcony waiting for you."

"Then I get no pay from Henry. He calls me yesterday. Tells me the picture was fine, but to get the four hundred now I got to drive up here to your place and deliver that envelope to you. A message, he called it. It was the only way for me to get paid! I figured I was probably risking my life—"

"You were." Frank was not kidding. He had been angry.

"Anyway, Henry tells me if I want to be paid—even do better, go fifty-fifty with him—I gotta drive up here, give you a message, he says. We got two people in that picture, he says. Let's see what we can get on the other one. The guy, Henry says, is stealing funds by computer from banks."

Frank sat frozen, silent.

"More power to you, I say, you doing that. I hate the fucking banks. So I came up here. All day driving in that blizzard. Then today Henry shuts me off, tells me to take a hike. My services aren't needed. Forget about the four hundred even. Says he's pissed at me, he's going to send that evidence to my parole officer. I can't let that happen!"

Frank poured more coffee. Paul nodded for a refill.

"I figure, he's after you, he's after Jean, and he's after me, too, blackmailing me. Maybe we can stop this guy if we get our heads together."

Facing tomorrow, it struck Frank this guy might be some help right away. With him and Frank trying to follow Fallon, Jean could be out of it.

"One other thing. Today I made a delivery back down to Boothbay and who do I run into again but Cheryl. She was the receptionist who'd moved up to some big office when I made that first pickup from Fallon, only she's back now at the door. Had a drink with her after work, some barroom close by the factory. We're in there, she's telling me about this boss of hers, Sam something, how he ran her through the wringer. He's one of them likes to hurt women. She says this guy is into some project having to do with some new medicine. Then he shows up, Mister Cool, with her so-called friend on his arm. I can see that this guy, he thinks the sun was made to give him a tan. This is the character Fallon was delivering some secrets stolen from somewhere else, using me as a cutout." Paul stopped, waited for Frank to speak.

"What company was this? Where this Sam worked?"

"Boothbay Chemicals."

"When you came by here last night, I was on the phone then, remember? It was Jean Newman."

Paul was startled. He was certain that woman would never call Frank, not after ending an evening like that.

"Fallon called her and she was calling me. She had no one else to turn to. So she called me, said, if he's after me he's coming after you, too. When I remembered where I'd seen you before, just after I hung up with Jean, I knew she was right. So I drove up, went to see her today. She explained what he was after her for, which was, for her to copy some stuff her husband had in his briefcase, get the copies to Fallon. Then, just before I saw you tonight, I did get a call from Fallon."

"Where's her husband work?" Paul asked.

"Bonnell, New York, big conglomerate that makes drugs, among other things."

"Big drug company?"

"Sure. Paul, this Fallon, he's working with someone inside Bonnell, has to be, because when he called Jean the caller knew her husband had left the briefcase at home. We think there's an inside job going on. Jean says that a few months ago half the designs were stolen. Now they want the other half. This guy Fallon's using that picture you took of us as leverage on her." Frank paused. "On me, too, matter of fact, he says I'll never get work in the security game if a picture like that gets out. He's right. So the deal is, Paul, this guy is planning to pick up these copies that Jean did make from her husband's case tomorrow at eleven at some mall up there. He's supposed to give her back the picture and negative." Frank got up, poured more coffee. "I don't believe it. I think this bastard's going to keep bleeding us as long as he can. So."

Paul refused the last of the coffee.

"You mean, she called last night, today you went up there to see her, and tomorrow she's making the exchange, the deal? How come you came back here?"

"Had an emergency back here. My wife's taken a turn, had to get her to a hospital for treatment. It's a long story, but . . . shit, her doctor got her addicted to pills. I had to come back here and get the kids settled, get Michelle checked in."

"Last thing you need now, this whole hassle with Fallon, right?"

"Thing is this. Tomorrow I'm going back up there, and meet Jean before. We're going to try to follow this guy after the exchange." Frank leaned close to Paul. "You can come along, and help us follow this guy. I bet the stuff he claims he's got on you is somewhere in his place. You help us with this exchange, I'll help you lift the evidence from his place."

"Shit." Paul was frightened, realizing he really did have to get this so-called evidence back. "Frank, this guy Fallon's a very bad dude. He spent about twenty years on the Newark Police Force. Even back when he started, not too long before the big riots there in the sixties, he was cited for brutality on some black people. He may have had something to do with firing the whole thing off. Then, later on in his long career, he shoots five people! Two he kills, both shot in the back. Three others wounded during B and E's. In both cases, he was alone, but headquarters supported him. He said self-defense and proving anything else is hard. He finally got thrown off the force when it was made public that he had been in a ripoff with other cops skimming off the rackets on some of the after-hours gang bars down there in the Ironbound district. I also found out he was called up on a departmental review, abusing his wife. Charges were dropped, but she divorced him a month later. There's a good whiff, also, the guy's still involved in some complex payoff scheme out by the Meadowlands Sports Complex. I also heard that when he was a cop he got in real tight with certain sleazy bankers up there. This is not a gentle man, Frank.''

''I see that.''

''Scary person, this guy.'' Paul shuddered, thinking, Me, help out on an exchange with Fallon? ''He knows what I look like!''

''Yeah. Well, don't worry.'' Frank thought for a moment. ''We'll set you up, a good disguise. You drive the getaway car with Jean, wait out in the lot. It's Jean who'll have to face this guy straight on. He'll never see you.''

''Oh, I don't know, man,'' Paul said, thinking, things are moving too fast, here.

''No, but I do. Now you're staying here tonight. We go up early in the morning. That's it.''

''Jesus.''

''Paul.'' Frank stood. ''This Fallon is tough, but we let him go on, he'll stay tough. He won't expect me to be backing up Jean. Let alone you. He thinks Jean's going to come to this thing like a wet noodle, shaking with fright. But this is one tough Jersey City broad. We got to stop him. He scares me, too, but I've been scared before, in the service. I get scared but I can still think.''

''I've never been in the service.'' Paul wanted to say, I get scared I don't know what happens.

''As I see it you still owe me, taking that picture, so I'll make you a deal. You sleep here. I'll make us breakfast in the morning. But you gotta help me here. I got a little picking up to do.'' Wait'll he sees the upstairs. Frank smiled. Paul was sure Frank was totally crazy. ''And you're gonna help.''

Paul stood in Frank's kitchen, staring at this horse-faced man, exhausted from his travels the previous thirty hours, tired and scared. And, of all things, hours of housework ahead.

"Sure, be glad to." I should have stopped at Cheryl's. We'd be snuggling down to bed about now.

"That's bullshit, but it gets you one of my last beers, anyway." Frank tossed Paul a beer from the refrigerator.

"My brand, even! Things are looking up."

"Stick with me, Paul. You'll be fine."

"That's what I'm afraid of."

"Shut up. Take the broom. The stairs are that way."

Chapter Eight

TUESDAY MORNING

Wentworth tried to open his eyes. He was blind! He could not see! A bolt of pure, unalloyed terror! What time was it? Why was it dark? What was that harsh buzzing noise? What had he done? Why did he hurt?

That grating sound. It's an alarm clock. My alarm clock!

Familiar pale green numbers floated, sickly, a foot away, reading ten after six. His clock. His bed! He was home! He had overslept! Why was he confused? How could it be time to get up and face another day? Without thought he swung his feet to the floor and sat up. A tremendous *thud* passed through his system. Then another and another. His heart, beating, thudding. Hangover, that was it. Hangover. Agony. Remorse. Fear. Confusion. Self-loathing. Physical pain.

He crawled to the toilet and threw up three times. He felt worse. Back lying on the bed, head securely resting on the pillow, he attempted to reconstruct the evening before.

What happened last night? How did it start? With Karen Frucci. That's it, Karen, she came to my office, apologized. We went to dinner. Windows on the World. She was impressed. She played footsie with me. We had wine. What did we eat? What did we eat? After dinner, there was a bill . . . over two hundred dollars! Then we went . . . where? A taxi, I remember a taxi, a warm smooth ear, her hand on my leg, stroking my leg, rising higher and higher from my knee . . . What happened then? It's a blank!

Wentworth again had to crawl to the john and vomit. His head hurt so much he could not raise it. He rested his chin on the cold porcelain lip of the toilet bowl, staring, from ten inches away, into his own vomit swirling in the bowl. He retched.

Trying to reconstruct the previous night's events tortured Wentworth through the tedious, seemingly endless procedure of putting himself together for the office. He was operating on autopilot, following his familiar procedures as he always did during the week. Except this time, for the first time in his life, he could not remember the evening before. He was confused, baffled, clumsy. In the shower he nearly fell after stepping on the bar of soap. When he bent down to pick it up, the rush of thick blood to his fragile skull was so intense he almost fainted. Only when showering did he realize he had slept in his underwear, now sopping wet around his hips. Somewhere in the rest of his apartment were his other clothes, cast on the floor, leading, he now saw, still dripping as he followed his trail, from the front door to the kitchen.

In the kitchen it appeared he had tried to make coffee. He had brewed a hot pitcher of water, having forgotten the coffee grounds, and the filter.

Back in the shower, rallying to turn the faucets to full cold and stand beneath the icy stream in pure, total chilled agony, moaning, he hoped such a blast would drive the residual alcohol from his pores.

After dinner, after the cab, where did we go? Did we dance? Did we talk? Did we come back here? Did we fuck?

What in the world happened?

Wentworth felt slightly fortified following the hot and cold shower, a close shave, a fresh cup of coffee and some juice, which stayed down with Alka-Seltzer Plus. He was unable to find any signs of passion either around the apartment or on the bedsheets.

He could remember nothing about his evening after he blacked out in a taxicab going somewhere with Karen!

The experience was terrifying!

He, Wentworth Randall, Junior, moderate, cool, had obviously had slightly too much to drink last night with someone he worked with, a female colleague out on a social occasion. Had it been a date? With someone who, in the cold painful light of a new, frightening day, could in fact be a dangerous enemy.

His biggest fear: Had he made a fool of himself? With her? Had he blown his golden opportunity?

And, worse, what would she be like today, when and if he saw her?

Should he call her? How could he do that? What would he say?

Then, still crushed by a splitting headache, but now able to face full daylight without squinting, having pulled himself somewhat together, having dressed with special care to draw attention away from his Visined eyes, he braced himself to confront the day. Until I see her, I won't know what happened. If I made an ass of myself, I'd better ignore her. If we were lovers, I must behave as if I recall it.

When he finally left the apartment he did his best to ignore the gnawing certainty that something wrong had happened last night. Something possibly terrible.

Karen Frucci arrived at work before seven o'clock, even earlier than usual. She immediately went down to Central Files on the thirteenth floor, where after some prodding she was given the phone records for certain managers—Wentworth included—for the previous one-year period. She said Drexell Aspin, chief counsel, Bonnell, needed the records to investigate whether the company was being overcharged for long-distance calls by its current long-distance supplier.

Actually, she could have said almost anything. The clerk in Central Files, a young man in his early twenties, still gritty-eyed from a night out the evening before, an evening of unrequited lust like most of his evenings, was far more interested in Karen's figure than the object of her visit. Karen surprised herself; after last night's exercise she rather enjoyed his stares.

Back in her office, with a fresh cup of coffee, the building not yet awake, alone, the door closed, she cleared her desk. First she reviewed her notes from their weekly special project team meetings, the Monday sessions chaired by Ironjaw. She listed on a separate sheet of paper the following dates: the days covering the weekend Horace Taylor lost his notes, the date Wentworth announced he was going to retain one H. Fallon as investigator, and those dates Wentworth reported anything about Fallon's subsequent investigation. Somewhere, she recalled, Wentworth had passed around the business cards for Mr. Fallon, and after some searching she found the card in her desk drawer: Henry Fallon. Investigations. Discretion Assured. Sounded like a dating service. An address in Newark, New Jersey. A phone number.

Karen wrote down the phone number. She studied the card. If I was Fallon I would minimize calls directly to my office. I would hire a blind service to screen them, give me a known-only-to-me-and-the-service-number, like what the dope dealers use. Or I would use a pay phone. I might use my home phone number for emergencies.

Am I being too devious? She called New Jersey information, asked for a listing for a Henry Fallon, at Two-Three-One Magnolia Street, Newark, an invented address rolling off her tongue as if she knew what she was talking about, and the operator said, "There is only one H. Fallon in Newark," giving a different street address. Karen said, "Oh, he must have moved. What is that listing, please?" and she had his phone number.

Next she pulled out a national industrial directory, looked for drug and chemical companies in the Washington–Baltimore area, where Wentworth had said he might be headed, area code two-oh-two or three-oh-one. She found three major firms listed and she copied the main number for each. It was her hope she could make a match between one firm and a three-digit exchange found on Wentworth's telephone records.

Now she had a list of three sets of numbers—Fallon's office and home, Wentworth's office and home, and three companies in the Washington–Baltimore area.

Karen carefully placed her list of dates and telephone numbers to the right and then began looking through Wentworth's phone records. She also looked through the records of the other project team members, but she was focusing on Wentworth. He, too, might be using pay phones, a blind service, or his home phone, but Karen thought him much too arrogant for that, careful in everything except his own ego.

Horace announced his loss of the plans Monday, May 23. The plans had been taken home, therefore, on Friday the twentieth.

Looking through Wentworth's phone records, Karen whistled. There. One call to Fallon's office number May 10! Then a call to his home, no, two, three calls, on the eighteenth, nineteenth, twentieth. Wentworth, at the meetings, proposed hiring an investigator in June, well after he had already been in contact with Fallon!

Had Fallon arranged to steal Horace's plans and copy them? Had Wentworth arranged it all and sent the plans home with Horace to enable Fallon to get them? Had those calls to Fallon just before the weekend been to tell him where the plans would be?

Karen looked again through the records. There were no area code two-oh-two calls, eliminating one prospect. Of the two remaining in three-oh-one, all Wentworth's calls went to a number not far different from the general number for Boothbay Chemicals, one of the three firms she had listed from the directory. In the middle of May there were several to a three-oh-one number with the same three-digit exchange. Two such numbers. Were these calls to someone within the Boothbay complex?

Karen considered the scenario. We let Wentworth suggest and then hire a private eye to investigate Horace's possible loss of the plans. This investigator turns up nothing, according to Wentworth, and we all buy it, even Ironjaw. But talk about a case of the fox in with the chickens! Even before we all said, good idea, Wentworth, fine, hire a private eye, he'd already started his deal!

Gotten half the plans. Those for the medicine itself. But not the binder; those were the second half.

And that second group? Are Wentworth and Fallon now trying to get the other half of the plans? Is that why all of us, me, Norman, Emily, Arthur, have taken home copies of the plans with us? On Wentworth's suggestion?

"Holy cow." Karen circled all the calls made to Fallon, all the calls to three-oh-one, copied the entries, and returned the logs to Central Files.

She knew she still had to nail down where those three-oh-one calls went. It would help, if she could prove Wentworth was taking a big position in, say, Boothbay Chemicals stock.

Karen finished her coffee, now cold. Through her closed door, she heard her secretary, Millie, arrive. Bonnell was starting another day. Now what would she do?

Karen smiled. Chances were that Wentworth hardly remembered much after dinner. Within a half hour of arriving at her place he was nearly out cold. Karen had put him back in his coat, called a cab, virtually carried him downstairs. After all was said and done, she hadn't rifled his pants at all. It hadn't been necessary, not after he made that comment about leaving for a position around Washington. She couldn't have rifled his pants even if she wanted to, he was so drunk. It didn't matter. The evening was a success. It started her down the trail of tracing his phone calls.

How would she handle this information? She needed more. She knew that. And she needed it fast. She wanted to confirm some things before she brought it up to Drexell, Bill, or Mr. Maroules, Ironjaw himself.

She decided to call Wentworth and ask him to lunch, to act as if they'd made mad, passionate love, see how that one went with him. Flatter him again, and get the name of his

Boothbay connection if she could. But Wentworth wasn't in yet. Poor baby. Must have a little headache.

Jean rose early Tuesday morning. She still had not told Norman what was happening with her. She was unable to, not after making peace with him the night before. It would have been perfect, then, last night, to cement their truce by making love, but she couldn't do that, not after the afternoon with Frank. She had lied to him, saying it was her time of the month. Another lie, she now thought, busy in the kitchen making a nice breakfast, and watching Norman appear, dressed for work. Norman grinned when he saw her peace offering on the table, French toast with real Vermont maple syrup.

"Jean, that's full of eggs. It'll make my cholesterol count go up!"

"I thought you had a choice, now, about that," Jean said, smiling.

"I have a choice, all right. But not Choice!" Norman laughed.

They both laughed.

Norman ate two small pieces of French toast, that was all, saying, "Maybe soon I can eat whatever I want but I can still get fat."

Jean ate silently, thinking, how do I tell him about the copied plans without bringing in how the thing began?

I don't.

"So you think Nauset's got the answer on this blood thing?" she asked.

"I'm betting on it," Norman said.

"Good." Jean watched Norman silently.

They laughed. How do I tell him? I don't.

She did not tell him. They had a quiet breakfast. By the time she dropped him off at the station her fear of the morning ahead was back, stronger than ever. After telling Norman she would deposit his bankbook in a money market account to beat the less than five percent the savings accounts paid, she made a few phone calls, went by the bank, withdrew the money, and called a broker with specific instructions. She had faith in her Norman, that she suddenly knew. Then she drove over to the Friendly's in Chatham, ordered coffee, and waited for Frank. As the clock on the wall went past eight-thirty, the possibility that he wouldn't come occurred to her. What then?

Frank showed up at quarter to nine.

Jean gasped when she recognized the lounge lizard Frank had cut off at the pass in Baltimore.

"Easy, Jean," Frank said, placing a hand on her shoulder and sliding into the booth next to her. Paul sat opposite.

"Hi, I'm Paul Johnson." He smiled. The gold tooth glinted.

"Frank?" Confused, Jean turned to Frank. His eyes laughed but behind the amusement she saw tension.

"Jean, it's all right. We have a new partner."

"What!"

Frank nodded at Paul.

"This is Paul Johnson, Jean. Last seen approaching our table in Baltimore. No . . . actually, we may have seen his heels as he left the balcony up on the fifth floor . . ."

Jean stared. This guy? Him? This guy now with Frank?

Paul smiled, gently.

"Frank can explain all this, uh, Jean."

"Bullshit!" Jean reached back and let him have it, a hard open-palm slap across the face bringing instant silence to the restaurant. "Bullshit." Her hand hurt. Paul's cheek was crimson. "Now explain, please," she said to Frank.

"All right. Told you, Paul. Remember what I said last night? She's not going to take any of this lying down?" Frank leaned back and repeated the conversation he had had with Paul in his kitchen the evening before. "We drove up here this morning and I think we have a plan. You will meet Fallon. I will be in the area. He doesn't know what I look like. And Paul will be in the lot in your car—"

"Unless he just drives away!" Jean was still scared and angry.

"He won't," Frank assured her. "Actually Paul knows a

lot we don't know and when we put it together it starts to make sense."

"What makes sense?" Jean asked, wondering, did they know about Norman?

"It's an internal job. Someone in Bonnell, part of that special group your husband is on, hired Fallon to steal the plans last spring. Fallon then passed the plans, or copies of them, to Paul here for delivery to a Sam Dworskin, Boothbay Chemicals, in the Baltimore area. We think the Bonnell guy is selling the design to Boothbay. Fallon is now after the rest of the plans, which is where you come in." Frank paused, to see how Jean was taking it. She was listening. "Fallon used Paul here for the Baltimore thing because he claims Paul has been running drugs and he has the evidence."

Jean looked at Paul.

"He looks to me like someone who could run drugs."

"I wasn't, Jean," Paul said. "All I saw were envelopes. I never checked. The whole thing was a setup, for me to be a mule for the Fallon thing, threaten me." Paul's cheek was still red. "You hit hard."

"They all say that." Jean grinned. She had hit him hard.

"Now Fallon is squeezing Paul, and Paul thinks he's not going to be paid for the work he did in Baltimore—"

"He shouldn't be!" Jean said, remembering the moment up in Frank's motel room.

"Paul thinks, if he can get in Fallon's place up here, find the evidence, take it back, he can get clear of this guy. Now, Fallon did call me last night, as you predicted. He's after my knowledge of bank security systems."

Paul shifted in his seat.

"So he has a picture of me, so-called evidence on you, Paul, and a picture of you, Frank." Jean spoke slowly.

"Yeah. So what we got to do is stop this guy. Neutralize him, somehow. Paul and I cooked up a plan, sort of, but you have to agree. It could be risky."

"All this sounds risky." All Jean wanted was to be done with all this, risky or not.

"Somehow we need to follow this guy, find out where he goes to ground, learn about his base. One thing is very important. Paul and I talked a lot about this this morning coming up here. Fallon only has power over us so long as we have the plans and he has the pictures. He won't release the pictures, or your evidence, Paul, without getting the plans first. I personally don't think releasing that picture will mean much. Who really looks at those pictures anyway? So until we give him the copies we have the power, even if he thinks he does. But for all those reasons, if you give him the copies of the plans today, he definitely will not give you the negative for the picture. He needs it to pressure me."

Jean said to Paul, "Are you crazy? This guy Fallon's nuts!"

"And dangerous. But even more dangerous if we don't stop him."

"We ought to just shoot him!"

"Jean." Frank was patient. "We can't do that. We just need to stop him."

"She's got an idea, Frank," Paul said.

"Well, I learned a little more since yesterday," Jean said, straightening her shoulders. "Last night, I had a good long talk with Norman."

"Norman?" Paul asked.

"My husband. He works for Bonnell. He's a member of the special team working on this project. They're bringing a new medicine called Choice to market this spring. We were right, Frank. Choice is some sort of medicine that just dissolves the gunk that builds up in blood vessels. I wonder who thought up the name. It implies you can eat whatever you want. Whenever you want. Flushes you out. That means—"

Paul laughed. "Holy shit. You mean, eat anything, fats, ice cream, whatever, anything at all and this stuff cleans you out?"

"That's what Norman says." Jean smiled. "Good news for all you cholesterol sufferers."

"Wow. And here I was just starting to worry about it, get

myself checked up." Paul laughed again. "Sounds like bad news for the heart bypass industry."

"Among other things. Norman said last night that in May, one of the staff lost a plan for a while. It might have been copied—"

Paul slapped the counter.

"I bet it was! That's just when I first met Fallon, picking up a big envelope for this Sam Dworskin, Boothbay Chemicals!"

"Norman says they all concluded the plans had just been misplaced, but . . . what you tell me, it fits with the theory that someone on the inside at Bonnell is arranging this." Jean paused. "Also, last night, Norman and I had a talk. I couldn't tell him about this thing here with Mr. Fallon, but Norman did say he's been told to take these plans home a lot. So are other staff, all by this Wentworth guy."

"Like he's creating excuses to blame others." Frank was nodding.

"So he can blame your husband?" Paul asked.

"Yes, except Norman's going to go to work for another company—Nauset, it's called. He's taking the job almost immediately. He says Nauset's also trying to make a cholesterol drug, but not with bacteria. He's going over there tomorrow, matter of fact, so he'll be all right. We'll be all right."

"You said Nauset?" Frank asked, recalling that one of his bank clients said to him, about a month earlier, watch out for this little company in Jersey. It's got a great future. He remembered it had a name like a Cape Cod beach.

"You didn't tell Norman about, er, this?" Paul asked. "Does he know, uh, about . . . er . . . ?"

"No. Nothing." Jean glanced at Frank. Frank was intently studying the clock on the wall. "Frank. You there?"

"Huh? Uh, yeah, let me make a phone call here." He got up and went to a pay phone in the back of the restaurant outside the corridor leading to the rest rooms.

"Who's he calling?" Jean asked.

"Huh?" Paul added more sugar to his coffee.

"Do you have any teeth left? I never saw anyone put so much sugar in their coffee."

Paul grinned. The gold tooth flashed.

"Most of 'em. Who's Frank calling? I dunno, but I expect, the hospital. At least I think so. We stopped once on the way up here. He had to call, he said, to make sure his kids were all right. He called the hospital from his house, too, before we left."

"What, you spent the night at his house?"

Paul nodded.

"At his house? What did his family say to that?"

"Well, only Frank was there last night. I went up there last night to talk to him."

"I thought he was at a motel here!"

"He was, but his father's real sick, you knew that? But something else, none of my business, his wife had to go to the hospital last night, a treatment center. Problem with prescribed tranquilizers."

Jean remembered the phone call to Frank in his motel room, a very upset wife calling because she couldn't find a tool at eleven-thirty at night, strange behavior. She had thought it strange even then with her mind on other things. And, sitting there, she wondered—a father in the hospital, a wife in treatment, self-employed, he must be very worried about money. Worried enough to profit from all that bank knowledge?

"You mean he went home last night, had to get his wife settled in a treatment place, probably had to get the kids set up somewhere, and then you showed up out of the blue?" Jean stared toward Frank, now speaking quietly into the phone. "What's he even doing, bothering with this?" But she thought she knew.

Paul shook his head.

"Must be, Fallon's got Frank really pressured, too."

Jean felt the fear return. What was the plan these guys had cooked up? It was a quarter to ten.

Here I am, part of a gang, what a gang. One suburban

wife, somewhat fitting the yuppie category. One lounge lizard who probably lives alone in some seedy apartment and spends all his spare change hustling women. He probably does very well indeed. He is attractive—lovely sleepy eyes. One middle-aged security expert with a dying father, a hospitalized wife, and something big to hide. Otherwise he wouldn't be up here right now. A yuppie, a wastrel, an ex-marine. What a crew. Up against this Henry Fallon who Paul tells me not fifteen minutes ago has already shot five people.

Nice. Real nice. The One-Night Stand Gang.

"What's funny?" Paul asked.

"Not much. This is all so ridiculous. Truly."

They waited for Frank to finish his call.

"All right." Frank sat down.

"What was that all about?" Jean was confused.

"Oh, I called down home, a hospital there. My dad's ill."

"Your wife, too, I hear."

Frank glanced at Paul.

"Um. Yeah. Last night I had to put her in a treatment center. I think her doctor got her addicted to pills."

"Frank, did you know this yesterday afternoon?"

Frank shook his head. They both ignored Paul.

"No. Got a call late yesterday from my son, Brad, after I'd already checked out the mall."

"Yesterday was a long day."

"Been a long week." Frank signaled for more coffee. It was ten o'clock. "Likely to get longer, too. Now listen, Jean, you can't give the plans to Fallon this morning. Don't even bring them with you. Bring a rolled-up paper that looks like plans." Frank reached inside his jacket, pulled out an eighteen-inch tube of rolled design paper. "Here are your plans. What happens is, you get there, hide these in your coat. Don't show them unless he shows you the photo and the negative. Both of them."

"Which you say he won't."

"I doubt it. Now you must not let this guy suggest somewhere else to go and do this. Say, here or not at all to him. Let him know you're not going to be easy. If he shows the photo, then I'll come by, maybe try to grab it, but don't give him the plans. If I grab the photo, he'll have to chase me. You take off with Paul. If he does not have the photo, then you say, we must meet later, you get no plans until I have proof this is the only photo, you say, give me a number you can be reached. I'll call you. Then leave. I'll run interference for you, give you time to get outside, in the car with Paul, away from the mall. Paul will drive you back to Friendly's and I'll call you here.''

"Great! I do all the easy stuff!" Actually, Jean was feeling a flush of anticipation. She surprised herself.

"We have to follow him and trace him to where his base is. To do that we must get you clear of him, so he gives up and goes home.''

"This guy shot people, right, Paul?" Jean asked. "I might get shot!" All the same, she thought, I'm a pretty fast runner, now I know why Frank told me to wear loose pants and good fast sneakers, a waist-high jacket that won't catch on anything. "What do you mean, interference?"

Frank glanced at Paul.

"Just act like you never saw me before, Jean. Pretend you don't know me if you see me.''

"Tell me again why we're doing all this?"

Frank was patient. "Point is, we've got to take the momentum away from this guy. If we roll over and deliver, we'll never get him to do what we want, to go where we want. Assume he needs those plans. If he has the photo and negative, it might be different, but I guarantee he won't have them! So be tough. He'll expect a scared, dizzy housewife, not a Jean Newman.'' Across the table Paul nodded as Frank spoke. "He'll expect a scared rabbit before a wolf—''

"Not a bad description," Jean muttered.

"You show him he has to meet again and make a trade. That gives us time to trace him. Then we can figure a way to search his place.''

"You should hear yourself."

"Jean, the plans don't matter, not here. Only that picture matters. No picture, no plans. Either we toss his place later today and find the stuff or he makes a trade tonight. At a place we set up."

"You better be right or maybe I'm dead."

"Relax. This is just industrial espionage, right, Frank?" Paul looked at Frank. Frank raised his eyebrows and watched Jean.

"Okay?"

"You'll be nearby?"

"Yeah, very nearby."

"Okay." Heart hammering, hands clammy, Jean went to the ladies' room. The coffee had run right through her. She took several deep breaths staring at herself in the mirror.

Frank and Paul spoke together.

"What if—"

"If he—"

They stopped. Frank said, "What else can we do?"

Paul used the men's room. Frank paid the bill for the coffees, two-ninety, left a big tip.

"Okay." Frank helped Jean with her jacket. She stuffed the "plans" down the front, zipped the jacket shut.

"What about the real plans?" she asked. She had brought the copies she had made with her.

"Where are they?"

"Under my front seat."

"Leave them there. He's never seen your car, has he?"

In the parking lot Frank said, "Now. Jean and Paul, you go ahead. Paul, drop Jean off at the other end of the mall from where she'll meet Fallon. Follow me, I'll show you. When she gets out, you follow me around and I'll show you where to park. Jean, be a minute or two late for the meet. Let him see you coming from the other end. Later on he'll think you're heading back to your car at the other end of the mall, which you won't be. I'll put Paul in a spot right across from the Bloomingdale's entrance. You won't be able to miss him.

When you take off, go like hell through the store, jump in the car, he'll take off. I'll be slowing him down behind you.''

Jean said, ''What about you?''

''Don't worry about me,'' Frank said, thinking, I'm doing enough of that already. ''I'm going to be around, close by all the time. Don't ever look at me like you know me. Oh, Paul, here.'' Frank rummaged in the back of his car, pulled out a felt watch cap and a pair of sunglasses. ''Wear these. If Fallon sees you he won't recognize you. Just don't smile!''

''No chance of that,'' Paul said. His face was pale, eyes darting back and forth. He had to use the bathroom again.

''We all set?'' Frank asked. They nodded. ''All right.''

Paul drove over toward the mall, with Jean. They followed Frank, a five-minute drive.

In the car Paul said, ''How do you do this?''

''What?''

''You're so goddamn calm, Jean.''

Jean was flattered.

''Give me one of your cigarettes, will you, Paul?''

Paul lit her a Kool, surprised she smoked.

''I'm not calm at all,'' Jean said, coughing, exhaling. ''But this situation—''

''I know.''

When they got to the mall Frank stopped up ahead. Jean turned to Paul.

''Listen! I'm getting out here. See Frank waving? Now you drive my car carefully. I like my car, all right?''

''I'll be careful. Jean, you be careful.''

Frank then led Paul around the mall complex after Jean got out of her car. She didn't even look back toward them, just marched into the mall, back straight, yellow scarf trailing behind the blue jacket. Determined.

Frank indicated the place, at the other end, for Paul to wait, a vacant parking space for the handicapped right across from the Bloomingdale's entrance. Paul nosed into the parking space and left the engine running. Frank shook his head and parked his own car farther down, close to the main entrance, hoping that Fallon had parked at this end or he'd never trace him.

Something was wrong, the way Paul waited. Frank figured it out after a minute. *I'm rusty at this, been almost twenty years, and then we were setting up ambushes in the leaves and heat. Not fucking around shopping malls.*

He walked over quickly to Jean's car. Paul sat, hat pulled low over his ears, sunglasses perched on his nose. He looked like a homeless vagrant. It was a great disguise.

Frank tapped on the window. Paul jumped a mile.

"Open the window."

Paul rolled down his window.

"What you going to do here? Jean comes running out, jumps in the car, what are you going to do? Floor it, in reverse, before turning around? Floor it straight ahead and bust over those eight-inch curbs you're against?"

Paul swallowed.

"I, uh, didn't think of that."

"Just turn the car around, heading out, that way, Jean gets out here, you're gone." Frank started to laugh. Paul looked like some bug, the big black sunglasses just under the dark rim of the blue knitted cap. "Relax, Paul, your own mother wouldn't recognize you today." He leaned down, arms on the door, face close to Paul. "And, Paul, when you take off, don't run over another shopper, all right? Don't speed. It would be pretty ridiculous to get stopped by a cop right beyond the entrance, having to explain why you were racing off while Fallon takes a good bead on you."

"Whaddya mean, takes a bead?" Paul's voice almost squeaked.

"Sorry. Wrong thing to say. Now relax." Frank slapped Paul on the shoulder. "See ya." He looked around, then walked into Bloomingdale's.

Jean, as soon as she entered Alexander's, staggered and stopped, taking a huge breath and unclenching her fingers. *That was hard, acting like I was not scared, walking like that. I'm plenty scared.* Her watch showed ten to eleven. As Fallon had asked, she wore a blue and yellow scarf, not a blue dress but a blue jacket, fainter blue jeans, and blue Reebok sneakers. Running shoes. What had Norman told her once, about racing, running? Find where you're going, look ahead at it, head up, and run using your arms like pistons. Never look back. Or to the side. Of course then he was speaking of strategy for a high-school four-forty, not running away from some ex-cop gone bad.

The rolled "plans," stuffed in her belt under the jacket, scraped her lower abdomen with each step. Frank had said to arrive a few minutes late and to look as serene as you can. Easy for him to say.

I'll think of this as a rehearsal for the school play, I was nervous then. Fifteen years ago! But when the curtain went up back then somehow the fear was gone. Think of this thing here with Fallon as a performance. Here she is, the lone female member of the notorious One-Night Stand Gang, loose in the Short Hills Mall, up to no good! Costume all set? Check your reflection as you stride past the glass-walled shops. Scarf tied properly. All in blue. My, who would ever think this pretty young lady is part of a terrible gang? Here, perhaps, to rob that store there, steal that fur from this store here. Here on bad business!

Jean almost smiled halfway through the mall, imagining she was entering from stage right, thinking, this isn't so bad. And then ahead on the second level, at the top of the stairs, she saw Frank's unmistakable form casually window-shopping, blending with the scattered shoppers, and she felt a calm descend as she walked on, unaware of her straight neck, head up, long stride, approaching the waiting area just outside Bloomingdale's.

Think of this as a bad blind date. Use the same philosophy. Be courteous, pleasant, totally noncommitted, and dump the guy as soon as possible.

Use my Jersey Shore beach club tactics, Jean thought.

When she reached the waiting area Henry Fallon, sitting on one of the half-couches beneath the stairs, at first failed to recognize this clearly confident, strong-willed woman in blue with a yellow scarf. She wasn't the frightened, timid, cowering housewife in a dark blue dress he expected.

Jean reached the waiting area, stopped.

There he is. He's huge. Exactly the mean face I expected, but maybe five years younger. He's about Frank's age. God, Frank, you're going to have to protect me from this one.

Fallon rose insolently and leered.

"Mizz Newman. Is this the east end?" When he stood Jean looked up, a mile, it seemed.

"Yes." Jean stopped a good four feet away. To her left, she knew without looking, just past the stairs were one set of outside doors. To the right, straight ahead, the open doors to Bloomingdale's. Her route, if she survived this.

"We have, I believe, an exchange to make?" Fallon gazed down from an impossible height.

"Perhaps." That was me, saying that? That tough, crisp, unwavering voice? Me?

Fallon blinked. Jean planted her feet, crossed her arms beneath her breasts.

"If you're the creep who's been calling me, you have a picture. Let me see it."

"My, my." A slow, sinister smile crossed Fallon's face. "What have we here?"

"The picture, dammit." This guy was huge but he was just a guy, Jean thought. A creepy guy. "Let me see the picture."

Fallon reached to a coat pocket, pulled out a three-by-five photo, handed it to Jean.

"This should resolve your doubts, Mizz Newman."

He watched her as she carefully took the picture. Jean could see, at the extreme upper left-hand corner of her peripheral vision, Frank slowly descending the stairs. She turned the picture faceup, looked at it, and stiffened, felt a rush of hot, terrible shame. Panic.

It was worse than she feared. She, twisted to face the camera. Frank, head turned away but face reflected in the

174

mirror over the headboard, just to the right of the flash's glare. A picture taken at just, just the critical moment.

Definitely publication material.

Jean thrust the picture in her jacket pocket. Henry Fallon waved a hand.

"Now, Mizz Newman, your share of the exchange?" He leaned forward.

"Where's the negative?"

Before Jean could step back Fallon grabbed her arm, even as she was speaking. He was lightning fast for such a big man. He spoke fast and quietly through his teeth, "Listen, you bitch. Give me those plans and then you get the negative. Not before. Now you don't want to make a scene here. Let's you and I go outside to my car—"

Jean could feel her hand going all pins and needles from Fallon's grip, but she set her jaw, shook her head.

"Let go! Asshole! You want me to start screaming? I'll start screaming here! Until I get that negative, forget my share of the deal! You bastard, let go!"

Jean took a deep breath, a huge breath. She was going to scream the mall to the sky, get the attention of some security guard. She had forgotten Frank, the plan, everything but the vise on her arm and Fallon's rank odor as he stood over her. Starting to panic, she reached in her jacket, pulled free the rolled plans, waved them in front of Fallon's face.

"Here are the plans, you creep! Now you get me that negative and then you can have these!" But, in a flash, he dropped her arm and snatched the tube.

This was all going wrong! Now that he had the false plans, he would know in a second it was all a setup. And where the hell was Frank?

Fallon raised the tube of rolled plans above his head where Jean couldn't reach them. Jean, unaware that Frank had started his move just behind her, drove her right knee up as hard as she could, grunting with the effort, all hundred and thirty-five pounds of her driving into Fallon's unprotected testicles. *Balls*. As hard, as absolutely hard as she could.

No question about this one, feeling the soft tissue strike the pelvic bone and then roll off, under her kneecap. Fallon froze, then went all still, staring at Jean with astonishment. Jean, terrified, kneed him again. Gasping, Fallon made a weak lunge for Jean's neck but started to bend instead, dropping the plans and cupping his groin with both hands. Then, eyes shut tight, mouth working trying to get air, Fallon fell to the floor.

Jean, seeing Frank beside her, muttered, "Where were you?"

Fallon, now huddled on his side, retched. Frank touched Jean's elbow.

"Take off, Jean. Now." He jerked his eyes toward Bloomingdale's.

Jean reached down, picked up the false plans, glanced at Frank, and bent down. She said into Fallon's ear, "You men, you think you have enough balls so if one or two get hurt it's no big deal, well, how about this? I want that negative, asshole. I know who you are, too, Mr. Henry Fallon. I'll call you at four this afternoon. Asshole!"

As she spoke Frank hesitated, then stepped deliberately on one of Fallon's hands, twisted his foot, hard, using all his weight, while Fallon's eyes were still closed. Something grated and snapped. Jean marched into Bloomingdale's, walked rapidly through the store, and exited outside, spotting her car parked directly across the traffic lane, Paul sunk low in the driver's seat.

When Paul saw Jean emerge from Bloomingdale's, at first he was sure the guy never showed. She looked so calm and deliberate. Then he saw her eyes focus on her car and she broke into a run. Paul threw open the passenger side door. Jean jumped in, slammed the door, sank down in the seat.

"Let's get out of here!" she whispered.

Expecting any moment to see Henry race in front of him carrying a cannon twice the size of Frank's, Paul forgot all Frank's caution about not speeding. He threw Jean's car in drive and floored it, slewing out of the parking lot, scattering gravel, nearly striking an old lady patiently pushing a shopping cart loaded with packages. When he reached the light on the exit road, he raced through the intersection, barely missing a car turning into the mall.

"Jesus! Easy!" Jean, head low, had both hands braced against the dashboard.

Paul remembered to slow down. Behind him, in the rearview mirror, he saw no one resembling Fallon, and as they passed under the Route 24 overpass he relaxed.

"We okay?" he asked.

Jean sat up.

"I'll take another cigarette."

"You smoke?"

"Shut up." Jean twisted around, checked behind her. The road was empty. Paul turned off toward Chatham and in two minutes he had parked the car at the back of Friendly's.

Beside him, once they had stopped, Jean began to shake. Paul pulled her close, hugged her. She was quivering, taking short little gasps, as if she couldn't draw a breath.

"Easy. Easy." Paul did not know what to say.

Jean began to talk against his chest.

"I got there and, oh, he's so big, so mean. He wanted the plans. He showed me the picture. You take a good picture, you bastard. I have it in my jacket—and no! you can't see it, ever—but he didn't have the negative like Frank said he wouldn't and then he grabbed my arm. It hurt and I—I—I kneed him good in the balls. He fell down. He was puking, I hit him so good—and Frank told me to take off and oh Jesus oh Jesus oh Jesus . . ."

"Easy, Jean. Easy." Paul tried to comfort her, keep his voice steady. He who had nearly pissed in his pants waiting in the lot. He'd been so scared. How could he comfort this person who had, singlehandedly, taken Fallon out?

Jean took several deep breaths, gripped Paul's arms, sighed, sat up, looked over at him. "We'll go inside? Wait for Frank to call?"

Paul looked so silly with that outfit, now facing her and looking like one of those beatniks a generation and a half out-of-date. Jean couldn't help it, suddenly she started to laugh. She laughed until she cried. She cried a little, then stopped. She had been scared.

When they walked into Friendly's—the best customers so far this Tuesday morning, that's for sure—Jean again felt the way she had connected with her knee, it was even a little sore.

What a feeling that had been.

Fallon, eyes shut tight, retched, one hand between his legs, the other hand, the hand Frank had just stepped on, now cradled by his side. Before Frank got out of there and hid behind the stairs, he ran his hands rapidly through Fallon's pockets. Nothing.

Then Fallon partially opened his eyes, began to struggle to his feet. Swaying, half bent over, he looked around wildly. Behind him, through the mall exit doors, Frank saw Jean's car speed past, leaving the lot. Fallon, confused, in pain, perhaps not aware Frank was running interference, lurched toward first one exit, then another. Then he turned, stared back down the mall corridor, made a decision, and ran—hobbled, really— toward the mall exit, the twisted thumb held stiffly by his side. He raced outside, stared around the parking lot, head swiveling. By then Paul and Jean were long gone.

Frank, staying well out of sight, watched as Fallon went all still, breathing hard. Then he turned, fast, impossibly fast, and stared back into the mall, toward Frank.

Frank was not sure whether Fallon saw him or not, whether he remembered Frank's frisk while he was on the ground, but Frank could tell, watching Fallon, that this guy would not give up, not yet. And the next time, if there was a next time, he'd be an even more dangerous adversary.

Fallon shook his head, looked at his thumb, and began walking out toward the parking lot. Frank immediately ran through Bloomingdale's, passing, just beyond the waiting area, two young teenage girls, probably playing hookey to smoke cigarettes and pretend to buy furs in the mall, staring at him as he went by.

Reaching the Bloomingdale's exit, he could see Fallon heading toward the far corner of the lot. Frank waited until Fallon got into a simple, late-model, dark sedan, a perfect vehicle for stakeouts or tails, a dark green or blue Chevy, license, New Jersey, ELO 948. As Fallon struggled to handle the shift column and steering wheel with a virtually useless right hand, Frank walked fast to his car, got in, and waited for Fallon to pass him on his way out of the mall lot.

Frank, too, put on sunglasses and a hat. When Fallon went by, Frank followed, keeping well back, and when they took the ramp up to Route 24, toward Newark, Frank made sure to keep one or two cars between them as cover.

Frank followed Fallon down 24 to 78 to the New Jersey Turnpike, the section leading to the Holland Tunnel, and stayed well back as Fallon drove off the Bayonne exit. Fallon then traveled south to Thirty-third Street, Bayonne, turned right, stopped. Frank pulled to the curb around the corner.

Fallon lurched from his car, protecting his injured hand, and walked rapidly to a residential doorway. Frank saw the small sign: Dr. Sturgis, General Practice. Frank nodded. Probably one of those doctors that fixes gunshot wounds without saying a word.

Fallon was at the doctor's, getting his thumb fixed.

Frank figured Fallon would be in there awhile, getting a cast. He must live down this way. If he has anything hidden, it's around here.

There was a pay phone further up the street, in the corner of a gas station. Frank, pulling the hat low over his eyes, strolled to the booth, opened the door, and dialed Friendly's in Chatham, the pay phone near the rest rooms. He could see the doctor's doorway through the streaked, dirty glass.

After two rings Paul answered. He and Jean must have been sitting close by in the extreme rear booth.

" 'Lo?"

"Paul? Frank."

"What's going on?"

"How's Jean?"

"Still shaking. Says she took him out."

"Did she ever. That lady's got a kick like a horse. Otherwise Fallon would have broken her in two! I sort of stepped on his hand just to help out. Jean's a real street fighter."

"That's what I'm afraid of," Paul said.

"Listen. I'm in Bayonne now, at a Sunoco station on Thirty-third Street. Fallon's gone to a doctor here. Just went. I'm watching the door. He'll be a while, I think."

"You hurt his thumb?"

"Might have broken it."

"So, that's it, right?" Paul asked hopefully. "Isn't it?"

"What are you talking about, Paul? We just got started. I figure once he gets his thumb fixed, he'll go to his place. Must be nearby, somewhere here in Bayonne. What I think is, you drive down here and meet me. There's a lunch shop across the street from this gas station called Tony's Lunch. I'll meet you there. You can be here in twenty minutes, half an hour." Frank rubbed the dirty glass with his thumb. "We'll follow him to his place and see if we can get in when he leaves."

"Jesus, Frank! Jesus!" Paul paused, breathing heavily. Then he asked, "What if he comes out, before I get there?"

"I'll follow him, you wait for me at Tony's. Wait awhile. I'll try to call you if I get tied up." Just then Fallon emerged from the doctor's door. "Shit! Listen, he just came out! Paul, meet me, or wait for me, Tony's Lunch, Thirty-third Street, Bayonne! Just you, Paul. Leave Jean out of this!"

Frank raced to his car and followed Fallon, already in his car and turning right at the next block. Two blocks farther down, one block to the right, Fallon stopped again. He ran up some stairs to a narrow row house: number one-twenty-six, two stories, dark windows, no name on the door. A one-family row house.

Frank waited. This must be Fallon's secret place, hidden in

Bayonne nowhereland. Not his residence, that's for sure. His main hidey-hole.

Less than ten minutes later, Fallon came out, looked up and down the street, headed for his car. Frank saw a big bulge under the jacket. Hardware, a gun, probably a forty-four, for Christ's sake. Frank noticed a slight change of clothes. Fallon was carrying a small bag. Taking a trip?

Fallon then drove past a twenty-four-hour teller window, transacted some business—getting cash?—and pulled onto the main thoroughfare heading back north to the New Jersey Turnpike extension.

Frank followed.

This time Fallon was in a big hurry. If his thumb was broken, it wasn't bothering him now. That or he had no pain nerves at all. He pulled onto the turnpike, east, and within minutes was heading down the ramp to the Holland Tunnel.

Frank, several cars behind, waited until Fallon had passed the last cross street, and was committed to the tolls and the tunnel into Manhattan. Frank turned right on the cross street and began wending his way back to Bayonne.

Fallon had business in New York. He was in a hurry. Frank doubted he was heading to an airport, although he might be. In any case there was no way for Frank to follow him on a plane. Chances were, even if he was just going into the city, he'd be an hour, maybe two. Frank turned on the radio, got a traffic report—no delays going in, but twenty to thirty minutes outbound, both tunnels.

Fallon would be in the city at least two hours.

Plenty of time to search his place. Maybe the only chance.

Chapter Nine

TUESDAY MORNING AND
EARLY AFTERNOON

When Karen met with Drexell Aspin at nine-thirty Tuesday morning she had been unable to reach Wentworth, so she left a message. It was a handwritten note she left with his secretary:

> Wen, I had a lovely time last night, especially dessert [drawn smile]. Today I will take you to lunch. Twelve-thirty? Call me.
>
> Karen

She and Drexell had scheduled the meeting the week before to go over the status of the licensing review for Choice. But Mannie's call yesterday for an early-morning meeting Wednesday, with the inclusion of a late-minute item for the board meeting, forced them to deviate from their agenda.

For twenty minutes they discussed assembling a package for Mannie to bring with him to board meeting. Aspin told Karen that Ironjaw wanted to use this board meeting to announce Choice; that is, tell the board Bonnell would be bringing a new medicine to market within four months that, according to early projections, would within two years triple Bonnell's net profits.

"Mannie told me late yesterday, Karen, that two of the board members, Hutchinson and Quigley—the accountant types?—asked in a formal memo for a detailed explanation about why we took over that plant in Iowa. Because that can only be explained by taking the lid off Choice, Mannie feels he might just as well use this as the occasion to announce the whole program."

Karen blinked.

"Is that wise? Based on our meeting just yesterday" —was it only yesterday?—"can we be sure we will have an approved, registered, proper shelf life material by April?"

"We must be sure." Drexell Aspin shifted uncomfortably. He was a corporate officer who never, never counseled haste.

"They asked about the plant in Iowa?"

Aspin nodded.

"But Iowa's giving us that plant!"

It was true. The state of Iowa, desperately seeking economic development to save small towns devastated by the farming decline, had embarked on a program whereby the state would, in exchange for new jobs, give, for one dollar, idle factories to relocating or new companies. Norman Newman had learned of this from a real estate hustler friend of his and he had pursued it. Bonnell had arranged to take over a former meat packing plant, refrigerated, 105,000 square feet, to use as the manufacturing base for Choice.

"True, but we must still invest substantial funds to bring the plant up to standard. Actually, the thing that probably triggered Hutchinson and Quigley was the fact that the factory was free—that's so unusual!"

"I see."

"Bill Doane will join us in a few moments to outline a series of major points to go over at tomorrow morning's meeting."

Karen made some notes.

"Drex, I have a concern."

"Yes?"

"What would be the consequences, to Bonnell, if, despite our efforts to track down Horace's loss last spring, the plans were copied? Another company brings out Choice first?"

"Well. To start with, it would not be called Choice because we have the register for that name, and the patent for the process—"

Karen waved her hand.

"Yes, but—"

"But you are asking what would happen if our medicine were beaten to market by another?"

"Exactly."

Aspin steepled his fingers.

"That doesn't bear thinking about, Karen. Ah, here's Bill."

They plodded through the morning, making notes, arranging outlines, preparing for the meeting the next day. Karen assisted, contributed, but throughout the morning she was trying to figure out how to tell about Wentworth. First, she must confirm that he was doing what she thought he was doing. Then, who to tell? When and how?

It had to be before the meeting tomorrow. If Wentworth was in fact engaged in a theft, and Mannie went to the board ignorant of this fact, his head would roll.

Not before hers, though, if she had knowledge she hadn't shared. Or even suspicions? Did she dare to bring it up now?

Karen smiled. That didn't even bear thinking about. With these two, Drexell and Doane, she needed absolute proof. Or she would be the one who lost, seen as a hysterical female. These men were smooth, gracious, urbane, polite. But under the skin, she knew they'd be quick to write her off as an overeager, paranoid, inexperienced, overly ambitious young woman.

She needed proof, not circumstantial evidence.

And if, tomorrow, she had no proof? What then? What *did* she have?

Just my wits, an upcoming lunch, and a certainly hung-over Wentworth.

The meeting finally ended. It was eleven-thirty. Karen returned to her office. In her message box, no call from Wentworth.

Karen called him. She was growing desperate and she knew it.

His secretary said, "Mr. Randall went to the bank this morning. He might not return until—oh! here he is now!"

"Randall." His voice was a croak.

"Wen?" Karen came on as nice as she could.

"Uh, Karen. Karen!" There was a long pause, then, "How, er, are you?"

"Oh, Wen, I'm so hung over!" That's it, start with this. "My head hurts, I can hardly remember some of the things we did last night!"

Things? What things, Wentworth wondered. Head still pounding, he longed for a good Bloody Mary.

"But I do remember some things, Wen." Karen let the silence grow. See what he says.

"You do?"

"Don't you?"

"Of course, Karen."

Of course not, Karen thought.

"I would be most upset, hurt, and annoyed if you didn't remember. Not to mention insulted." Karen was thinking, How much of this can I get away with? How long before he gets nervous, uneasy? "You do remember my coffee, don't you?"

Wentworth tried a knowing chuckle.

"And your remarks about the pattern on my sheets, really!" Karen waited. On the other end, Wentworth's hopes rose. He had apparently not made a fool of himself. Quite the opposite. She was cheery and acting just as if . . . Sheets? He had commented on her sheets? "I'm sorry I had to send you home last night, Wen. It was so late."

"What time was it?" Wentworth asked. He had no idea when he got home.

"Oh, three? four? You weren't paying attention to the time, were you?"

"Of course not." Wentworth, from deep within, summoned a rally. He was, perhaps, recovering. "Karen, how about lunch, today?"

"Didn't you get my note? I sent you a note! I asked you!"

"Uh, no, haven't managed to go through my in-box yet. Not with this meeting tomorrow." Wentworth had been unable to do much more than keep up appearances; that and listen to Ironjaw's ramblings for two hours this morning. He had a list as long as his arm to accomplish before tomorrow came.

"Good minds think alike," Karen said. "Twelve-thirty? One? The Salad Bowl? Thirty-eighth and Sixth. You know it?"

"About one would be good, Karen, and yes, I'll find it. The Salad Bowl?" Wentworth wondered, her sheets? Her sheets!

In her office Karen put the phone down, laughed, and buzzed her secretary. "I'll be out to lunch, Millie, one to about three, at the Salad Bowl. Yes, with, uh, Wentworth Randall. Can you make me reservations, please?... Now, Millie, where'd you get that idea? I don't hate him. Not at all." Karen listened, smiled. "Yes, an olive branch." Actually, a switch.

Wentworth looked at the list of tasks assigned by Ironjaw, the items for him to coordinate and assemble as preparation for tomorrow's meetings. He had a number of calls to make— William Doane, Drexell Aspin, Horace Taylor. There were a series of panel presentations to be developed by the graphics department. All arranged to allow Ironjaw to present the board with a positive, upbeat picture of Bonnell's future with Choice as the company's new anchor product.

A lot of work but, he saw, nearly all possible to delegate to others. Wentworth had a theory of management: the cleaner the desk, the less work obviously done, the more efficient, effective, the manager. Or assistant. A few calls, a few orders passed from Ironjaw through him to others, this was management at its best. By now the headache was nearly gone, the morning-long thirst slaked. He saw that in fact he could direct most of this list to others, leaving himself free to continue his recovery.

He began making calls, running through the list rapidly, working through the lingering pain, continuing with black coffee, plenty of sugar, doing the job he did best—delegating.

By twelve-twenty Wentworth had assigned most of the list. Karen's call and her invitation to lunch had revived him. Maybe he would avoid beers altogether when he reached the Salad Bowl, assuming of course the place served alcoholic beverages at all. Based on Karen's dietary habits, this Salad Bowl was probably one of those vegetarian palaces. Perrier water and apple juice.

How could he not remember a moment on Karen's patterned sheets?

Wentworth buzzed his secretary, told her he was going out to lunch at the Salad Bowl. If Ironjaw needed him or if there were any urgent matters, he would be there. He received a call from Sam Dworskin just as he was heading out the door.

"Randall!" Wentworth heard noise in the background. It sounded like Sam was at the Baltimore or D.C. airport, a public address system or something.

"Sam. Glad you called."

"You hear yet?"

"Nothing. I expect to right after lunch. He ought to be at Kearney's late this afternoon with the document."

"Well, I'm coming up there as we planned. I'm at the airport now. You and I should get together before we meet Fallon with the plans. We have some urgency here." Dworskin was speaking fast but clearly.

"Urgency? What's wrong?"

"Wentworth, you did tell Fallon he was through, yesterday?"

"I did, but—"

"I believe that after we get the plans he should be removed from this project. The man is a loose cannon."

"I agree."

"Any idea of when he might want to make the delivery?"

"We agreed he will never contact me during office hours, so after work, I guess."

"Fine." Sam paused, adding more coins to the phone. "All right. My other business in New York, the new stock issue?"

Wentworth knew what the stock issue was for. Like the Bonnell issue, it was Boothbay's way of raising the funds for the marketing and production battle ahead, except that since the plans had been stolen last May, Boothbay was working on a timetable for rollout a month ahead of Bonnell. And some of the stock issue had to do with his, Wentworth's, deal. He would get five thousand shares. Their value, at twenty-one a share, was over one hundred thousand dollars. With the delivery today of the second portion of the plans, for confirmation of Boothbay's binding strategy, those five thousand shares should be worth over two hundred thousand after rollout, doubling his money in three months.

"I'll be in the city by two," Sam said. "Got that meeting with Dixon, Bruns. They're preparing the issue. They're down at Twenty-two Wall. After that I'll get on up to Kearney's. Be there about three."

"Good."

"Yeah. When you hear from Fallon, make sure the exchange is set for after we have some time to talk."

Wentworth said, "I went to the bank this morning, got the money. It's a lot of money, Sam. Not to mention the stock he says he wants." Henry Fallon had demanded, over and above the twenty thousand dollars, the same number of shares Wentworth and Sam were taking: five thousand each.

"That's an issue," Sam said flatly.

"Sam, this ten thousand I have, it's most of my savings!"

"I'm bringing cash, too, we'll offer him that. It's my savings, too. It's worth it. The stock he wants? We have to talk about that. If we get Fallon truly off this project, perhaps

188

the stock he expects won't be such a problem. Or, for that matter, the money."

Wentworth wondered what that meant.

"All right, Sam, Kearney's? After work?"

"I'll be there by three, maybe even earlier. I'll wait for you."

Wentworth left the office and walked up to the Salad Bowl. He felt the cold December sun against his face, a nice day, a bright day. Maybe too bright. All around him, on the street, hundreds of people coming and going, a lunch-hour crowd, suits and secretarial outfits, all the young professionals networking.

By the time he reached the Salad Bowl he felt normal, hangover finally gone. Once again he was in control. Everything was coming together.

The Salad Bowl was a classic. Brown wooden panels, brass railings, groups of tables set on small raised platforms, four tables to a platform, plants of all kinds hanging from the ceiling, a virtual forest. Wentworth hated it.

No smoking anywhere.

Karen was already seated near the back, a nice corner table. She looked great. Wentworth wished he remembered what she looked and felt like without clothes.

This thing developing with Karen Frucci would be a nice diversion for the next two or three months, someone to focus on and forget the tensions concerning Boothbay, Sam, the plans. His stock. His vice presidency.

A nice diversion, and next time—Wentworth never questioned there would be a next time with Karen Frucci on her patterned sheets—he would not forget what she was like out of those nicely fitting clothes.

Initially Wentworth looked fine to Karen, though on closer study there was something behind his eyes, a hollow look. His skin was just a little gray. He must have had a terrible morning.

Karen rose to greet him. She kissed him, almost on the lips but not quite, let him think her aim was off.

"Wen. Are you feeling as bad as I feel?"

She looked fine to Wentworth.

"I'm feeling fine, Karen." He stared at her. How could he not remember bedding a woman like this? This was alarming. Wentworth stepped back, trying again to remember what had taken place the previous evening. He could not remember much after the hazy cab ride to—to—where? He certainly remembered no sex.

"Karen. I forget. What exactly was the comment I made about your sheets?" he asked, smiling a big smile, eyes intent. A slight, almost imperceptible shadow crossed Karen's face. She looked away, and in that moment Wentworth knew something was not right here!

Karen, caught off guard with no ready answer, tried to recover, but she could see his face tightening now with suspicion. She had better come up with a good answer. On the defensive, and therefore attacking, she became indignant.

"You don't remember!"

Wentworth, in an agony of suspicion, doubt, and continued sexual longing, shook his head.

Karen had planned the lunch this way: Wentworth, hurting, would have the well-known hangover horniness and for a while be eager to believe he had slept with her. In hopes of a rematch, perhaps even an afternoon delight, he would again have a drink—hair of the dog, loosen up—and somehow she would get the name of his Boothbay contact, which she felt would truly confirm his treachery. Wentworth, who also had plans for this lunch, in some ways exactly as Karen suspected, now smelled a rat. He was suddenly unable to believe he had had a total blackout. He struggled with his own unslaked lust and his sense that all was not well. Karen was up to something! Pumping him. She knew!

What had happened last night?

What had he said?

"Mr. Randall. Telephone call for Mr. Randall," came over the restaurant's public address system. Wentworth and Karen were still standing.

"Excuse me." Wentworth was relieved to depart the scene if only for a moment. Expecting to hear from Henry that all was in order, and with it confirmation that he was still in control, he found the telephone by the receptionist desk and took the call.

"Wentworth!" It was his secretary. She sounded agitated. "A man just called for you. He was so insistent. So rude!"

"Who was it?"

"He insisted he had to speak with you. He would not give his name! He said he had urgent business with you! I tried to put him off!"

"What did he want?" Wentworth's eyes darted. Panic bloomed in his chest.

"He said it was urgent he see you. He said he had an extremely important message for you, and I, uh, I hope it was all right, I gave him the phone number there to reach you but he said he was going to see you! I hope it was all right?"

It was not all right! It had to be Henry Fallon. If he had the plans, he would just call and make arrangements for the delivery after work. Something must have come up! Something bad!

If Henry Fallon came to the Salad Bowl, Karen would see him. If she was suspicious, Fallon's presence might confirm those suspicions!

Wentworth beckoned toward the receptionist.

"There's someone who may come to meet me here, and I, ah..." The receptionist was cute, in a bright red dress, blond, with nice blue eye shadow. Wentworth turned on the charm. "...need to meet him privately, without my lunch companion knowing. Can you ask him to wait in the entryway and come get me? I'm at that table over there. Can you do that, discreetly?" He passed her a ten-dollar bill. Her eyes widened, seeing the money. This nicely dressed young executive, something wrong with his skin, was engaging her in a plot, and she smiled, nodded.

Wentworth returned to the table. Now to deal with Karen.

All he had to do was remain pleasant, smile, say nothing, and find out how much she suspected.

Karen had used Wentworth's absence to recover her poise. She would brazen it out. If necessary, she would rifle his pants, tonight if she could. She set about being as nice as she could be.

"I ordered us drinks," Karen said. Wentworth took a sip. A martini. He usually hated martinis, but this time the gin went down well.

"Karen, what are you up to?"

Karen, facing the front of the restaurant, was not listening. She was looking in amazement over Wentworth's shoulder toward the door. There was commotion. Wentworth could hear it, and even before he turned to see what was happening he knew it was bad.

The receptionist, trying desperately to earn her ten dollars, could not believe it when a horrible man with some kind of bandage on his hand thrust her aside and plowed past her to the dining room. Karen saw someone who appeared crazed approaching their table, glaring at Wentworth. Wentworth, beginning to stand, face white, eyes darting, obviously knew this person.

Wentworth saw the intent glaze in Henry's eyes, the concentration. He was about to open his mouth, speak, try to head Henry off before he said something in front of Karen that would give the game away for good, when Fallon grabbed Wentworth's arm, digging his broad fingers into Wentworth's bicep. "Come on, sonny boy. We got something to do."

Karen watched incredulously as Wentworth Randall, Junior, was literally dragged from the Salad Bowl, without even a word to her. What was going on? Somewhere in the back of her mind a small voice said, follow them, and another voice said, that's crazy. By then she had grabbed up her coat, left a ten on the table to cover the drinks—too much but she was in a hurry—and walked rapidly after them.

Out on the street Wentworth was being hustled into the

driver's seat of a sedan. Karen could not hear what they were saying but there seemed to be a lot of yelling. Then the car pulled away. Karen memorized the license number, thinking, what now? even as she flagged down a cab.

"You see that car up there with the Jersey plates turning left? Follow it!"

The cabbie laughed and pulled away from the curb.

"Sure, anything the customer wants. What'd they do, rob a bank?"

"They stiffed me for lunch!"

"Why? I'd buy you lunch." The cabbie studied Karen in the rearview mirror. Up ahead, the car Wentworth was apparently driving turned left again, uptown. The cabbie grinned.

"This on the level?"

Karen nodded, swallowing.

The cabbie reached over, turned off the meter, sat up straight, sped after the car.

"My shift's over, miss, and tell the truth, in two years driving a cab, no one's ever said, 'Follow that car.' My big chance, today."

Karen, half-listening, almost smiled. This was sort of silly, but she was trying to think, too. What was happening?

"You do this often?"

Karen glanced in the mirror. The cabbie was looking back at her. He was about her age. Pleasant enough. Probably one of those struggling actors doing this to make a buck before just doing this to make a living. Was that maniac who just kidnapped Wentworth Randall, Henry Fallon? Is this the proof I need? Or is this a wild-goose chase?

The car they were following began repeating its route and they went by the Salad Bowl again.

"These guys are going nowhere. You sure about this? My guess, they're gay. That's my guess."

"Just keep following!"

Wentworth had trouble believing what was happening to him: first when Fallon grabbed him, and then when Fallon dragged him from the restaurant. Wentworth's arm was in agony. Somewhere he had torn the pants of his new seven hundred–dollar suit. And as Fallon dragged him outside to a car, Wentworth fleetingly wondered what Karen was doing back at the table.

"Get in! You drive!" Fallon jerked open the driver's door, manhandled Wentworth into the seat behind the steering wheel. Wentworth, too stunned to resist, gasped for air. Henry Fallon slammed the door, walked fast around the car, entered on the passenger side.

"Henry! What the hell are you doing? I'm not your enemy!"

"Shut up! Drive."

"Drive? Where?" Wentworth was getting his breath back. The reaction was setting in now. "Know what you just did? Do you know who that was I was with? That was Karen Frucci, the deputy chief counsel of Bonnell! The number two attorney! Not financial officer, not personnel department, but attorney! And you know what? She was sniffing around, Henry. Asking questions! Now her questions are answered!"

"Shut up." Fallon thrust keys in the ignition. "Drive!"

"Fuck you!" Wentworth raged. Fallon's hand, his left hand, moved so fast Wentworth felt nothing for a moment, only heard the sharp slap. Then the side of his face exploded in pain.

"Don't you 'fuck you' me, sonny," Fallon said, half turned, looking behind. "Now you listen to me. We got some business to take care of, so start the car. Drive!"

Wentworth started the car, pulled out to the street. In all his life he had never been hit in the face. Always before, style, charm, and words were adequate.

"Left here!" Fallon leaned back and rubbed his knuckles. Wentworth could see, from the corner of his eye, that Henry's right hand was bandaged.

"Henry? Listen." Wentworth started slowly. It hurt to talk. He thought his jaw might be dislocated. "I don't know what is happening here but that scene back there may have tipped

Karen off! And I have work to do this afternoon. We have a very important meeting in the morning with our chief executive officer. It concerns Choice. If I am not properly prepared, my position will be at risk! And now, that scene with Karen, Christ!''

"Left again!"

"I take it," Wentworth continued, "you had a problem today? We weren't supposed to meet until later!"

"Left once more."

"What happened?"

"Listen to me, sonny." Fallon leaned close. "That cupcake Jean Newman sandbagged me. She had help. She didn't have the plans with her. She said she'd call me at four today. Know what that means? That means she knows who I am which means she's got to have help! So we got us a problem!"

"We have a bigger problem, what just happened in the restaurant."

"Her?" Fallon glanced in the sideview mirror. "She's been following us in a cab since we started. Now you follow my directions. We got to lose the bitch. Then we'll go to your place."

Wentworth felt real fear. Was a gun making that bulge in Henry's jacket?

Behind them, the cabbie sat up straight. The dark sedan suddenly jerked left on a cross street.

"Wow! They're trying to get away!" He grinned, eyes flashing in the mirror. "No shit."

Karen, leaning forward, swayed back as the cabbie floored it. "Don't get too close!"

Ahead, the car swung left again; this time the cab had to run a red light to stay close. Karen saw, through the rear window of the car ahead, a pale flash as Fallon looked back.

Another left, on a broad avenue running north and south, Ninth Avenue? Tenth? Not much traffic. They ran through several lights, working the greens as they flashed up ahead, and Karen thought, what is this accomplishing? At that moment a large Pepsi van turned into their street just in front of them. The cabbie stood on the brake, tried to swing past around the van, but by the time they were clear there was no one in sight up ahead.

Karen slumped back. Was what she just saw proof? Did that incident in the Salad Bowl affirm that Wentworth was working with Fallon, if that even was Fallon? It had to be. What else? Maybe they *were* lovers, the whole thing was a spat. All Karen had heard was, "Come on, we got something to do." It seemed proof enough for her, but . . .

The cabbie was watching her in the mirror.

"Listen, I'm sorry to lose them."

Karen half smiled.

"Jamie Giari. That's me." He passed her a card. "I know you and I, we're living in different time zones, same city. But give me a call if you want to reminisce about my first car chase." Karen liked Jamie's smile. This time she really smiled, digging in her purse for a card of her own, what the hell.

"I'll go back to work now, I guess. Put the meter on, please." She gave her office address and handed her card over the seat.

Before driving Paul to Bayonne, Jean thrust the plans in a large manila envelope and left them under her name at the public library in Chatham. She didn't want to be anywhere near Fallon with those plans under her seat. This was the second straight day she had not been in to work. She had called in sick yesterday. Today she had forgotten to call at all.

As they pulled away from the post office Paul said, "Frank told me to come alone. Insisted."

Jean was driving.

"Did he?" she asked. "What would you have done, gone in your delivery van—the van you must have left down at Frank's house? Before he drove you up here today? How exactly did he expect you to get to Bayonne? It's a long walk." She pulled onto Route 24, moved over to the passing lane, driving fast. "This thing we're in now, let's get it cleared up."

Paul said, "Frank wants me to go with him and see if we can get in this guy's place. You better stay put somewhere else." Paul stared over at Jean. "You and Benson, you're both crazy. Crazy!"

"You really think so?" Jean asked, teasing. She'd better call work, cover her hind end.

Paul let Jean drive, trying not to dwell on what they were driving toward. The way he saw it, simple breaking and entering, B and E, was a felony in some states. Even worse was a felony against a former cop gone bad, hurt, especially if Frank had broken his hand. Paul saw the light in Jean's eyes, she was liking this! Paul gnawed a knuckle.

They found the gas station and the lunch shop in Bayonne easily, pulling into the small parking lot less than forty minutes after Frank had called them. Frank was parked along the curb in his car, wearing a hat. He frowned at Jean and gestured for Paul to get in. Through a rolled-down window he said to Jean, "You park here and wait. Maybe go inside and have some coffee. Wait."

Pulling away before she could argue, he said to Paul, "What's she doing here?"

"Only ride I had," Paul said. It was nice to see that Frank, the take-charge marine, forgot details, too. Frank nodded.

"We don't have too much time. Half hour? Fallon went in through the Holland Tunnel. Been gone about, let's see, thirty-one minutes, that's when I left him entering the tolls. Whatever he's doing in New York, will keep him there for a while. There are pretty long delays on the crossings leaving the city to Jersey. I figure we got maybe thirty, forty minutes clear."

"Clear?" Paul's hands were sweating.

"I followed him from the doctor's to a row house place. At first I thought he lives there, but I think maybe it's a safe house for him. It's pretty unprotected as far as I can see. We'll start there."

"Start there?"

"Yeah, I figured we'd wear these caps, look like maintenance guys. Say we're with the sewer company."

Paul tried to laugh and choked instead.

"Little obvious, don't you think? Two guys, marching up to a place, going in?"

Frank glanced at Paul.

"Listen. This guy Fallon's a strong, nasty son of a bitch. We got to neutralize him with the time we've got, when he's hurt. Let's make use of it."

"What if someone's in the house?"

Frank had no answer.

They parked directly in front. On the stoop, Frank said, "Good. No alarms, nothing. Maybe this is nothing, here."

It took Frank just a moment to jimmy the lock to the door and push it open. Inside was a tiny hallway with a narrow stair rising to a second level. Some entrepreneurial landlord had taken a narrow one-family row house and divided it into two tiny apartments, with the second floor reached by a narrow steep stairway.

"Come on," Frank said.

They climbed the stairs. A narrow door, with nothing on the nameplate, faced them on the tiny second-floor landing. Frank carefully examined the door, the wall around the door, and the new carpeting. It looked to Paul like Astroturf, that indoor-outdoor plastic material. Frank saw no wires or alarms.

He knocked, twice.

"Hello? Mr. Fallon?"

Upon hearing the words echo in the stairwell, Paul froze. The house was silent. If anyone was in the place downstairs, they were either asleep, listening silently, or gone to work.

Frank, feeling around the door, was surprised. There were no special security precautions whatever. He whispered to Paul, "Maybe this place is not Fallon's hidey-hole. Maybe he's got a woman stashed here."

"No," Paul whispered, "No woman would live here."

Using a small pick from his key chain, Frank slid open the locks on Fallon's door. The door swung open. Frank and Paul entered cautiously but fast, closing the door behind them. They stood in a single room, a cramped, studio-type apartment, one poorly made bed along the wall under the window, a hot plate and tiny refrigerator plugged in by the sink, a television set on an upended wooden crate at the foot of the bed. A small filing cabinet stood on the room's far side.

"This looks like his hidey-hole after all," Frank said.

Paul stared around the room. It smelled rank.

"You check the bed, Paul, the bathroom area. Look in the toilet tank, under the rug. I'll tackle this little file cabinet over here."

Paul, heart thudding, went through the room. Nothing under the rug. Nothing under the mattress. Nothing in the pillow. In the bathroom, nothing either in the small medicine cabinet over the sink or in the toilet tank. Paul worked fast, as quietly as he dared. He kept glancing toward the door. He was certain Fallon was going to break in, guns blazing.

Frank saw at once he had to be careful with the file cabinet, a small one-drawer unit eighteen inches square. The cabinet was wired to some kind of whistle-scream alarm system, which in turn seemed connected to someplace else—the police station? Fallon's car? His home?

Probably a beeper on his belt. He'd have the thing rigged up so if someone came in here and jimmied the file, the beeper with Fallon would go off wherever he was. Except the person working on the cabinet would not know that, continuing to work while Fallon hustled back here and broke his balls.

Frank traced the wires along the wall to a small closet, where Fallon had installed the system for the beeper, the charger, and the signals. He had done a good job, a slick job, and if it had been someone besides Frank—Paul, for example, now clumsily thundering around the bathroom with the grace of a hippo—the alarm would have been triggered as soon as the file was touched.

Working carefully in the dark closet, Frank disarmed the system. Checking first to make sure there was no backup, he then worked open the cabinet with his Swiss Army knife.

Paul emerged from the bathroom.

"What's in there?"

Frank glanced through the files.

"Jesus, this Fallon has a lot of stuff here. We don't have much time! We got to take the whole cabinet!"

"The whole thing?"

"Yes." Frank, glancing at the files as he spoke, saw at once there were a lot of juicy opportunities here. There were files on a number of police officials in the New York metropolitan area, especially the Newark force; a lot of files with names, probably husbands or wives; some certificates or something for the Meadowlands; a lot of stuff.

"Oh, man." Paul was sweating.

Paul opened Fallon's door and held it while Frank lugged the cabinet down to the car. There was no one on the street. It seemed like one of those semi-residential, semi-industrial areas probably occupied by individuals who worked for the ILA or one of the shipping companies.

"Come on, come on!" Paul said, as they shoved the cabinet in the rear seat and started the car. Frank pulled away slowly, looking to Paul exactly like he should look, like someone who had every right in the world to march into an apartment, remove a cabinet, as if it were a normal part of a day's work.

When they turned a corner and left the street behind Paul let out a huge breath. They had been in Fallon's place eleven minutes.

"Jesus."

The cabinet in the rear seat shifted as Frank turned the corner.

"That's gold in there," Frank said. "Gold."

Jean was working on her second cup of coffee when Frank and Paul walked into Tony's. One look at their faces told all.

"You got it."

Frank touched her shoulder.

"We don't know. Right now let's just get the hell out of here. He's going to come back any minute."

"Did you find it?"

Frank sat down. Paul kept looking outside.

"Don't know yet. We took a file cabinet he had hidden. The place seemed to be his bolt-hole. We have the files. We better head back and go someplace to look the stuff over."

"And if we have our files, what does that mean?"

Frank and Paul looked at each other.

"If they contain all the stuff connected to us, including the negative and your stuff, Paul, we're clear of this guy. Unless the guy's a pack rat and has other copies somewhere else." Frank smiled.

Paul said, "Shouldn't we get out of here? This is Fallon's area."

"In a moment." Frank watched Jean, who took the photo Fallon had handed her, blushing bright red. She glanced at Frank and tore it into small pieces. Frank went on, "We have to make some decisions after we look at these files. Do we just ignore him, act like whatever he has is in that cabinet out in my car? Do we just say, the job's done?"

Jean was shaking her head.

"Whenever he gets back here, it'll be obvious, won't it, that someone's been by?"

Frank nodded. Paul's eyes opened wide.

"And now that we have the files, if they're the only files he has, he'll be unhappy, won't he?"

Frank nodded again. Paul, sitting next to Frank, pressed his hands against his forehead. Jean reached across the table, tapped Frank's forearm.

"In fact, he'll be real pissed, won't he?"

"Man's already got a pair of sore testicles. Maybe a broken thumb. He loses all his blackmail files, which looks like his main business. Plus he won't have the plans he's trying to get. But he probably still has the negative. Yeah, he'll be pissed.''

Paul scratched his head, mumbled, "So we can't just sit here, say, great work, folks, we're all set, we have what we need, assuming it's in that file drawer we stole. We can't just quietly fold our tent, go back to our normal lives yet.''

Frank and Jean said nothing. Paul went on, head bowed under his hands, "You mean, we aren't done yet, don't you?" He looked up, through his fingers. "In fact, unless we can get this guy Fallon off the case it may be worse than ever if he comes after us, is that right?''

Jean and Frank nodded. Paul shivered and swallowed. He looked like he wanted to cry. Frank stood up. "Back to that Friendly's, people? We can look through the files there.''

"I'm so sick of that place, Frank.''

"Better than your house. Fallon knows where that is, Jean. Remember, he called you there?''

"Oh, shit.''

"Good." Fallon faced forward. "She's history.''

Wentworth, driving, glanced in the rearview mirror. Tenth Avenue was empty behind them. His jaw ached. It felt like a tooth was loose. His headache was back.

"All right, sonny. Let's go to that place.''

"Where, Kearney's?" They weren't supposed to meet with Dworskin until late afternoon.

"Let's go. We got some business to discuss." Fallon twisted his shoulder, stared at his bandaged hand. He looked at Wentworth. "Who was she again? The classy broad?''

"Her name is Karen Frucci. She's deputy general counsel, Bonnell Corporation. She's the number two lawyer. She's on the special project team, the Choice team. Ever since the start of this, last spring, she has been suspicious of me. And you.'' Wentworth had to proceed carefully here, it would not do for Fallon to know what happened last night. Whatever did happen. "Yesterday, the weekly meeting, she started asking questions and almost derailed everything. I had everyone convinced you had found nothing. Ironjaw—Mr. Maroules, the CEO—told me, after the meeting yesterday, to call you off, which is what I called about yesterday, among other things. He ordered me to fire you. But, Karen, she kept at it, invited me to dinner last night, tried to seduce the truth out of me. She's suspicious.''

"Did she?"

"Did she what?"

"You tell her anything?"

"No!" I hope not. "But she's persistent. She smells a rat somewhere. That's what the lunch was about . . . Now, what you did, grabbing me in there, she'll know for sure!" And she'll tell Drexell or Bill Doane. What happens if they believe her?

"Listen." Fallon reached over, tapped Wentworth on the shoulder. Wentworth cruised his street, looking for a parking space. "Remember our deal? You and your friend pay me twenty thousand on delivery and then come up with my shares. As we agreed."

Wentworth parked the car, then turned to face Fallon, wincing.

"Now, boyo, you call in sick at work. Then when your partner gets here, we'll meet him, get set, then make the trade tonight."

Wentworth opened his mouth.

"Don't you and Sammy play games with me. I know he's going to be up here to make the pickup himself. So when he shows up, we make a new plan. When's he gonna be here?"

"How did you—"

"Jesus! It only took one call to his office. He's on his way to New York, business they said. So, when's he gonna be here?"

"Uh, three. Sam won't like this."

"Let's go."

It was two-thirty. Wentworth led Fallon to Kearney's. Fallon walked stiff-legged, holding his injured thumb away from his body. Wentworth rubbed his jaw. He wondered what Karen was doing.

Back in her office, extremely hungry, the first thing Karen saw on her desk was a list of assignments from Wentworth, delegated activities to prepare for the early meeting tomorrow. Millie must have received the list just after she left for lunch. Busy work. Karen looked at the list, shook her head. She had other things to do.

Holding the list, she went upstairs to Wentworth's floor. Whatever was happening, she doubted he would return to his office very soon. Karen was virtually certain that Wentworth's kidnapper—it certainly had looked like a kidnapping—was Henry Fallon. If, as she suspected, Wentworth and Fallon were up to something, the incident at the Salad Bowl told her it had gone wrong. When things go wrong, the pressure rises and mistakes are made.

On Wentworth's floor, Karen said to his secretary, "Grace, Wentworth gave me this list to do. I need to check some files in his office for the necessary background material. He told me at lunch to come on up here, take a look."

"He just called! Was he all right at lunch?"

"What do you mean?"

"He called in sick, said he'd come down with a bug."

Some bug. A two-hundred-forty-pound ex-cop.

"Well, he did mention he was not feeling well." Karen went on, improvising, "He asked me to use his files to help him prepare for this meeting tomorrow morning."

Wentworth's secretary unlocked his office door. Karen closed the door behind her once inside. She immediately started through his Rolodex, under *B* for Boothbay.

Nothing.

She began, then, riffling through the cards, starting at the beginning, looking for an anomaly, a clue.

Nothing.

Karen checked the file drawers. Wentworth was well organized. Neat. Moderate. In control. The only desk drawer

locked was the tray drawer at the center of the desk. She
checked the corners of the green blotter on the desk. No key.
Feeling under the desk she felt a stiff paper packet taped to
the underside. In it was a small key.

The key opened the drawer.

In the drawer, one passport, a list charting Boothbay
Corporation stock values since May and copies of a form,
signed by Wentworth, for options for five thousand shares of
Boothbay stock. The form was also signed by one Samuel
Dworskin, vice president, Business Development, Boothbay.

Aha. Boothbay. Karen telephoned Boothbay's main number, the number she had found through the directory that
morning.

"This is Karen Frucci, Bonnell Corporation, New York. I
am trying to reach Samuel Dworskin."

"I'll connect you."

"Please, if I get cut off, what is his number, please?"

Cheryl, the receptionist, back on the main desk, gave the
number. Karen wrote it down, then waited for the connection
to be made.

"Business Development. Mr. Dworskin's line."

"Samuel Dworskin, please." If he was there, what would
she say?

"I'm sorry, Mr. Dworskin is in New York for the day. Can
I take a message?"

"Thank you, no. I'll call later."

Karen replaced the phone. Samuel Dworskin, the name on
the stock option forms, happened to be in the Boothbay office
of business development. Karen guessed if a company were
working on a new product and had an office of business
development, the new product would come from that office.
Chances were good that this Dworskin was Wentworth's
connection. Karen pulled out her copies of Wentworth's
telephone calls during the past several months, ran her finger
down the list of area code three-oh-one numbers. There. And
there. In all, she counted eleven separate calls from Wentworth's
line to Dworskin's office line.

Quickly replacing the papers she had pulled from the files, she copied the stock option agreement on Wentworth's copier—how the hell did he rate a personal copier?—and, to the best of her memory, replaced everything in the tray drawer as it had been when she opened it. Replacing the key in its hidden pocket under the desk, she gathered her material, left the office, thanked Wentworth's secretary, and returned to her desk downstairs.

She had tied a lot together—the phone calls, the stock options she had found, the name of the guy at Boothbay. It should be enough.

What had Drexell said this morning, when asked what if Horace's plans had been copied? That, he'd said, didn't bear thinking about.

Perhaps, now, after what had happened since that comment, Drexell might want to reconsider.

Her intercom buzzed.

"Karen, there's this person on the phone." Millie was laughing.

"Who is it?"

"He says, he's a recent acquaintance of yours. It's a personal call, he says. He said to me he has been auditioning with you for a chauffeur position?"

Karen laughed, picked up her line.

"Yes? Karen Frucci."

"Deputy general counsel, just like your card says. Reads like you have the keys to the kingdom there at your company. Are you as important as your title suggests? Because if you are, we aren't on different levels. We're maybe on different planets."

"I'm just a gopher with a fancy title," Karen said, grinning, fishing in her purse. There it was, Jamie Giari. He'd called her within two hours of dropping her off.

"I'm off duty, just like I warned you I would be." He got right to the point. "When are you off duty?"

"You're being a little precipitate, aren't you?"

"Life is short. I am aging fast. I apologize for losing your quarry this afternoon."

"That's all right." Karen leaned back. Jamie had a nice telephone voice. It went with his eyes. She remembered his eyes in the cab mirror.

"So. Are you one of those workaholic women, slaving seventy, eighty hours a week with no time to play?" He was laughing.

"Sometimes ninety," Karen said, realizing the truth as she spoke it.

"Well. How about tonight you and me have a meal? You'll need a break from the office pressures before you return to burn the midnight oil. You can tell me all your dreams and desires and I'll tell you about my theory of close pursuit."

"I hope it isn't related to dodging Pepsi vans on Tenth Avenue, because your close pursuit was just a little rusty today."

"I'm not talking about chasing cars."

"You *are* precipitate."

"Can you break away?"

I can use the break. An evening with a charming, funny character like this guy would be nice, she thought.

"What do you do, Jamie, when you're not driving a cab?"

"But that's what I do!" He was laughing again. "You think, maybe you hope, this guy, when he isn't driving a hack, is studying law nights at Columbia or taking an MBA at NYU or working as an actor, right?"

"Ah . . ."

"Thought so. I'm a cabbie, Karen. Before this job I was a New York City fireman, but I got a disability, injury on duty. Been out for two years. Now I run a cab. You want to see my scar?"

Karen laughed. "Tell me, Jamie, where to meet you. Let's have dinner. I could use the break." My friends would howl if they knew I was about to date a cabbie. What a contrast to Wentworth. Though they'd have howled about him, too.

"One other thing, Karen. When we meet tonight, if I get a little tongue-tied, don't worry about it. It's just, you're the first woman I've ever seen, up close in person, that takes my breath away."

Karen blushed. If this was an example of close pursuit, Jamie's version, it was an interesting theory he had. The way she was feeling listening to him, it was an effective theory, too.

After arranging to meet at a small Italian place three blocks across town from the office, Karen called Drexell Aspin and made an urgent appointment to meet with him and William Doane at four-fifteen. A very urgent meeting, she stressed.

Then she began outlining and summarizing everything she knew or suspected on her word processor. She had just over an hour to prepare.

Chapter Ten

TUESDAY, LATE AFTERNOON

Frank led Jean and Paul back to the Friendly's in Chatham for their third visit of the day. The shifts had changed. All the help were different this afternoon. Paul and Jean sat at the same corner booth in the back, waiting for Frank, still at his car getting some files. Paul shook his head.

"This seat should have my name on it."

Jean ordered three coffees. Frank came in, carrying an armload of files. He dropped them on the table.

"Here. This is a start. We got to look through these and see what's here, how strong this stuff is. See if stuff on us is here, the negative, anything on you, Paul."

The brown manila file folders covered the table.

Paul and Jean started looking at the files.

"What's this?" Paul asked, pulling a photograph from the first file he had grabbed. "Jesus! Don't look, Jean!" Jean looked, twisted her mouth, stared at Paul.

"Fallon must have thought he'd died and gone to heaven when he saw the picture you took, Paul. A lot better than this here. Or worse, depending on how you look at it." Frank looked at the picture, grinning.

"Listen!" Paul was excited. "In this file, Fallon has the

goods on this muck-a-muck town official patronizing an escort service in Fort Lee. A photo, the works!''

"Divorce?" Jean asked.

"Don't know. And, look! This file here!" Paul gestured. "Same kind of stuff on one of his brother policemen in Newark! Only here, the picture looks like a drug sale. See those packets? Jesus!''

Frank nodded, head bent as he studied files of his own. "This guy had a real business going. It seems like he's got leverage on practically all the law enforcement and other officials in northeastern New Jersey!''

Jean held up a file. "City officials, too. Look at this. Here's photocopied evidence of a payoff to the Board of Adjustment for a sewer contract! Two contracts!''

Paul sat back, sipped coffee. "What's his deal?"

Frank frowned. "It looks like Fallon took a lot of stuff with him when he was dropped from the force. Got a lot more since. I bet, with all this stuff on people, he's set up to be what they call a fixer."

"A fixer?" Jean asked.

"Maybe they use another word, now. Let's say a developer wants to put a shopping mall somewhere, needs some variances or an endorsement. He comes to Fallon. For a fee or a percentage of the take, whatever, Fallon delivers. Like this file here—what I've got in my hands now. Fallon has the goods on some poor bastard who's attorney for the Township Committee, a town in Morris County. This poor bastard's been caught receiving payoffs from municipal contracts. Fallon has all the evidence right here! Say a developer wants to get a project built in that town. Fallon uses this lever to get the legal opinion he wants to sway the committee.''

"Nice." Paul was impressed.

"Nice? Nice!" Jean was almost shouting. "It's shitty! Talk about sleaze! These are supposed to be public servants!''

"Just business," Paul said. Jean shook her head angrily. Frank spread his hands.

"Look. What Fallon has here is a network of levers,

points, and pressure spots he can use or turn to and get a client what he wants. For a fee, of course. The guy's quite well established in the blackmail business.''

Jean kept going through the files as they talked.

"But there's nothing here on any of us! Not the negative. Not whatever Fallon says he has on Paul.''

"Not this batch, anyway.'' Frank pushed the stack of files aside, gathered them in his arms, and carried them to his car. He returned with a smaller stack.

"This is the rest of it. I bet there's nothing here either, but let's check.''

They checked. There was even a file on the mayor of a north Jersey town, one of the upscale communities up by the New York border. The mayor had a financial interest in an "adult" movie theater and used his wife as treasurer. Jean couldn't believe it.

Toward the bottom of the stack, under *T,* they found a file, titled, simply, "Ten." Frank began to smile, a wide toothy grin. In the file was a telephone log, listing, by time and date, calls made to several numbers, with either *W.R.* or *S.D.* entered after the number. There were also concise directions to someone's apartment, with information regarding the security system, an apartment in the name of Horace Taylor. Notes made concerning the whereabouts of one Jean Newman the previous Tuesday, followed by "one hundred," which had been crossed out, replaced with "four hundred," and a sheet of paper headed "plans" followed by "twenty thousand cash."

"This is it," Frank said. "Right here. This file here tells it all. He'll want this back.''

"Any negative?" Jean wanted the negative. Period.

"No.''

"What about me?" Paul asked.

"Only this note, raise it to four hundred. Oh, no, another thing, marked 'Dworskin says, envelopes, through a Cheryl, coke.' Gives some dates.''

"Oh, Jesus. It *was* coke.''

"Listen, Paul, this file is evidence, not only on all of Fallon's activities, but also on the deal we've stumbled into. This file lists both the Bonnell and Boothbay connection. If I got it right, Fallon expected to pick up twenty thousand dollars in exchange for the plans tonight. That's money we should get!"

Frank was looking a little wild to Paul. Jean thought so, too.

"Whaddya mean, we should get that money? Shit!" Paul couldn't believe it.

Frank was patient, explaining, "Think about it. Chances are Fallon will still want to pick up the plans and if I were Dworskin or Randall I'd want to be close by when the delivery's made. So if they're going to be up this way, I figure we'll make Fallon see it's worth more to him to get his filing cabinet back than some money for a bunch of plans he's delivering."

There was, however, no negative in this second stack of files.

"Frank," Jean asked, "when Fallon went to New York, leaving his hidey-hole, did he have a briefcase with him?"

"I don't think so, but maybe he had one with him."

"Or he has another duplicate filing system elsewhere," Paul suggested.

"Oh, God!"

"Easy, Jean, think about this." Frank smiled. "Aside from us three learning more in the last hour about public officials than we ever wanted or cared to, you know what we do have here?" He leaned forward. "We have Fallon's main business. These files are it for him, the main event, his gold mine. With these files, he'll survive, no matter what! He'll make more money, squeeze a few more guys. He'll get back the twenty he's going to give us from his partners tonight in no time at all. These files are his life, Jean. The stolen plans from Bonnell don't compare to that!"

"And he'll kill for that, won't he?" Paul asked.

"Perhaps." Frank paused, thought. "We have the lever we

need to clear this up. He must be carrying the photo negative on him, but look what we have here. Any of this stuff gets out, he's finished! Finished!''

"Finished? Like, dead?''

"Well, Jean, these files get out, either the law locks him up forever for all his bad deeds or, more likely, one or several of these lovely people he has the goods on decides to take him out! For some of them, that would be both a pleasure and, I suspect, no problem.''

"Yeah.'' Paul was thinking hopefully about the chances that one of Fallon's "clients'' might take him off the face of the earth. He smiled wistfully.

Jean gestured. "What if we, for example, just mailed these files back to the people they are about, sent them along with a note saying 'Enclosed please find a file on your activities brought to you by one Henry Fallon, ex-cop, address such and such'?''

"Yeah.'' Paul's tooth flashed.

"I know we can't just go to the law, but tell me why again. I forget.'' Jean was confused.

"What, how? Paul and I stole these files from Fallon's place! That's breaking and entering. Anything we find, if we're not locked up for theft, would be inadmissible in a court of law. If you're found holding these plans, what are you going to say? Oops, I picked them up from my husband's briefcase. I'm selling them here to get back a picture of me and this guy committing adultery—''

"All right, fine.'' Jean remembered now. "So what do we do?''

Frank stretched. "You'll call him, Jean, like you said you'd do this morning, at four o'clock. Tell him, or dictate to his service, when and where to meet us. At the meet, we do a double trade. First, for the negative, we give him the plans. Then, for twenty thousand dollars, we give him the file cabinet. But''—Frank went on, raising a hand before Jean could interrupt—"first we copy at least the best of these files. Hell, all of them. And we let him know, if anything comes back on us later on, we'll release the copies to the proper people." Frank grinned. "Standoff."

"And so, what if, at this meet you propose," Paul asked, "he just blows us all away?"

"He won't, can't, at a public place with a lot of people around. That mall again. We can lie in the shadows. This way, we can get what we want—the negative and his promise to pay off. Plus, we might get some cash and we'll be protected with copies."

Paul was troubled. "Yeah, but what if he doesn't have the cash? Do we give him the files then?"

"Sure. But we let him know, we have copies. See how he likes being on the other end of a little blackmail. I think he went in to New York today to get help! He was hurt. He's probably heading back to his place about now, where he'll see the files missing and get your message. We do this right, neutralize this guy, involve his partners in a way we got some leverage on them, we're in the clear! Just like the last week never happened."

"It's only been a week?" Jean asked.

"I don't like it." Paul knew Henry, feared him.

"Neither do I," Frank responded, "but what's our choice? If we can identify Fallon's partners as well as Fallon in this Bonnell thing, then we can turn the law loose. Or the security forces of Bonnell, whoever, let them handle it."

Jean stared at Frank. "That's not very nice."

Frank chuckled. "Nice? Huh. Nice isn't part of this deal."

"Well?" Jean glanced at Paul.

Paul raised his eyebrows. "Whatever. I guess."

"Okay." Jean stood. "What number do I call? More important, what exactly do I say?"

Frank reached up, pulled her back into the seat.

"Sit down, Jean, we better write the message out. We're almost done here. Just a few loose ends still. Then you call, all right?" He leaned forward.

Paul said, "Oh, boy." Frank had that glint in his eye, same as when he answered the door with that cannon in his hand the night before, that half-wild look. All of a sudden Paul had to take a leak. Nerves, it had to be nerves. Frank and Jean, they made him nervous. They'd make anyone nervous.

On the way to the men's room, Paul stretched and tried to relax. Not easy.

Wentworth sat, facing Henry Fallon, facing the door, his back to the wall mirror in Kearney's, one of those smoky dim Irish pubs scattered throughout New York. Fallon's eyes were on the mirror all the time.

Waiting for Sam.

Wentworth fidgeted. They had been silently waiting for a half hour. It was close to two-forty-five. Wentworth's mind raced. When Sam comes in, he'll be thinking, as we planned, we'd meet first before connecting with Fallon. We'll figure out a way to get rid of this guy once we have the plans, and a way to avoid giving him this money I'm holding here burning a hole in my jacket. And how will we ever get any stock for Fallon, let alone ten thousand shares? Jesus, he's big, an animal, totally uncouth without anything but the streetwise brutality so common in all uniformed officials. How did Sam and I get tied up with him anyway? Jesus. My jaw feels broken. The bastard hit me, just like that! We had it planned out so well, a nice, simple matter. Transfer the designs to Boothbay, an interested buyer in the market, be reimbursed in untraceable stock, not cash. Then I make the move over there, to vice president. Who would know? Young professional graduate of Princeton, seeking career development opportunities, moving to a new company, same general field, after three years at Bonnell, what's unusual about that?

Wentworth remembered he had been referred to Henry Fallon by Sam. Not that Sam knew him. Just that Sam's company had used his "services" for a discharge permit at a small plant they had been operating in Elizabeth, now closed. Sam said, call this person, he's done work for us. I hear good things about him. He gets results.

And what about Karen? What must she think? How suspicious was she? Wentworth reran the aborted luncheon in his mind. She came on all cozy, familiar. He had to think they had been intimate. Was it all a setup? When he asked her what remark exactly had he made about her sheets, she froze. Just as if there was nothing there, no comment to remember. Maybe he never saw the sheets at all. Two hundred-plus dollars, he remembered that, and the cab ride. What then? Avoiding Fallon's eyes, Wentworth remembered he had been hearing alarms ringing somewhere off in his brain. Why had he had so much to drink? He never drank too much.

And what was Karen doing right now, at this moment? She had tried to follow them, for Christ's sake! What would she say, back at the office? She couldn't even know Fallon, not by sight anyway. She had never seen him and he didn't give his name at the Salad Bowl. Maybe she thought he had been kidnapped. All she had, really, were suspicions. Unless he had said something last night. But then why was she trying to get information today?

All was not yet lost. It's never over until it's over, the curtain drops, and we're far from the final act on this one. If Sam and I manage to neutralize this guy and get the plans as arranged and then shut Fallon up somehow, I can report tomorrow at the meeting that Fallon's out of it. I'll say there was a theft. I found out about it. I was even kidnapped yesterday by the thief, whom Fallon identified. He was working for—let's see, I sent those plans home with most everyone at one time or another—why not lay it on Karen? I'll explain what happened at lunch today, say I was kidnapped. That explains why my jaw is the size of a watermelon. I can even make myself a hero, a tough guy, say I escaped.

His mind racing on, Wentworth imagined: Sam and I get the plans tonight, we'll copy them, still get them to Boothbay, but I can appear at the meeting tomorrow, tell my story, then say, here, here are the plans, returned to us with no damage done. He liked that picture, the special projects team open-mouthed in awe, Ironjaw naming him vice president at that moment. Karen looking foolish, humiliated with her suddenly hollow accusations.

Wentworth took a breath, relaxed. The situation was not so dire. We'll get the rest of the plans. Sam must have some specific idea of how to shut this guy up, some way to buy his silence. All we need here is a little breathing space, a few weeks until Boothbay hits the street with its version of Choice: earlier than Bonnell, just different enough chemically to be clear of patent infringements. For that, the chemical difference in the vector, or binder, this segment of the plans, was desperately needed.

Breaking the long silence, emboldened by his kidnap fantasy, Wentworth asked, "What happened today? The plans?"

Fallon grimaced and shook his head. Wentworth pressed.

"I arranged it all this weekend! Called you Sunday morning, told you Newman had left his case at home. It gave you all day to get to his wife, scare her into making the copies. You told me yesterday she had copied them!" Wentworth was pushing, he knew it. Fallon stiffened.

"Shut up."

"What happened? Did some scared Maplewood housewife get the best of you?"

Fallon reached over and gripped Wentworth's cheek, the bad side. He squeezed. Wentworth gasped with pain.

"The delivery got screwed up, my man. She's going to call at four, leave a message with my service, because I'm not there. I'm here with you. We make the transfer tonight." He still held Wentworth's cheek. Tears flooded Wentworth's eyes.

"That hurts," he managed to say.

"Does it?" Fallon removed his grip. "We wait here. When your partner gets here, we'll all go make that pickup."

Wentworth rubbed his eyes. He said, staring at the table between them, unable to meet Fallon's eyes, "We need those plans. We get them, we all get paid off. But you are the intermediary. I should be back at the office, keeping Karen off base."

"Huh." Fallon watched the door through the mirror.

Wentworth was silent.

At half past three, Sam Dworskin came through the door, dressed for Wall Street stock issue meetings, formal, nice dark gray suit, neat, carrying an Argentinian leather briefcase, eyes scanning Kearney's looking for Wentworth. As soon as he noticed Wentworth had company, as soon as he spotted Fallon's broad angry back, he turned on his heels and made for the door, that fast. Fallon was faster. One moment he was facing the mirror, and then in a two-step flash he was beside Sam, towering over him, guiding him forcefully back to the table. Sam threw off his hand, wriggled his shoulders to straighten his coat, and sat down opposite Wentworth. Fallon sat beside him.

"Wentworth." Sam's eyebrows were raised, asking, what's this?

"You never met, did you, Sam?"

"Let me guess." Sam, to Wentworth, appeared immune to Fallon's looming threat. "Henry Fallon, am I correct?"

Fallon almost chuckled.

"Now let me get you young professional men a beer. Make yourself comfortable, Dworskin. We got to wait until four. You won't go anywhere, will you?" He rose and walked across the room to the bar.

Wentworth said, in a low voice, "Christ, Sam, this man kidnapped me almost three hours ago! We have a problem! A big one!"

Sam frowned, eyes locked on Wentworth.

"What happened?" At the bar Fallon waited for the bartender to finish taking an order from a waitress working the food section of Kearney's. "We were supposed to meet first!"

"I know! But he just appeared, dragged me from a lunch meeting!"

"Did he get the plans?"

"No."

"Oh, shit." Sam glanced toward Fallon.

"He says another meet will be set up with a phone call at four. Then we all get the plans!"

"I see."

"Do you?"

They looked at each other.

Fallon returned with beers.

"Now." He drank half his beer in one swallow. "Let us get a few things clear, here."

"Yes, we should," Sam began, but Fallon cut him off.

"First, we all go to get the plans. My deal with you, I get you these plans, you get me twenty thousand, cash. You have that on you?"

Sam nodded slowly. Wentworth followed his lead.

"Now, about the stock."

"Stock?" Sam was all innocence, surprise.

Fallon reached over, grabbed Sam's shoulder, squeezed. Sam's face drained of color.

"Listen, sonny, don't you go and get all smart with me, all right?" Fallon gestured toward the briefcase Sam held on his lap. "Open it."

"This? I just have a bunch of legal forms, no significance whatever."

"Open it."

Sam opened the briefcase. Fallon poured through papers, memos, and files.

"I see you got Shearson Lehman to underwrite a nice new stock issue. Let's see, almost a million shares. What are you raising: thirty, forty millon? Nice fee for Shearson. Oh. And what's this, these, here? Stocks! Actual stock certificates!" Wentworth was staring at Sam, who slowly rolled his eyes and shook his head. "Five thousand shares for Sam Dworskin and options for five thousand more for Wentworth Randall! However, I see no certificates for me."

Sam was silent. Wentworth waited, tense. Fallon turned his head slowly from Sam to Wentworth.

"Nothing for me, eh?" His voice went all slow and cold. "I smell me a cross here, my men, and I better remind you who is working for who here. It's clear you boys have a nice little partnership, but my guess is, once you get the plans, I'm history, right?"

"Absolutely not," Wentworth and Sam spoke together.

"Don't matter. See. I'll just keep these." Fallon shoved the stock certificates in his jacket. "Makes an even ten thousand, as we agreed. Right?"

"Wait a minute!"

"No, you wait! You still need those plans or your schemes are history, not to mention your jobs. You get the plans, you'll have money, power, all the glory and stock options you ever want. Me, I say, a stock certificate or two in my jacket are worth any number of stocks in the bush, so I'll keep these."

"Those documents are not in your name!"

"Big deal, Dworskin. I'll just hold these, as security, until tonight when you boys pay me. Then we'll talk. Besides, I can get a dozen guys to forge over their transfer to me."

Sam slumped, caught Wentworth's attention, shook his head slowly. Wentworth, seeing his one hundred thousand dollars worth of stocks disappear in Fallon's jacket, felt sick.

"Fallon, listen to me. You can play the tough ex-cop to Wentworth here, but at Boothbay we have firm evidence on what you did for our factory in Elizabeth. I can make a few calls and make things very hard for you!"

Fallon laughed.

"Dream on, sonny. You're all right. You seem to have a little more spunk than your reedy partner here, the clotheshorse. But the fact is, getting right down to it, you have a lot more to lose than me. So for the rest of this little adventure, you're both working for me. I'm the one who has everything on file back at my place. That gets out and you'll both be in jail so fast you won't believe it!"

Sam lowered his eyes.

"All right. Let's just get the plans."

"Now let me make a call and arrange the meet tonight. She should have called in by now." Sam and Wentworth watched

Fallon silently. "One more thing. The problem I had this morning trying to get the plans? That lady Jean Newman had someone with her, a big asshole who I think did this job on my thumb after she let me have it in the balls. Tonight we got to be ready for anything." Henry Fallon stood to go to the phone. He leaned over them. "And if you're starting to think of a cross, think about this. I was on the force twenty years and more and in that time I shot my share of people. Two died. Know what?" He leaned closer, spoke softly. "Killing is easy! You boys don't understand that. You're too slick for that and that's the reason I'm running this show, not you!"

"Oh, shit." Wentworth watched Fallon walk to the phone.

"What happened today?" Sam's eyes followed Fallon.

"I don't know. Just what he said now, the woman must have taken him out or something, her and this ally of hers."

"Listen, Wentworth." Sam spoke fast. "What I wanted to meet with you on before we met Fallon was to figure a way to take him out. He's the only thing linking us and the stolen plans! Tonight, after we go to this exchange and get the plans, somehow we have to neutralize him, silence him!"

"What do you mean, take him out?" Wentworth was afraid he knew exactly what Sam meant.

"He's the guy doing all the hustling on Newman. He's the guy stole the plans in the first place! He's the guy made the copies and delivered them to that stupid ex-con mule you used! It's this Fallon who's the link between us!"

"What do you mean, take him out?"

"Decision time, Wentworth. How much, just how much, do we want this deal?"

"You serious?"

"Dead serious."

"Well." Wentworth inhaled, sat up straight. "I'm dead serious, too. Dead. Serious."

Some corners, when you have to cut corners, they're bigger than others, Wentworth reflected. Sam was nodding.

* * *

At four o'clock, Jean, some notes in her hand, called Fallon's number. Frank had drafted the demand in longhand, exactly what she would say.

The phone rang twice, then the service cut in.

"This is four-oh-six-six. You know what to do." After a short pause there was a beep.

Jean spoke as Frank held the paper and moved his fingers. "Mr. Fallon, this is Jean Newman. Meet us at seven o'clock. Alone. We will meet at the exact same place as this morning. I have the plans. I will trade them for the negative. I also have one file cabinet from Bayonne. I will exchange that for twenty thousand. Cash. If you think I may have protected myself with copies, you are right. Seven o'clock."

"That was nice." Frank crumpled the notes. "Short. Spoken slowly. Clearly."

"Oh, Jesus," Paul said, "he's gonna be pissed!"

"We gotta bet, Paul, this Fallon's a survivor. Above all else, he'll behave at least until he gets that file."

"I'm not so sure." Jean remembered how Fallon's eyes flashed when he grabbed the plans this morning in the mall.

"We got three hours," Frank said. "Where's the nearest copying machine?" He was looking at Jean

Paul said, "You know, coming up here, I'm probably fired from my job."

"Call in sick. Make some excuse. I've been sick for two days." Jean touched Paul's arm. "I'll be right behind you in the unemployment line, Paul."

Frank paid for the coffee. Outside the early December afternoon was fading. Night was falling. "Now." Frank left a tip. "Jean, you and Paul go make copies of those files. Here." He pulled two fifties from his wallet. "Use this to pay. The copies, once made and stapled together, should be a couple of big stacks. Then mail those copies to my address. I wrote it here. You ought to just have time to make the copies and get them mailed in an envelope, regular mail, to me." He paused. "This time, you'll bring the real plans, but you ought to copy them, too. He knows we know the mall and the area better than him. He heard you saying 'us' over the phone. He knows there's more than just you. Our deal with him, he gets the plans and his file system back. We get the blackmail material and maybe some money. He may have another blind file, but he'll know we have made copies of his file, so, I hope, standoff.''

"Now that we have his files," said Paul, "maybe he'll forget about your negative and my envelope stuff he says was coke. Or, at least he'll leave us alone.''

Frank nodded.

"All he'll want, Paul, once he gets that call, are his files back.''

"And our hides," Paul added.

"Chance we have to take. Now go get the copies.''

"Meet back here?'' Jean asked.

"Sure.''

After Paul and Jean left for the copy shop, Frank went to the phone and made some calls.

He was thinking: Jesus, we should pay these folks here at Friendly's rent, all the time we spent here today. I wonder what some of the help think. Who cares what they think? I got to get these calls made. Then back over to the mall and hope for the best. What a thing, to spend the best part of a week trying to unravel from a one-night stand, especially during the same week my wife's gone to a rehab and my father's due to come home to die. To die. Jesus, sitting here with Paul and Jean, worrying about this Fallon, this negative, these plans for this miracle drug, it's kind of easy to forget what's really important. Which is, get out of this mess here so you can go back to Philadelphia and live a normal life.

Frank first called his broker-bond trader, the person he had been able to place the returns from the scam with in a way that appeared safe. He caught the guy just before the close of business, telling him, cash in the bonds at once, to hell with the small loss. Yes, all of them. Here's what you do with the money.

Then he reached Sue Kitchner's house, asked for Suzie.

223

"Are you at home, Dad? Did you get the house picked up?"

"I'm still up in Jersey, honey. A job up here has run a little longer than I expected. It was good you kids went over to Kitchner's. Yes, the house is picked up. With luck"—a lot of luck—"I ought to be back home late tonight, and I hope that by tomorrow you can come home. I'll let Sue know. So, how's the boyfriend front at school?"

"It's crummy, Dad. Boys are so shallow."

Frank laughed. Suzie was absolutely right, even talking about big boys like himself.

"Got anyone in mind?"

"Really, Daddy." Suzie paused. "Any word on Mom?"

"Not yet. Don't worry, she'll be fine. I spoke to a nurse this morning, she's doing fine." Was it only last night she was signed in?

"Here's Brad."

When Brad came on he was out of breath.

"Dad! Mr. Kitchner's just got this new kind of bicycle machine, you sit down with your legs out in front of you, sort of, pedal using straps over your toes, it's hard!"

"How far'd you go?"

"Four kilometers!"

"You can show it to me when I get back, all right?"

"Sure! Oh, and Dad!" Twelve-year-olds were interested in everything, Frank remembered the feeling. "I got an A on my science test!"

Frank finished his conversation with his son and then called the hospital to check on Michelle and his dad. His dad, no change. Dr. Andros felt he could be moved, anytime. He had left a list of what he thought was needed for home care. Michelle, from the rehab, had left a message for him. She would like him to call sometime Wednesday. Frank suspected Suzie might have packed the wrong outfit for her. The nurse, when he spoke to her, said Michelle was doing very well. Can you say that after less than a day? Frank asked. Sometimes, she said, they understand right away what they're here to work on. She's very lucky, your wife.

Then he called his broker back and made sure his instructions were being followed.

With yet another coffee in hand, to go this time, he went to his car, got in, and peeled from beneath the front seat a paper bag in which he had wrapped his pistol. He shoved the pistol in one of the deep pockets of his parka.

They had Fallon's filing system. He ought to be reasonable. But if he comes at us all, guns blazing, I better be ready. Best thing would be for me and Paul to meet him, to somehow get Jean out of the way. Forget it. Jean has a mind of her own. If she wants to be there, she will be.

Chapter Eleven

TUESDAY LATE, LATE AFTERNOON

When Henry Fallon returned from the telephone, it was obvious to Wentworth that something was wrong. Fallon's eyes were wild. He was almost foaming at the mouth.

"Problems?" Sam amazed Wentworth. How could he be so cool in the face of such rage? To Wentworth, Fallon had the look he imagined the bad guys in maximum security cells practiced before mirrors.

Fallon spoke, hissing through his teeth. "Tonight! Seven o'clock. Same fucking place, that mall out toward Summit. Now come on! We got to move fast here. I got to go by Bayonne and check something. That bitch! *Bitch!*"

Fallon was shaking, he was so angry. Wentworth grabbed his coat and followed Sam and Fallon to the door.

"Not so fast, there!" The bartender rushed from behind the bar, caught them at the door. "One of you has to pay the bill!"

The bartender, not a small man, appeared little next to Fallon. The furious ex-cop glared at him for several seconds. The bartender stood fast.

"Pay," Fallon said to Wentworth.

Wentworth paid. They walked back to Fallon's car where he ripped a ticket off the windshield.

"You drive," he said to Wentworth. To Sam, Fallon said, "You sit in front. Now get to the fucking Holland Tunnel fast!"

As they waited to enter the tunnel, the rush-hour crush already started, Fallon said from the back seat, "All right, we have us a problem."

"What did she say?" Sam asked.

Fallon muttered in the back seat, grinding his teeth. Wentworth could hear him. "She said . . . she said this. Meet at that mall, same place, at seven. Said she has the plans, but we got to bring the negative. She also said—and this is what I got to check in Bayonne—she said she's been in my place there and has my files! My fucking files!" Fallon leaned forward, head thrust over the back of the front seat. "Included in those files, boyos, were detailed notes about this little caper, including some notes about the twenty thousand you're going to pay me! So now, to get the files back, she wants the twenty! She says, otherwise, she'll make public the stuff in those files!"

"You mean Sam and I are implicated in those files?" Wentworth was horrified.

Fallon snarled with disgust, "Jesus Christ! You do have the money, don't you?"

Wentworth glanced over at Sam, thinking, that twenty thousand is our money, not from any big corporate account. The stakes have gone up, here.

"Is she with anyone? This Jean?" Sam asked.

"Gotta be." Fallon was almost shouting. "This morning when she gave it to me in the balls—I admit I wasn't ready for that—some big guy 'helped' me except he was just slowing me down. She got away. But she knew my name. And my filing system, in Bayonne! It's out of the way. Nothing listed anywhere. Someone had to follow me and check the place out, probably broke in after I came into New York to get you assholes. I had that filing system wired up to my beeper here. Anything disturbs it, I'd hear it, and I'd be back there. But today, nothing. Whoever got into my place knew something about security." Fallon was raging. Suddenly he slammed the back seat. Wentworth jumped. The car veered. "Fuck! Of course! That son of a bitch that was in the sack with that broad in Baltimore. Frank Benson works in security. He's the guy ripping the banks off. It's gotta be him!" Fallon sucked air through his teeth.

"Whaddya mean, that guy was in the sack with her?" Sam asked.

Wentworth was confused. "What did you do, Fallon, go after him, too? Is that why we got these problems now? Christ!"

Sam caught Wentworth's eye, shook his head, and said, "So, now the plan is, instead of giving the twenty thousand to you, we hand it over to these people for the files, right?"

"Right!" Fallon started to smile. "Because of that asshole and because of the loss of those funds to get my files back, I'll just keep these stock certificates. We'll call it even!"

"*Even?* Shit! Those certificates are worth ten times what the twenty thousand was worth!" Wentworth couldn't believe it.

"Cost of doing business, sonny." Fallon leaned back, tapping his fingers on his knee, his good hand, waiting to get to his place in Bayonne. Sam, watching Wentworth drive, raised an eyebrow.

At four-fifteen, Karen gathered her material, walked down the hall to Drexell Aspin's office. William Doane arrived just as she did, saying, "Something urgent, Karen?"

Karen sat in one of the stitched antique armchairs opposite Aspin's desk. She was tense. Drexell shook his head when Doane sat down and gave him an inquiring glance. Karen placed her neatly typed file on her lap. She handed a copy to Aspin and another to Doane. Without opening the documents both men gazed toward her, waiting.

"Gentlemen. I asked for this emergency session to solicit your judgment and advice. I realize how pressured we all are to prepare properly for the breakfast meeting tomorrow." Karen paused, sat up straight. The level, unblinking stares from Aspin and Doane unnerved her. They were paying full attention. "Let me, briefly, summarize what I believe is going on, which I feel may well jeopardize Choice's rollout." Doane jerked upright and Aspin nearly dropped his pipe. "As you observed yesterday at our weekly meeting, I raised certain questions concerning the relationship between Wentworth Randall, Henry Fallon, and the possible copying of the Choice schematic last spring, when Horace Taylor misplaced the plans for some hours. I may have been out of line, but I have always wondered why we never saw anything written from Fallon, or any evidence of his work. Although I respect Wentworth's point, shared, a believe, by you, Drex, that such a lack of a paper trail was necessary, I thought I had better see what else I could find out."

Karen paused, took a breath. Aspin and Doane, sitting utterly still and attentive, waited. "Let me outline for you what is happening. You can follow me in the material I have provided you. First, in May, after The Event with Horace, we all agreed to retain a private investigator—keeping The Event even from our own security division—to pursue the chances that Horace's 'misplacement' might well have been a theft, allowing the plans to be copied by one of our competitors. Wentworth announced to us, at a meeting at the end of the month, that he had found Mr. Fallon after some searching. He told us that Fallon was a retired policeman, had even reached the rank of lieutenant and that he specialized in corporate investigations. Wentworth told us Fallon was familiar with industrial espionage, do you remember?" Doane nodded. Aspin looked confused. Karen went on.

"You can see, however, if you look at the first few pages in the packet I have prepared, that *Star Ledger* stories during Fallon's career show him to be a much-maligned and possibly corrupt policeman, who in the end did not resign, but was in fact fired. He was let go due to allegations that he was collecting payoffs to 'facilitate' certain approvals at the city level. I have also copied several stories about five different incidents where he shot people, two of whom died. This is the man we hired on Wentworth's assurances.''

Aspin was frowning. Doane looked uncomfortable, as if hearing about these sordid details left a bad taste in his mouth.

"Now, on the next pages, I have listed dates and telephone calls made on those dates. This morning I got Central Files to give me the telephone records for Wentworth's phone. I explained, in fact, that you, Drex, were examining records concerning our long-distance carrier, and it was from these records that these lists you have before you were taken. Although we authorized Wentworth to hire Fallon about eight days after The Event, and he claims he found Fallon after a search that did not begin until that time, you can see from these records that he called Fallon several times in the weeks before The Event, with three calls made in the days immediately before Horace Taylor took the plans home with him! I went back through my meeting notes for the meeting just before The Event, and my notes indicate that Wentworth had maneuvered Horace into taking the plans home. Horace did not want to, but Wentworth insisted, claiming, I believe, that we had serious time pressures facing us. My conclusion, from these records and my notes, is that it looks as if Wentworth had retained Fallon, but earlier than the rest of us knew, and, in fact had retained Fallon to steal the plans from Horace.''

William Doane and Drexell Aspin bent over the telephone logs.

"Then, if you recall, Mr. Maroules specifically prohibited the plans, or any version of the plans, from leaving the Bonnell office structure, for any reason, a command routinely ignored by Wentworth. In fact, he had many perfectly good and sound excuses for dispatching the plans home with Arthur Stein, Emily Mott, Norman Newman, and myself! Also, I believe, Bill, once even with you!''

"Yes." Doane spoke quietly, remembering.

"On the next page you will find further records of telephone calls made from Wentworth's line. These calls were to several numbers in area code three-oh-one. That's the area down around Maryland. Monday night, after our staff meeting, because I was concerned, I managed to wrangle a dinner out of Wentworth. He had too much to drink—''

"Our Wentworth Randall!" Doane looked baffled, even amused. He obviously had great difficulty imagining Wentworth Randall, Junior, inebriated.

"With the liquor in him he made a slip, muttered something about how it would be too bad to leave New York. At first I thought Mannie might be sending him out to Iowa to work in the management of the Choice production facility. But Wentworth said no, he had a job offer elsewhere, around Washington. Same area code as these numbers, which, you will see, predate The Event by quite a few weeks!"

Karen took a deep breath. Her throat was dry from talking.

"Today I managed to go to lunch with Wentworth. I wanted to pursue this, try to identify a specific firm or name that could be linked to these numbers, especially as on several occasions he had called Mr. Fallon within minutes of these three-oh-one numbers. We went to lunch, at a place called the Salad Bowl. Just after we sat down a big, rough, monster of a man stormed in, grabbed Wentworth, and virtually kidnapped him! Wentworth knew him. It was obvious he didn't want to be seen with him. This man said, 'Come on, we have some business to discuss.' ''

Doane stared at Karen, his mouth open. Drexell Aspin, head lowered, was fiddling with his pipe.

"So I followed them in a cab. The guy who had Wentworth forced him to drive. They lost us. So I came back here, made a call, checking out the license plate. It's registered to one Henry Fallon, Newark!"

By now she had Doane and Aspin's total, undivided attention.

"And then Wentworth, some time after being taken away by Fallon—it had to be him—calls in sick! Did you know that?"

They shook their heads.

"So I went on up to his office, talked his secretary into

letting me in his office, looked around. In the drawer of his desk, if you turn the page, you will see the copy of a letter, for a stock option agreement, five thousand shares, signed by one Samuel Dworskin, Business Development, Boothbay Chemicals.''

Doane stiffened. Aspin's documents slid off his lap to the floor.

"So I called Boothbay and asked for Dworskin's number. Dworskin's private office number is the number Wentworth has been calling in area code three-oh-one since early May!"

Karen sat back, spent.

"Your conclusions, Karen?" Aspin asked gently.

"I think this shows Wentworth had an arrangement with Dworskin to steal the Choice design and sell it to Boothbay. He used Fallon as the operating agent on the ground. In exchange, Wentworth has both the stock and a position at Boothbay. What does this mean? It means, Boothbay may very well be ahead of Bonnell's rollout schedule for a drug of their own. And if I guess right, Fallon and Wentworth are still at it, probably for the vector and binder element of the plans!"

Doane pursed his lips, said, "So when they roll out their version, the substance is chemically different enough to be clear of patent problems."

"Yes, Bill, correct."

Aspin lit his pipe. His hands shook slightly.

"Good work, Karen. William and I don't shoot the messenger, but we must speak at once to Mannie, so he doesn't. Most distressing."

"I'm sorry, Drex, Bill."

Doane said, "All may not be lost here, grim as it seems at this moment. First, Boothbay may well still be behind us. They are likely to be, in fact. Second, and worthy of consideration, there may be another explanation for this."

"Like?" Karen asked.

"Well, you said it looked like this Fallon kidnapped Wentworth today, correct? Perhaps, and I am not defending him by any means, but just perhaps Wentworth can explain all this in a more favorable light. This is, ah, Karen, a most startling story." William Doane exchanged a glance with Drexell Aspin and sighed, then went on, "Perhaps this is tied to one of the other team members, for example." Aspin was nodding as Doane spoke.

"Let's see what he says, tomorrow, eh?"

"Yes, Drex. However, we should try to reach Mannie tonight, if we can."

"Thank you, Karen." Drexell Aspin placed Karen's document on his desk, rose, and began walking toward the door. Karen realized she was dismissed. This would now be a matter between the three men, without her. If what was said earlier was correct, maybe she did not want to be there anyway. Not if the messenger was likely to be shot.

At least this left her open tonight for a dinner date.

Wentworth, caught now in a haze of throbbing pain and fear, drove in the traffic down the New Jersey Turnpike extension to the Bayonne exit, wiggling a loose tooth with his tongue as a form of self-torture.

When they reached Bayonne and parked the car, it was fully dark, a cold December night. The snow from the weekend storm was piled high along the curb, not yet discolored with grime. Fallon gestured them toward a narrow two-story row house on a street lined with similar buildings, apparently largely vacant. The area looked to Wentworth like a mill town residential area, probably built to service one of the refinery complexes over in Newark. Fallon fumbled with a key and they entered a narrow hallway and were directed by Fallon up the stairs.

The door to the small one-room apartment on the second level stood wide open, unattended. Wentworth and Sam, pushed from behind by Fallon, stumbled into the dark room. The light from the December moon illuminated a small bed, a hot plate, a threadbare carpet, and little else.

Fallon closed the door and turned on a naked overhead bulb.

"Right there. There!" Fallon growled. He pointed toward the corner. There was nothing in the corner.

"There's nothing there," Wentworth said stupidly. Fallon swung toward him, raised his good hand, clubbed him across the left ear. Wentworth staggered and fell. His ear rang with pain.

"Jesus! What was that for?"

"Shut up! There's nothing there! That's the problem!" Fallon bent down, pulled some wires from beneath the carpet. "See these here? My file cabinet was wired up to these here. There's an alarm system in the closet there, connected to my beeper, that was my protection. Those bastards took the whole fucking cabinet!"

Sam carefully sat on the bed, watching Fallon's every move. Against the wall Wentworth cupped his ear and moaned. Fallon jerked off his jacket. He wore a heavy shoulder holster. A pistol handgrip stuck from his armpit. He sat on the bed at the other end from Sam.

"Jesus," Wentworth whispered, staring at the gun.

Sam said, "What was in that file cabinet?"

Fallon said nothing for a moment, thinking, looking crafty. "I told you—among other things, a lot of other things, one file which included everything having to do with this plans deal here!"

"More specifically, what?"

Wentworth prayed for Sam to lay off, not be so demanding. It was Fallon here who carried a gun. Can't Sam see this character's likely to pull out that cannon and start blasting?

Fallon lowered his head, faced Sam.

"Like, telephone records showing calls made to you or to Randall here. Notes I made on our agreement, including that you would pay me twenty thousand cash for the plans. Enough stuff that, in a court of law, they'd put you away for years!"

"I see." Sam briefly caught Wentworth's eye. Wentworth

realized, head throbbing with pain, watching Sam and Fallon, that unless they got this stolen file back and the plans, it would be his ass and Sam's ass, both of them in the sling along with Fallon's. They would all go down, all three of them.

"But," Wentworth muttered, trying to think, "without the negative, how are you going to get the plans?"

"Who said I don't have the negative? That, at least, was not in the file, which is a good thing because then we'd have been truly fucked!" He pulled out the pistol. Wentworth froze. Sam stiffened. Fallon began to tap his knee with the pistol. *Tap-tap, tap-tap-tap.*

"Listen, boys, here's the deal. The negative's in my wallet. Now you two have the cash to pay me, right? As agreed?" As he spoke he raised the pistol and pointed it toward Wentworth, then swung it toward Sam. Sam, eyes wide open, slowly, ever so slowly reached in his coat and removed a thick envelope. Wentworth, matching Sam's motions, removed a similar envelope from his jacket.

Fallon said, "We got to use this money to pay that broad or her partner, to get the files back. That's the deal they told me over the phone." He sighted the gun toward Sam. On Sam's brow, sweat glistened. Wentworth stopped breathing. "We give this twenty to them and I'll let you off the hook for the twenty you owe me. I'll just keep these stocks." Fallon tapped the certificates jammed behind his belt halfway down the front of his pants. "We meet at this mall at seven."

"Where?" Sam could still talk.

"The Short Hills Mall, about twenty minutes from here out Seventy-eight and Twenty-four in Short Hills. Same place I met this broad this morning."

"Where at this mall?"

"Far end, by the stairs. There's a waiting area there. At seven, we meet there and trade the plans for the negative. Then they trade the files for cash."

"So how do we know they'll deliver?"

Fallon kept the gun pointed.

"They need that negative, sonny. They probably want that money, too. It's a lot of money. Once I get close to them, fuck it, I can pull out this"—he waved the pistol—"and besides, to start off, it'll be you two guys meeting them at first. I'll stay back and cover you!"

Wentworth felt his bowels go loose. This whole thing was looking worse and worse. No assurances on any front. Being forced to actually make a trade for these stolen documents. Henry Fallon firmly in the driver's seat and driving hard. Sam blinked, staring at Fallon. Both envelopes lay on the bed between Sam and Fallon.

Sam caught Wentworth's eye, nodded slightly. He said to Fallon, "Hadn't you better count the money? Don't you want to be sure there's twenty thousand there?"

"You count it!" Fallon waved the gun. Sam glanced again at Wentworth and started slowly going through the money. Fallon faced him. Wentworth watched Sam pull the bills from one envelope and begin counting them.

"One hundred. Two. Three. Four . . . One thousand . . . Two thousand . . ."

It seemed to take forever. Fallon finally said, "Come on! Move it!"

After an interminable wait, Sam completed the count for the first envelope. There were one hundred one–hundred dollar bills. Wentworth wondered why Sam suggested they count the money in the first place. Wouldn't it be perfectly obvious to Fallon that they would not ask for a count if they had intended to shortchange Fallon themselves? Wentworth did not understand what Sam was up to, but it was something.

"All right? Ten thousand here." Sam pushed one envelope aside, started on the second.

Fallon watched him. This time Sam worked much faster, really very fast. As Sam stacked the second pile of bills Fallon lowered the gun slightly, mesmerized by the growing stack of money.

Sam stopped, took a breath, said, "I only count eighty-two hundred here, eighty-two hundred dollars." He smiled at

Fallon and leaned back slightly, hands held above the pile of money.

"What?" Fallon, in a rage, lunged for the bills, forgetting for the moment the gun he had been holding. Sam, quick as a cat, kicked the gun from Fallon's hand. The gun bounced once on the bed. Wentworth immediately understood this had been Sam's intent all along: to lull Fallon with the counting, draw off his attention, and then zing him with a mistaken total. Moving so fast Wentworth almost could not see it, Sam grabbed the pistol, just as Fallon realized his mistake, roared, and jerked upright, lunging for the gun himself.

Sam leapt from the bed, the gun in both hands, held in front of him. Fallon rushed him.

Sam, standing rigid and calm, pulled the trigger once, then twice. The bullets whined. A tiny puff of dust leapt from Fallon's shirt. The gunshots, impossibly loud in the tiny room, clapped Wentworth's ear with agony. Standing behind Sam, frozen, Wentworth watched as Fallon staggered and clutched his upper chest. Then Fallon's shoulder blossomed red. He sighed and fell like a tree, sprawling facedown next to the bed.

Sam faced Wentworth. His eyes were crazy.

"He was right. Killing is easy!" Sam then handed the pistol to Wentworth. "Hold this while I get his wallet and the stocks."

Holding the hot pistol—it almost burned his hand—Wentworth gasped.

"Sam, uh . . ." Wentworth could not see if Fallon was still breathing. Some thick red blood seeped out from beneath his armpit.

"Shut up!" Sam jerked the stock certificates from Fallon's belt. He then pulled a wallet from Fallon's pants, snapped it open, and threw several bills to the floor before pulling out a small envelope which held a photo negative. "You get the money!"

"Jesus, Sam." Wentworth could not get enough air. He grabbed the piles of bills, stuffed them in his coat.

Sam said, "Keep the gun. Hold it for now. We'll ditch it at the mall. Come on!"

Wentworth, dazed and nauseous, tore his eyes from Fallon. He saw Fallon's chest shudder and heave, an impossibly deep rattle guttering behind Fallon's lips. Fallon's eyelids fluttered. Wentworth tore after Sam out the door and down the stairs.

They ran to the car, threw themselves in, and raced from the curb. There was no one on the street. The entire neighborhood appeared deserted, lifeless.

"Sam?"

"Listen!" Sam drove intently, below the speed limit. "It's after six o'clock. Relax, will you? Nobody's after us!"

"Relax! Not yet, nobody's after us!" Wentworth started to laugh. He surprised himself. He was hysterical.

"Listen, you think anyone heard those shots? I don't! There were no lights on downstairs. No one home there. None of the windows were open and I had closed the door. Maybe it sounded loud in the room but I bet anyone hearing it outside would think it was backfires. We're gone, out of there! Now look!" Wentworth could tell Sam was higher than a kite. A lot higher than Wentworth was, that's for sure. Wentworth was terrified, sick. So how come he felt so aware? "We have the negative now and we'll make the trade! We have the money and we'll get the files back."

"Yeah, Sam, but about Fallon—"

"Forget Fallon! He's history! When we get to the mall, you wipe off the gun and ditch it in a trash can. It's a long way from Bayonne and no one will make the connection, not in a million years. By then we're long gone!"

"Jesus, Sam, you just, just—"

"Shut up." Sam turned his head, spoke reasonably. "Think of it this way. We did society a favor, ridding the world of one blackmailer. Not to mention, Wentworth, we rid ourselves of a major problem!"

Wentworth listened, took a huge breath, leaned back. Maybe Sam was right. Fallon was out of the picture, and how else would he get out of the picture? Sam must have planned this all out, the money thing, right from the time they walked in the apartment. Wentworth was impressed. Now, with Fallon gone, there was no one to link them together with the plans. Once they got the files back, they'd be clear.

"Sam, today Karen Frucci really started getting on my case about Fallon and this whole thing. Like she was almost accusing me of being in on the deal. Her suspicions could be very dangerous. We have this huge meeting tomorrow morning. She saw Fallon grab me at lunchtime from this restaurant. The fucker kidnapped me, what'll I say?"

Sam, pulling onto 78, said, "You were smart on all this, weren't you? You laid off those plans on some of the others now and then, set it up so you could say they had the opportunity to sell them?"

Wentworth nodded. "Yes."

"So, if this Karen Frucci makes a big stink, can you lay off the blame on her?"

Wentworth thought. Images of Fallon's arm and the dark red stain spreading beneath ran through his mind. His ear, his jaw ached. He shook his head, tried to think. "Maybe. If I need to." I'll need to, all right, assuming I get through the next couple of hours. Wentworth looked behind him. No blue lights. Just like that, Fallon was gone.

Maybe it was a good thing. Otherwise, if he and Sam had met as originally planned, how would they have decided to neutralize Fallon? Glancing over at Sam, who now drove upright and tense out toward Short Hills, Wentworth realized maybe what happened was a good thing. At least for him and Sam.

"What about this gun?"

"We'll dump it after the trades. Not until then, though. Keep it in your jacket pocket." Sam laughed.

"Jesus."

"Come on, Wentworth. This is hardball here."

Wentworth wanted to weep.

Chapter Twelve

TUESDAY EVENING

Seven o'clock. The Short Hills Mall. At this time of the evening on a Tuesday night, there were not too many people, though the mall was busy enough.

Since six-thirty Frank, Jean, and Paul had been on station, ready. The file cabinet was stowed in the trunk of Frank's car, parked close to the Bloomingdale's entrance. Frank and Jean waited by the stairs, somewhat apart. Jean, wearing the same outfit as earlier, stood by the foot of the stairs, visible down the length of the concourse. Frank, carrying his gun, leaned against the wall between the Bloomingdale's doors and the outside exit, partly in a shadow. Paul, carrying the plans, wandered back and forth along the upper level, keeping a sharp eye out for Henry Fallon. He wanted to avoid being seen by Fallon as he was certain Henry did not yet know he was part of this.

When Fallon appeared, they would trade the plans for the negative. Then, after making that exchange, they would discuss the exchange of money for the files. Fallon would walk with Frank to the car, and there, once Frank had collected the money and handed it over to Paul, Frank would open the trunk and deliver the cabinet. As Frank saw it, the plans and negative would now be secondary to Fallon. His main play would be for the files.

Jean was so nervous she felt ill. Frank had said, once Fallon appears, sees you, you go up those stairs, get out of the way. Let Frank and me handle this. After what you did to him, no telling what he might do around you.

Waiting, now, under the stairs, shoppers passing, Frank said across to Jean, twenty feet away, "Been just a week, know that?"

Jean, listening, realized that just a week before, at about this time exactly, in fact, she had started hustling him at dinner down in Baltimore. Just a week?

"Relax, Jean." He was moving his head, trying to watch all directions at once, waiting for Fallon.

Jean wished she was just another shopper, here with her credit cards, an open account, here to buy, wander from store to store, trying on clothing, pretending to be rich or even buying like she was rich. She knew the Short Hills Mall would never be the same after this. Would anything?

One week? She looked over at Frank. He was standing there so quietly. Steady.

Paul, upstairs, saw no one who resembled Fallon. As soon as Fallon appeared and Jean came up the stairs, he would pass her going down. He would face Fallon with Frank.

At ten past seven Frank started to think Fallon wouldn't show when he saw Paul, up above, gesture and point, mouthing something. Paul was waving toward a thin, dark-haired man about thirty years old carrying a briefcase. Dark-eyed and suspicious looking, he was wandering slowly toward the waiting area, intently watching Jean. Frank tried to read Paul's message.

Jean jumped when someone she had never seen before said to her, "Jean Newman?"

Frank moved fast. He realized Paul had been mouthing "Sam." This must be Sam Dworskin. Where was Fallon?

Jean said, "Who are you?" By now Frank was alongside, slightly behind her.

"Mr. Fallon was unable to make it. I am here in his stead."

Frank wondered what it was about this guy that rang a bell. He knew he had never seen Sam Dworskin before, yet there was something in his expression, body language, that he knew he had seen before.

"We have two items of business if you are Jean Newman. Are you?"

Frank glanced upstairs, warned Paul off with his eyes. Not yet, Paul.

"What business do you mean?" Frank asked.

Dworskin switched his gaze from Jean, straightened up.

"My business concerns plans, first, and a file cabinet, second. Mr. Fallon was to meet you here at seven."

Jean reached back, grabbed Frank's hand.

"All right." Frank pushed Jean away and she turned and walked rapidly up the stairs. Paul hovered about halfway down. "You deal with me, not her."

"Of course." Dworskin smiled. His eyes were empty.

Wentworth, farther down the concourse, watched Jean Newman go up the stairs and out of sight. Sam gestured with his hand. Wentworth approached, as did Paul.

Frank saw a second guy, behind Dworskin, his face looked like a melon, it was so puffed up. One side anyway, and the other ear was cherry red.

"Shall we go in there, sit down?" Frank gestured toward the small restaurant just beside the exit, offering nonnutritious, traditional food. Sam nodded. Frank, studying him, again wondered about him.

They all sat at a booth by the door, Paul and Frank across from Wentworth and Sam. Sam and Frank sat opposite each other on the inside.

"You been in an accident?" Frank was speaking to Wentworth.

Wentworth said nothing.

"Now." Sam placed the briefcase on the table. Frank saw dark stains on one cuff, looked like rust. Or blood. And then he remembered, recognized what was so familiar about this guy. Sam's eyes, mouth, movements, and body language were exactly like soldiers he had seen that had just killed the enemy up close. The unbelievable relief, the high of surviving, that was it. Frank leaned back. Careful now. He knew where Fallon was. These were the two guys who had hired him. These were the main players. They wanted the plans. They needed the file.

Frank smiled. Paul, beside him, waited, afraid.

"All right, Benson." Sam leaned forward. "We have two trades, here. One, a negative for some plans. Two, cash for some files."

"That's as we said, over the telephone this afternoon." Frank was calm. Paul watched this Dworskin character. He looked like a lizard, eyes all hooded and bright. The other guy looked like he'd crashed the wrong party.

"The negative first?" Frank asked.

Sam Dworskin opened the briefcase, reached in, pulled out a small envelope.

"Here."

Frank pulled the negative from the envelope. It was the picture all right.

"Is that it?" Sam asked, smiling. Paul could tell he was enjoying this.

"Yes." Frank nodded to Paul, go ahead. Paul pulled the plans from his coat. Both Sam and Wentworth were transfixed as Paul handed the documents over.

Frank waited while Wentworth glanced at the plans and nodded to Sam.

"All right?" Frank asked.

"Yes."

Frank, smiling slightly, slowly tore the negative to tiny shreds, piling them in the ashtray.

"Now," Sam said, "the file."

"The money first," Frank said.

Wentworth glanced toward Sam and pulled the corners of

two thick envelopes from his coat. Paul leaned close. He could see hundred-dollar bills under the torn corner.

"There are two hundred-dollar bills here," Sam said. "Now our business is nearly done. When you give us the file, this money is yours."

Frank grinned tightly.

"Out in the parking lot, opposite the Bloomingdale's exit is a gray Nova off in the back, with a dented driver-side fender. Your man here and Paul will go out there and make the trade. You and me, Mr. Dworskin, we wait here."

Sam stared toward Frank and smiled.

"No," Sam said. "You see how my associate has his hand by his side under the table? He's holding a gun on your balls. We'll get the file by ourselves and leave the money for you in the car."

Wentworth gulped. He had left the gun in the car, beneath the back of the front seat. Frank noticed Wentworth's expression, stared at Sam, and after almost a full minute shook his head.

"Then we have a standoff, Dworskin. I have a gun on your balls. How about that? See how my right hand is down in my pocket? Now, you willing to have your bluff called?"

Sam swallowed. Wentworth shuddered, sweat beading his brow. Sam said to Wentworth, "Go out there, make the trade." He tossed Wentworth some keys. "Then wait for me in our car. You'll drive."

Paul rose to follow Wentworth.

Wentworth walked from the restaurant to the exit doors. He waited for Paul to lead the way to the parked Nova. Jean Newman, who had positioned herself just outside the restaurant in case she might be needed, watched as Paul led Wentworth across the parking lot. She hid in the shadows under the overhanging roof outside Bloomingdale's. Through the glass wall facing the restaurant she could see Frank facing Sam Dworskin, both motionless, each tense.

Paul reached the car, backed into a space under the light, and, watching Wentworth, thrust the keys in the trunk. The trunk opened. Inside, resting on a blanket, stood the file cabinet. Paul stood aside, gestured. As Wentworth bent forward, Paul said, "The money, pal."

Wentworth handed over the envelope. The cabinet was heavy. Face and ear throbbing, he carried it to Fallon's car, which he and Sam had parked some distance away deep in the shadows. He put the file on the back seat. Paul was behind him. As Wentworth was ducking into the car, adjusting the cabinet, he caught a gleam of gunmetal shine and noticed the gun he had dropped earlier behind the front seat. Praying Paul would not notice, Wentworth carefully shoved the pistol in a coat pocket. Behind him Paul, who now had the money, was walking rapidly back toward the mall.

The gun sat heavy but warm in Wentworth's coat. Wentworth had vague notions of revenge, of somehow getting his money back, and he followed Sam back across most of the parking lot before he remembered what Sam had said, to wait in the car. Impatient to be away from here, Wentworth returned to Fallon's car.

Wentworth, opening the car door, saw and heard again in his mind the shockingly loud reports when Sam shot Fallon. He shuddered. For an instant Wentworth wondered why the dome light wasn't working; it had gone on just a moment before when he had stowed the cabinet in the back seat. He started to slide into the driver's seat.

Paul, back inside the restaurant, nodded toward Frank. Frank waited. Paul felt the thick envelopes of cash against his chest. Sam Dworskin began to rise.

"You two wait here ten minutes before you leave. Let's consider this business done. Don't be stupid and make any calls."

Frank said, "Fine." His right hand, holding the gun, stayed in his pocket.

Sam, now standing, said, "I see why you needed that negative, Benson. It was some picture. Perfect timing, in fact. It got you right at the moment, didn't it? I'm impressed, older guy like you, looks like you hit that mirror over the headboard of the bed, you can still shoot pretty far, huh?'' He had a feral glint in his eye.

Frank looked at this guy. He was lucky to be thirty years old, eyes as empty as space. Some high-paid executive hustler running a race to glory, playing as low and dirty as it gets. Frank said, ''You got your file. Now fuck off.''

Dworskin left the restaurant.

Frank and Paul watched him leave and start across the lot toward the car. Frank said, ''You all right?''

Paul, still remembering the feeling when Sam had said, there's a gun pointed at your balls, shuddered. ''How did you know they didn't have a gun?''

Frank sighed. ''A gun makes a bulge the size of a lunch box in a sport coat. That Wentworth's coat hung perfect. He's a guy who never wears coats that hang wrong. I could tell, looking at him, guns aren't his thing. Unlike the other one, Sam. If he had a gun, by now we might be dead.''

Jean walked in the restaurant, sat down. Frank gestured to the ashtray.

''One torn-up negative, right here. And Paul here's holding a pile of cash.''

Jean said, ''That was Wentworth Randall, the guy with Sam, wasn't it?''

''Where was Fallon?'' Paul asked.

Frank shook his head.

''I bet Fallon's a goner, Paul.''

''What do you mean?''

''I think Sam and that Wentworth met with Fallon, and Sam took Fallon out of the picture. Sam had the look of a guy who's killed and likes it, finds it fun. I don't think Fallon will bother us anymore. He must have made another mistake, like he did with Jean this morning. He got so excited he left himself open. I'll bet he dropped his guard with these two guys and Dworskin let him have it. Fallon's likely dead somewhere.''

* * *

Wentworth shut the driver-side door, fumbling for the car keys, taking a huge breath of relief. They were almost finished! Then he sensed something rising behind him and a hard calloused hand grabbed his throat. A cold circular pressure twisted just beneath his ear.

Someone was strangling Wentworth! Far off, across the parking lot, he registered Sam standing and starting toward the car. Then, just behind his vision, he heard a ragged breath. Wentworth smelled a sickly sweet odor and knew it was blood. The voice, when it came, was terrible. "Stay silent, boyo, not a fucking word, not one peep!"

"Fallon! Uh, Fallon! How did you—" Wentworth's neck was breaking! Sam, now running, raced around the front of the car, looking back toward the mall, and lunged into the passenger seat, yelling, "Let's get the fuck out of—" Then he froze, seeing in the back seat the rising form of a disgusting, bleeding Henry Fallon, shirtfront wet with blood, one eye bruised and shut, other eye crazed.

"Drive, boyo! Drive!"

"How did—? I thought—" For once Sam Dworskin lost his cool. Henry Fallon chuckled, a wet flubbery gasp.

"I got more fucking lives than a cat. All I had to do was steal a car and drive out here, sneak in here when pretty boy looked the other way. All you did, asshole, was drill me through the shoulder. Now drive!"

Wentworth, in a panic, twisted the keys. The engine roared to life. Totally terrified, Wentworth stabbed with his foot, flooring it. The car screeched forward, bucking, fishtailing. Henry Fallon, perched on the forward edge of the rear seat, surged back as the car leapt ahead. The sudden acceleration threw the gun from Wentworth's coat pocket onto the front seat. Wentworth, literally driving for his life, had forgotten the gun. Sam Dworskin, seeing a sudden gift from God before him, grabbed the gun and, in a flash, thrust his arm across the back seat, emptying the pistol into Fallon's chest just as Fallon fired his own gun toward Sam.

Wentworth, at the wheel, screamed, certain he was dead.

The car, filled with an acrid sweet cordite scent—the smell of hot blood, and, now, shit—was suddenly silent. Wentworth, steering blindly under the Route 24 overpass toward Chatham, dared glance to his right, asking, "Sam?"

Sam Dworskin's form, limp and slack, slid quietly beneath the dash toward the passenger wheel well. His cold eyes, open, reflected the passing streetlights. Sam's mouth hung open.

From the back seat Henry Fallon said, in completely normal tones, "Aw, fuck it."

Wentworth, certain he was next to die, hunched his neck desperately into his shoulders. He drove, rigid, waiting for death. The silence lengthened. Wentworth drove ahead, well under the speed limit, instinctively seeking unlighted streets. To his left across a worn cement bridge he saw a small sign—River Road—and he took it, following a narrow winding street past some worn frame tenement homes approaching a railroad overpass. Then, the road turned sharply and started past a park by the river bottom. As the headlights swung across some naked trees, Wentworth dared look up into the rearview mirror.

Henry Fallon's head, outlined against the rear window, lolled. Black blood dribbled over his chin. Suddenly Wentworth turned sharply into the park, seeking shelter, a place to hide, forcing the car over the snow and around some bushes and trees. As he turned Fallon's body fell to the side.

Wentworth maneuvered Fallon's sedan even farther away from the road, almost to the river itself. He turned off the headlights and the engine. The car engine ticked in the cold. Passing cars out on River Road could not be seen, could not see him. Wentworth, gagging and shaking, could not believe it.

He was alive!

Then as relief washed over him his mind started to race. They're both dead! I've got to get away from here! If I wash up in the river a little I can walk back, catch a train in Chatham to New York! Get back! Get away!

Somehow before he left the scene, after washing his hands in the cold river, he remembered to wipe the steering wheel, door handles, and file cabinet with a rag to remove his fingerprints. He retrieved the bloody files concerning their operation from the cabinet and he remembered to grab the stock certificates from Fallon's coat. These, too, he washed in the river. Then in a flash of inspiration he started the car, headed it toward the river down a short slope, and jumped out, leaving it in drive. The car nosed into the water and stopped, bubbling.

Christ, it was cold.

"So you think we're clear?" Paul asked, eyes alight.

Jean took a deep breath.

"Let's call the police, give them a tip."

"A tip?" Paul asked. "We don't want any attention here, do we? We call the cops to check Fallon's place, maybe there's a body there, couldn't it get traced back to us?"

"I think, make a few calls, leave a few tips around, that'll be all right," Frank said. "I bet that Sam's heading straight for the airport."

"Can I make that call?" Jean asked.

"Jean, listen. I gotta drive Paul back home and get back to work, handle my personal business. I know your husband's wondering where you must be—"

Jean, rising to go to a telephone, stopped, realizing that they were about to split up, forever, just like that. She stopped, staring at them both. Then she reached out, shook Paul's hand, Frank's hand.

"Thank you."

Frank smiled.

"Thank you, Jean. You're a tough lady. A tough, lovely lady."

"I'll send you all a postcard, my round-the-world cruise with all the money I'm about to make," Jean said, smiling, eyes shining. She turned, then swung back. She hugged Paul. She hugged Frank. She laughed. "Know what?"

"What?" Paul and Frank spoke together.

"This morning, when I had to meet Fallon the first time, I thought, we're a gang. The One-Night Stand Gang, that's how I've been thinking of us. We made a pretty good gang, huh?"

"That we did," Frank said. He kissed Jean. Paul's tooth flashed.

"So you think we really got away with it?" Paul asked.

"Good chance, Paul. This whole operation, the way that Sam and Wentworth tried to run it? It was too rich for their blood, know what I mean?"

Jean laughed.

"All right, gentlemen. We'll handle the rest of our business as planned, correct?" Jean winked at Frank.

"First thing in the morning," Frank said.

"Shouldn't we split up this money?" Paul asked.

"Tomorrow, we will," Frank said.

"Huh?" Paul asked. He thought they would split the money up now. Frank nodded to Jean.

"Paul, why don't you hold that money until we get to a bank tomorrow? You'll be with me. Jean trusts me. Besides, won't that pile of cash feel good, so heavy in your coat?"

"Now that you mention it." The cash was heavy. Jean smiled.

"Well, then." She kissed them both again, fast, and started walking over to the telephones on the concourse.

"That's some woman," Paul said, wistfully.

"I know." Frank watched her. "I know."

Back in Maplewood, just after eight o'clock that evening, Jean opened her front door. Norman was sitting at the kitchen table, facing an empty bottle of beer, brow furrowed.

"Norman."

"Jean! Where the hell have you been? I was worried!"

Jean reached in the refrigerator, pulled out a beer. She handed Norman a fresh bottle.

"Norman." She sat down, faced him. "I have a lot to tell

250

you about . . . a lot." She reached over, touched his cheek. "Just hear me out, all right?"

Norman stared at his wife. Jean knew she looked great tonight, tired but great. She'd taken a lot of time at a gas station. He'd listen to her, hear her explain about what she had done with their money.

Jean started in, holding Norman's hand.

Heading down the turnpike, sipping coffee, relaxed, it seemed, for the first time in a century, Paul leaned against the seat and stared, mesmerized, at the road. Frank was driving. On the radio, a classical station, nice soft music, a concerto.

"Paul?" Frank finished his coffee. "How do you stand with Ryan Express? The delivery company."

Paul laughed.

"How do I stand? Out in the cold, after these past two days!"

"Got a suggestion. My business, it's not bad. I could use some help if you're interested, could train you up fast."

Paul stared at Frank, shook his head.

"I'm a fucking ex-con, Frank. On parole! How'd that look, working security systems with a parolee? Especially one who used to kite bad checks?"

"Let me handle that. Think about it, all right?"

No more 7:00 A.M. wakeups freezing in the van waiting for the radio assignments? No more driving around? A new line of work?

"Give it some thought," Frank repeated. "Next few weeks, I'll need help, nothing too specialized, mostly just paperwork. When I get back home tonight I have to arrange to bring my dad home. He'll take a lot of care and a lot of my time, his last days on earth. I can do that, now, with Michelle at the hospital being treated for her problem. She's going to be a month or so in the rehab, and I got the kids to take care of. You could help me covering some of my road calls, get your feet wet, see how you like it."

"You hungry?" Paul asked. He was ravenous.

"Yeah, but I stay away from road food. It's too greasy. It kills my cholesterol count." Then Frank paused, listening to himself. He laughed. "I'll cook you up a good meal when we get to my place. Late dinner. You can spend the night. After we finish cleaning the house—still have some work to do—"

"Shit."

"And then, first thing in the morning, after we finish our business, get by a bank and finish that up, you decide by then, all right?"

"Frank, about this cash I'm carrying? What—"

"Jean and I made a plan back there at Friendly's one of those times you had to go pee. Here's what we're going to do . . ."

Chapter Thirteen

WEDNESDAY MORNING

Wentworth Randall, Junior, facing the performance of his life, arrived at his office before seven, and assembled some files and papers to further bolster his case in the event he needed it. He then proceeded to the Executive Dining Room where Ironjaw was holding the breakfast meeting. For this meeting, Wentworth's most important ever, he had dressed in his most elegant, understated rising executive suit, a nice charcoal gray with blue highlights supported by a yellow shirt and dark blue tie, a gold tie clip and gold cuff links. He was dressed to kill.

The night before he had caught a late train from Chatham to Hoboken and New York. It had taken him thirty minutes to walk to the Chatham station. When a train finally arrived, Wentworth had scuttled to the last, virtually empty car, and then sat beneath a section where the overhead lights were out. The conductor, thinking him drunk, paid him no mind.

Wentworth rode back to the city on PATH from Hoboken and returned to his apartment, still shaking, mind racing, not quite convinced, despite the graphic evidence he had left behind in Fallon's car, that he was in the clear. After showering for what seemed like hours, he struggled to develop, then lay out, a theory to explain himself, head Karen off at the pass. By the time he tumbled into bed, he felt some security. He had the plans back in his possession, at least. And he had manufactured an explanation to offer.

It was thin, but better than nothing. Wentworth was sure there were no connections between him and Fallon now that the files were back in his possession. At least there were no identifiable connections aside from his earlier reports on Fallon's investigation to the Bonnell special projects team. When Fallon and Sam's bodies were found, there would be nothing, Wentworth believed, to connect their demise to him.

Be confident, Wentworth told himself. Believe your case of Karen's duplicity. Wentworth would claim that, acting on his own initiative, he had been in contact with Fallon even before The Event. Even then he had been concerned about Karen's role. He had noticed that Karen had urged Horace to take the plans home. He wanted to be sure Fallon would be watching Horace's apartment to observe and then follow whomever Karen had arranged to steal the plans. Wentworth was certain no one would remember who had told Horace to bring the plans home. It had been so long since those early meetings. He would say Karen arranged the theft and that he had been using Fallon as a lead, knowing Fallon was crooked. He, Wentworth, had been documenting the links between Fallon and Karen. At a dinner with Karen, she had tried to enlist his aid, even seduce him. He had refused. At lunch the following day, which she had arranged, Karen must have called Fallon, told him they would be eating at the Salad Bowl, and arranged for Fallon to come there and kidnap him, to take him away to neutralize him. Kill him.

Wentworth would say that Fallon began to beat him. That would explain his swollen face. Fallon forced Wentworth to call in sick, then dragged him off to someplace where he was going to kill him. But Wentworth escaped.

It might work. If necessary, if his link with Dworskin had been found during Karen's searching, he would say he had been stringing Dworskin along to satisfy his belief Boothbay Industries was behind what Karen was up to. Sam Dworskin was Karen's Boothbay contact.

Christ, it looked even thinner in the morning light. Wentworth knew, in a case like this, it would be Ironjaw who ruled. He felt he had a good rapport with Ironjaw. His only mistake, he would argue, was being initially fooled by Fallon, but he had not been involved in anything else improper. Karen's accusations Monday were a classic red herring, throwing the scent from her onto him.

All these thoughts, remembrances, swirled in Wentworth's head as he pushed open the doors to the Executive Dining Room, entering the chamber with mustered confidence, alertness, and, most of all, style. Wentworth took his seat to Ironjaw's left, but to his surprise Ironjaw wasn't there. Everyone else was—Drexell Aspin, William Doane, Horace Taylor, Emily Mott, Arthur Stein, and Karen Frucci. Wentworth nodded to each, smiling, looking them in the eye. He could brazen this out. Someone else was missing, Norman what's his name, the computer nerd. Why was William Doane sitting at Ironjaw's place?

"Good morning, Karen," Wentworth said, smiling tightly.

Silence. There was total silence. No one was speaking, or even, for that matter, drinking juice or buttering muffins. Everyone was motionless, staring toward the door. No one spoke. What was going on? Wentworth felt his palms start to sweat. Where was Ironjaw?

A waiter entered, pushing a small table on rollers, upon which was a television set. The waiter plugged the television cord into a socket, handed Doane a hand-held remote, and left.

William Doane, implacable, spoke.

"Mr. Maroules will not be joining us this morning."

Silence. Wentworth saw confusion in everyone's faces.

Doane pulled a magazine from his briefcase. Wentworth was wondering what was going on. What does this have to do with the agenda Mannie and I agreed on yesterday? Doane tossed the magazine lightly upon the table. Somewhere glass tinkled against china plates. The magazine, Wentworth saw, was the latest issue of the *New England Journal of Medicine*.

"This will appear on newsstands today. I got this copy late last night. There is an article in here about a new medicine developed by Nauset Pharmaceuticals, a small company in Elizabeth, New Jersey. It says they have developed a medicine that is not based on biogenetics. A medicine called Passage."

Doane spoke slowly, clearly. Wentworth struggled to understand what was going on.

"You'll have plenty of time to read this."

Doane thumbed the remote switch and the television flickered on. Everyone was looking confused. It was 7:30 exactly. Doane changed channels to stop at "Good Morning, America."

"I was informed of this on the late, late news, just after the chairman called to inform me the board had suspended Mr. Maroules, effective at once." Doane paused and sighed, then raised the volume so everyone could hear.

". . . and as is reported in today's issue of the prestigious medical journal, the *New England Journal of Medicine*, a small drug company in New Jersey has completed testing and development of a pill that appears to actually dissolve the plaque that forms in veins and arteries from too much cholesterol in our diet! Nauset Pharmaceuticals, developer of this drug, announced today that their new drug, Passage, will be offered for sale as early as January first. Joining us now from his office in Elizabeth is Nauset's president, Richard Platt. Mr. Platt, thank you for joining us at such an early hour. Can you tell us how you discovered this amazing drug?"

All Wentworth could think, hearing the reporter and the official being interviewed, was that this changed everything about Choice. Whether or not plans were copied, sold, or given away, everything with Fallon was unimportant!

Karen, sitting across the table, still glowing from a long, wonderful, entirely unexpected night with Jamie Giari, was speechless. She caught the glint in Wentworth's eye, the tiny movement of the thin lips toward a smile, and she surprised herself. Who the fuck cares what will happen now to Wentworth Randall, Junior?

"... and although logic suggested we needed a biological agent, and I know several other firms are pursuing this, we were fortunate to stumble on a mixture that appeared to do the job using a vitamin and fish-oil solution—"

Wentworth felt his face throb.

On television, the female half of the news team chattered, "Well, it certainly looks good for cholesterol sufferers and bad for the anticholesterol diet market—"

Wentworth, watching the rest of the project team stare with shock at the television, couldn't help it. His jaw ached fighting to suppress the wild joy and elation rising in his chest. He gave in to it. Wentworth smiled a huge smile, bigger and bigger. He started to laugh. Sitting there, laughing until tears came, Wentworth remembered something his father once told him, many years earlier, which was: If you cut too many corners, my boy, you know what you end up with: a pile of shit.

Oh, Jesus, what a joke. He had pulled it off!

"That's him. Over there." William Doane spoke quietly. Wentworth, gasping, suddenly noticed the two policemen who had been waiting outside for Doane's signal, who were now headed his way with handcuffs!

William Doane's mouth twisted. Karen Frucci and the others watched in astonishment.

He was going to be arrested. Wentworth Randall, Junior, couldn't believe it. Actually, he could.

At 8:00 sharp, Frank and Paul were at the bank, confirming the orders telephoned in the day before. Up in Maplewood, Jean watched the same television show a great many others in the country were watching, thinking with comfort and a feeling of warmth how the twenty-four thousand in bankbook savings which she had used to buy Nauset stock the day before might possibly double by the end of the day.

Frank and Paul left the bank, wandered to a coffee shop. "You decide?" Frank asked. "Want a job?"

"Uh, yeah. I guess I could see what nine to five is like."

"Good. It won't kill you, Paul."

"That wasn't easy, there, handing over all that cash."

Frank laughed. He and Jean had agreed to let Paul have half the cash for the plans, give him a big surprise. Frank had directed his broker the day before to take all the cash from the scam and buy Nauset stock with it. He knew Jean had done the same with her and Norman's money. The previous day, at Friendly's, they agreed to let Paul keep ten of the twenty for himself.

"Listen. Nauset stock was at eleven and a half at the start of today. When the trading starts here in a few minutes you can watch it shoot up and up all day long. I bet by the end of today, it'll be over forty and I bet you that within a few days you'll have tripled, quadrupled, triple-quadrupled your money! Then, when the bigger companies, the Bonnells and Boothbays, make a play to buy Nauset, the stock will double again!"

"But how'd you know, last night, to do this?"

"Didn't! But Jean did it with her money yesterday. She figured, if Nauset's going to pay her husband over twenty grand just for information, it had to be a good investment. Me? I did the same thing. Took a chance, I guess."

"Jesus, Frank."

Frank grinned and looked for a few seconds at the menu board behind the grill. It was 8:10 in the morning. Frank waved for the waitress.

"You hungry, Paul?" They had not yet eaten breakfast.

"Sure."

"Good." Frank spoke to the waitress. "Two breakfasts here. We'll both have two eggs over easy, bacon, a steak."

"Bad for you, all that stuff," Paul said.

"And," Frank said, before she could close her book, "give us two pieces of pecan pie with vanilla ice cream and whipped cream."

The waitress blanched. "Lordie, mister, for breakfast? All that fat!" She poured them both coffee.

Paul said, "I thought you had a cholesterol problem, Frank."

Frank Benson laughed and reached for the cream. "Fat chance of that, bub. Fat chance."

A Tom Bethany Mystery

BODY SCISSORS

Jerome Doolittle

"A riveting political thriller written with an insider's savvy...Doolittle offers a polished performance... The Boston area scene is a lively backdrop, the dialogue crackles with fast repartee, and the characters make an assorted and colorful cast."
— *Washington Post Book World*

Available in Paperback from Pocket Books

And Look for

STRANGLE HOLD

Available in Hardcover from Pocket Books

POCKET
BOOKS

456